A GENTLEMAN WORTHY OF KISSES

A REPUBLISHED REGENCY NOVELLA DUET

GRACE BURROWES

GRACE BURROWES PUBLISHING

WHEN HIS GRACE FALLS

(Originally published in the novella duet
How to Ruin a Duke)

TITLE PAGE AND DEDICATION

When His Grace Falls

by Grace Burrowes

This story was originally published in the novella duet, *How to Ruin a Duke*, with Theresa Romain's story, Rhapsody for Two.

Dedicated to those fallen upon hard times

CHAPTER 1

"A duke cannot, of course, be *ruined*, except by his own folly, and
what an entertaining spectacle that is!"
From *How to Ruin a Duke* by Anonymous

"She is the personification of gall, the embodiment of presumption,
and a walking temple to betrayal." Thaddeus, Duke of Emory, made
a precise about-face at the edge of the library's carpet. "I'd sooner
share my coach with a viper than admit this family ever employed
Lady Edith Charbonneau. Stop swilling all the good brandy."

Thaddeus had been scolding and lecturing his baby brother for
more than twenty years, not that Jeremiah had ever listened.

"A lady's companion has a difficult lot," Jeremiah said, draining
the last of the spirits from his glass. "Have you considered paying
Lady Edith off? I'd be happy to act as intermediary."

Thaddeus made another about-face before the portrait of the
previous duke. "That's quite generous of you, but she hasn't
demanded to be paid off. She hasn't even acknowledged her authorship of the damned book. And what sort of woman titles a book, *How*

to Ruin a Duke? She and I barely spoke during the whole of her tenure as Mama's companion. What she knows about dukes wouldn't fill a toddler's porringer."

The mere sight of Lady Edith's compilation of drivel—already sold in a bound edition—made Thaddeus want to roar profanities and throw the book at the nearest fragile object. He'd been the butt of satire before—every peer was—but he'd never so badly misjudged a woman's character.

He'd liked Lady Edith, rather a lot, and he liked very few people indeed.

"What she knows about *you*," Jeremiah said, "handsomely fills nearly three hundred pages. Have you read it?"

"I wouldn't admit it if I had." Much less admit that he'd read it several times, word for word. Alone, of course, because on occasion—rare occasion—the author managed a humorous turn of phrase that provoked a begrudging laugh.

Jeremiah opened the book to a page at random and ran his finger along the prose. "'His nose is majestic, and those ladies in a position to comment knowledgeably—said to number in the scores—claim other aspects of the ducal anatomy are in proportion not only to His Grace's magnificent proboscis, but also to his considerable conceit.' This can't possibly be aimed at you, Emory. Your conceit surpassed considerable before you reached your majority. At the very least, your conceit qualifies as stupendous."

"Unlike your sense of humor." The footman had positioned a spray of daisies on the mantel, a half inch off center. Thaddeus corrected the error and realized the flowers were nearly out of water.

"Again, Your Grace, I suggest with all deference that if you'd simply wave a handsome *sum* at the woman, your handsome *person* would no longer be the subject of her literary maunderings. I'll search her out, handle the details, and nobody need ever acknowledge the source of the money."

Now that was a fiction approaching the absurd. Jeremiah was so inept at managing his funds, his allowance was disbursed every two weeks rather than quarterly. He was a good soul, but too generous with his friends and too reckless with his bets.

No misanthropic spinster would ever write a satirical tome about Jeremiah. Being a charming, impecunious courtesy lord had its advantages.

"Will you join Mama and the ladies for the carriage parade?" Thaddeus asked, using the pitcher on the sideboard to water the flowers. The day was glorious as only London in late spring could be.

"Isn't it your turn, Your Grace?" The polite form of address became mocking when Jeremiah adopted that tone.

"I rode with them yesterday and the day before," Thaddeus replied, returning the pitcher to the sideboard. "The ladies prefer your escort because everybody likes you."

Jeremiah saluted with his brandy glass, which was full again. "You really do need to work on your flattery, Emory."

"I am a duke. I need not flatter anybody. I'm simply speaking the truth. You are not only received everywhere, you are *welcomed* everywhere." While Thaddeus had long since reconciled himself to merely being invited everywhere.

He and Jeremiah both had the family height, blue eyes, and dark hair, but Jeremiah had perfected the air of a man amused by life's contradictions. Thaddeus could not afford that posture, which only made the damned book all the more vexing.

"I do have a certain modest social appeal," Jeremiah said. "I admit it. If I'm to squire Mama and the ladies about, I suppose I'd better change into riding attire. What pressing engagement prevents you from joining us?"

A dozen pressing engagements. The house steward was in the boughs over some comment the sommelier had made about the dampness of the cellars. The kitchen staff agreed with the sommelier, the footmen had aligned themselves with the house steward, and the maids were stirring the pot as maids were ever wont to do. Mama expected Thaddeus to make peace among the warring parties—a task that Lady Edith had somehow managed from time to time—but really, the cellar *was* damp. All London cellars were.

"My afternoon is not my own," Thaddeus said. "And it's your turn, Jeremiah." They had a schedule, so the escort tribulation was evenly divided between them, but the schedule was usually honored in the breach, and the breach was invariably on Jeremiah's part.

"Give my regards to whichever merry widow is claiming your time, Emory."

The tailor—a short, bald, nervous fellow who had no acquaintance with merriment that Thaddeus could divine—claimed that a final fitting for Thaddeus's new frock coat was absolutely imperative, the third such final fitting for that one garment.

The Committee for the Relief of Aged Seamen hadn't disbursed this month's funds, mostly because Thaddeus hadn't yet bullied them into it.

No less than four bills pending in the Lords required a judicious application of ducal persuasion in the direction of various earls and other tedious fellows, all of whom wanted to be seen having dinner with Thaddeus at his clubs.

"I will tend to the press of business," Thaddeus said, lining up the decanters on the sideboard in order of height. "Tending to the press of business is, after all, why I was born."

"Mama might attribute your birth to other causes." Jeremiah took a considering sip of his drink. "According to a certain scribbling spinster, your chief pursuits are nearly breaking your neck in wild horse races, consuming vast quantities of liquor, and disappointing mistresses after you've made their wildest erotic fantasies come true."

"No wonder I am usually in need of a good nap." In truth Thaddeus hadn't any mistresses to disappoint. At the beginning of the Season, he'd promised himself to engage the company of some friendly widow who didn't mind an occasional frolic, but that had been several months ago, and the press of business had interfered with even that pursuit.

"Enjoy the carriage parade," Thaddeus said, striding for the door. "I have an appointment with a certain publisher whom I hope will lead me to Lady Edith's doorstep."

"You intend to confront her ladyship directly?" Jeremiah set down his glass on Grandpapa's desk. "Is that wise, Emory? She can turn even an innocent meeting into more grist for her mill. Perhaps I should go with you."

This genuine fraternal concern was part of the reason Thaddeus continued to support his brother. Jeremiah spent money like a sailor in his home port for the first time in two years. He wiggled out of social obligations, and his naughty wagers were legendary in the club betting books.

But he was loyal to Thaddeus, and if a brother could have only one redeeming value—Jeremiah had many, in truth—loyalty was the one that would most easily earn Thaddeus's esteem.

"If I can locate Lady Edith," Thaddeus said, reversing course to put the empty glass on the tray on the sideboard, "then perhaps I will have you accompany me when I call upon her, but first I must find the woman."

Jeremiah gave the library's globe a spin, letting his index finger trail along the northern hemisphere. "Is there some urgency about this errand, Emory? Society is having a good laugh at our expense, but this is not the first such book to be published, nor will it be the last."

When Lord Jeremiah Maitland was the voice of reason, pigs might be spotted kiting about the branches of the plane maples.

"I'd rather it be the last such book published *about me*. The author is said to be working on a sequel, and if I allow a second book into print, Mama will disown me."

"Would that Mama disowned me. Why is it your fault that somebody has decided to immortalize your exploits for the delectation of bored clubmen?"

Thaddeus made for the door once again. "Immortality by way of infamy and ridicule is not a goal I aspire to. Shouldn't you be changing into riding attire?"

"Explain to me why you take such grievous exception to a harmless spoof. I always have time to lend a friendly ear to my dearest older brother."

This was true, oddly enough. "In the first place, the exploits are unfairly portrayed, as you well know. In the second place, the book is being read by far more than the younger sons and idlers lounging about the clubs. In the third,"—Thaddeus got out his pocket watch to compare the time it kept to the eight-day clock on the mantel—"this dratted book has Mama concerned for my prospects."

The two timepieces were in gratifying synchrony.

"Your *prospects?*" Jeremiah spluttered. "Mama thinks no decent woman will have you, a poor old homely fellow with only what—six or is it seven—titles to your name and a different estate to go with each one? Perhaps our dame is suffering a touch of dementia. We certainly can't let that get out or the sequel will devolve into a trilogy."

"This isn't amusing, Jeremiah. What decent woman wants to ally herself with a man who's the butt of a three-hundred-page joke?"

Jeremiah strolled for the door. "The book is merely a nine days wonder, Emory. Shall I place a wager on who will be the topic of the next such tome? I nominate old Moreland. He was supposedly a rascal in his youth."

"No wagers, if you please," Thaddeus said, preceding Jeremiah out the door. "That rascal has three grown sons who'd skewer you without blinking if you maligned their papa, and then the in-laws would start in." Besides, Thaddeus both liked and respected Percival, His Grace of Moreland, who had passed along more than a few insightful suggestions regarding the care and feeding of parliamentary committees.

"I fancy a bit of swordplay, now that you bring up skewering," Jeremiah said. "Shall we drop around to Angelo's?"

Nice try. "You shall change into your riding attire. I will send a footman to the stables to tell them you'll need your horse."

Jeremiah stopped at the foot of the staircase that wound up in a grand sweep around three-quarters of the octagonal foyer. Of the house's public spaces, this was Thaddeus's favorite. Marble half-columns created a series of niches wherein reposed classical urns, dignified busts, and splendid ferns. Ancestors scowled down from the portraits on the walls, and the mosaic on the floor—the family coat of arms—hadn't a single flawed or misplaced stone.

"One must concede the author has shown initiative," Jeremiah said, foot on the first step. "Don't you agree? She is enterprising enough to write all those pages, to find a publisher, to turn common human foibles into entertainment. That's not something just any idle fribble could do, Emory."

Jeremiah sounded genuinely admiring or perhaps envious.

"If another such book comes out, and I become a running joke from year to year, no duchess I could esteem would bother marrying me. That leaves *you* to secure the succession, my lord, meaning your bachelor days would be over."

"Good gracious, Emory. As dire as all that? Then be on your way, by all means. Nothing must be allowed to jeopardize my bachelor-hood. The good ladies of Mayfair would go into a decline and I would have to join them."

His lordship scampered up the steps all merriment and laughter, though Thaddeus was certain that Jeremiah's last expostulation was only half in jest.

Lady Edith Charbonneau sat on the hard chair, her outward composure firmly in place while she raged inside. Two years as companion to the Duchess of Emory had resulted in the ability to maintain her dignity, if nothing else. Little good that would do her when she had no roof over her head.

"My lady, I do apologize," Mr. Jared Ventnor said, from the far side of a desk both massive and battered, "but at present I am not in the business of publishing books of domestic advice. Have you tried Mr. MacHugh?"

"Mr. MacHugh has all the domestic guidance authors he needs. He suggested I proceed by subscription, but Mr. Ventnor, I am a lady by birth. I cannot be seen importuning my friends to support my publishing endeavors. The result would label my literary aspirations charity, and I will not be made into an object of pity." Moreover, the goal of Edith's considerable writing efforts was to earn money, not to perfect her begging skills.

When male authors drummed up support for a book yet to be written—much less published—that was business as usual. A woman in the same posture met with a very different reception.

Mr. Ventnor rose. "Leave me some of your writing samples. If I can't publish you, I might think of somebody who can once I have a sense of your voice and tone. Reading for entertainment is becoming stylish, and whoever can write the next *How to Ruin a Duke* will be assured of a long and lucrative career."

If I never hear of that book again... "Might I consider my writing samples and send you the best of the lot?"

Ventnor was rumored to be a decent sort. He had a wife and family, he paid his authors honestly—not a given, in London's publishing community—and he met with impoverished spinsters when he doubtless had other things to do.

And yet, paper was precious. Edith had only the single final copies of the samples she'd brought, thinking to pass them over for Mr. Ventnor's perusal while she'd waited.

"You may send them along," he said, offering his hand to assist her to her feet. "But promise me you will show me something. Too many authors claim they seek publication, and when I ask for a sample, they fuss and dither and delay, gilding the lily—or tarnishing it, more likely—until their courage has ebbed to nothing. Send me something within the week."

"I can make you that promise, sir."

He was mannerly. Edith gave him grudging respect for that. As an earl's daughter, she'd met many mannerly men. Only those who offered her courtesy when nobody compelled it earned her admiration. Ventnor could have been rude rather than kind, and Edith would nonetheless have applied to him for work.

He walked with her to the front door, past all the editors at their desks and clerks with their green visors. The air of industry here was unmistakable and fascinating. An earl's daughter was raised to be an ornament, idling from one entertainment to the next. A lady's companion might be kept busy, but she could not *look* busy.

These fellows gloried in their work, and in the challenge of making a business successful.

"Have you considered finding another post as a lady's companion?" Mr. Ventnor asked, passing Edith her cloak. "My in-laws move in polite society at levels above what a mere publisher can aspire to. I could ask my wife to make inquiries through her sister."

He really was kind, and Edith really did want to smack him with her reticule. She'd learned to keep a copy of *Glenarvon* in her bag the better to deter pickpockets and presuming men. Heaven knew Lady Caroline's book had few other redeeming qualities.

"I have had my fill of being a lady's companion," Edith said. "It did not end well." She put her Sunday bonnet on and tied the ribbons loosely. The day was fine, and even a poor spinster could enjoy a beautiful spring afternoon. "Companions are not generously compensated, and they are pitied when they aren't held in contempt."

By polite society. The servant class, much to Edith's surprise, had been far more tolerant and welcoming.

Ventnor bowed over her hand. "Send me those writing samples, please, and I will consult my family on your behalf. Necessity sometimes compels us into situations we'd otherwise avoid, but circumstances unfortunate on their face can end happily."

He spoke as if from experience, when to all appearances he was a contented and prosperous man.

"If you say so, Mr. Ventnor, though necessity has landed many a decent woman in ruin. Good afternoon and thank you for your time." Edith let herself out into the lovely day, the sun a benevolence and the London air enjoying a rare freshness. The day was a lie, promising pretty flowers and blossom-scented breezes rather than the stinking oppression of the coming summer.

A pretty lie, like much of polite society.

Edith set off down the walk, abundantly aware that she had not even a footman to accompany her. Women of the lower orders moved about as they pleased, but their freedom made them less safe. As a companion to a duchess, Edith had been safe on the streets, something she'd taken for granted.

She ought not to have said that part about decent women being brought to ruin to Mr. Ventnor, though the word haunted her. That silly book—*How to Ruin a Duke*—couched ruin in terms of stupid pranks, idiot wagers, and pleasures of the flesh. Those venalities were hardly ruinous to a duke.

True ruin meant horrors that gave Edith nightmares. Debtor's prison for Foster, worse for Edith herself.

She was so sunk in dread over those familiar worries that she didn't see the oversized lout who plowed into her right on the walkway. The instant after he'd nearly trampled her, she caught his scent, a particular blend of grassy and floral fragrances.

Such a beautiful, warm fragrance for such a chilly, self-possessed man.

The Duke of Emory steadied her with a hand on each of her arms. "I do beg your pardon, ma'am. I was at risk for tardiness at my next appointment and one is loath to inconvenience another who has—"

She stepped back, her reticule catching His Grace a glancing blow that he seemed not to notice. "Hands off, Your Grace. Please watch where you are going. Last I heard, gentlemen were to yield the way to ladies, but then—"

"You," he said, glaring down the ducal beak. "The very person who has authored all of my difficulties."

Emory was a monument to aristocratic self-possession, but unless he had changed very much in the past six months, he wasn't given to rudeness or wild fancies.

"Your difficulties are the envy of those who must work for a living. Excuse me, sir." She tried to maneuver around him, but for a big man, he was nimble.

"I do not excuse you. I hold you accountable for a wrong done to me and to my family, and I intend to seek retribution from the perpetrator."

"Then call him out." Edith dodged left only to again be blocked by a wall of fine tailoring exquisitely fitted to the ducal person. "That's what Lord Jeremiah would do." Then his lordship would probably delope, have a drink or six with his opponent, and go carousing onto the next potentially fatal lark. No wonder the duchess had been a woman easily vexed.

"Alas," Emory retorted. "My detractor, who stands before me in the most horrid shade of pink I have ever beheld, is a female. One cannot call out a female, which said female well knows and likely exploits at every turn."

"Are you tipsy, Emory?" Many wealthy men were seldom sober, but Edith had put Emory in the seldom drunk column. "Fevered, perhaps? Have you suffered a blow to the head? That must be it."

"I have suffered a blow to my reputation, and well you know it."

This conversation was attracting notice, which Edith could ill afford. "I'll thank you to spare me a litany of the slights you image yourself to have suffered, Emory. Having already earned the notice of a satirist, you should be reluctant to accost women on the street, much less lecture them about your supposed miseries. Good day."

She made it past him, but he fell in step beside her.

"Have you no escort, my lady?"

"Why would I need an escort when I can fly from one destination to the next on my broomstick?"

The hordes of pedestrians made way for Emory, and thus for Edith. Even an indignity as minor as getting jostled on the street had been an adjustment for her, an insistent reminder that she'd come down in the world, far down. She hated that Emory could see what she'd been reduced to, and resentment gave her tongue unladylike sharpness.

"And there," Emory said, "we have a pathetic gesture in the direction of the feeble wit that has apparently inspired you to make a living with your pen." He tipped his hat to a dowager mincing along on the arm of a young man. "You should have an escort because a lady does not travel the streets alone."

"And who made up that rule?" Edith mused. "Instead of limiting a woman's movements to those times when some hulking bullyboy is available to escort her, why don't gentlemen of goodwill simply cosh the heads of the parasites who presume to assault the gentler sex in broad daylight? Fellows styling themselves as gentlemen could have a jolly time bloodying noses and wielding their fists while the ladies accomplished their errands in peace. But no, of course not. Englishmen could not be half so sensible. The ne'er-do-wells wander freely, while the ladies are shackled to the company of dandiprats and bores, all in the name of keeping the ladies from harm."

Emory remained at her side right up to the corner. "What the *hell* is wrong with you?" He spoke quietly, and if Emory had one virtue—even his mother allowed that he had at least five—it was that he rarely used foul language in the hearing of any female.

Traffic refused to oblige Edith's need to cross the street. "What the *hell* is wrong with me?" Cursing felt fiendishly good. "I was nearly knocked on my backside by male arrogance bearing the proportions of a mastodon. That same mastodon has insulted my only warm cloak, and he has made me a public spectacle while accusing me of behaviors that he apparently disapproves of. You clearly need a change of air, Emory. I intend to turn north here, I suggest you strut off to the south."

She made a shooing motion.

He caught her hand and put it on his arm. "Literary notoriety has gone to your head. Her Grace would despair to hear you spouting such ungenteel sentiments. Perhaps you are the one in need of a change of air, my lady."

Traffic cleared and as the crossing sweepers darted out to collect horse droppings, His Grace accompanied Edith to the next walkway.

"What I need, sir, is a decent meal, peace and quiet, and to be rid of you."

"You do look peaked. All that flying about on broomsticks must be exhausting, but then, ruining dukes probably takes a toll on a lady's energy too. Perhaps your conscience keeps you awake at night?"

He sauntered along, tossing out insults like bread crumbs for crows, while the crowds parted for him as if he were royalty. He was merely 42nd in line for the throne and the last person Edith wanted to spend time with.

"Are you ruined?" Edith asked, untwining her hand from his arm. "You look to be in obnoxiously good health to me."

Both Lord Jeremiah and His Grace of Emory were attractive men, viewed objectively. Lord Jeremiah was the classically handsome brother, with wavy brown hair styled just so, a mouth made for drawling *bon mots*, and a physique that showed the benefit of regular athletic activity. His demeanor was congenial, his manner relaxed and gracious when in polite surrounds.

He could be an idiot, but he looked like a lord ought to look.

Without Lord Jeremiah as a contrast, Emory would have passed for handsome as well. Next to his younger sibling, though, the duke was two inches too tall for the dance floor, his hair a shade too dark and unruly for proper fashion. Those shortcomings might have been overlooked, but he was without his brother's charm.

And polite society valued charm exceedingly.

Edith had respected Emory when she'd been in his mother's employ. The duke paid well and punctually, and he did not bother the help. She'd learned to appreciate those traits. She could not, however, recall any occasion when Emory had relented from his infernal dignity, which made the book written about him hard to credit.

"Where are we going?" Emory asked after they'd crossed another intersection.

"You may go straight to perdition." Edith had another three streets to travel before she'd be home. The thought of some bread and butter with a cup of tea loomed like a mirage on the horizon of a vast desert.

"I find it odd that your pen has sent me to social perdition, and yet you offer me nothing but insults."

He wasn't making any sense, or perhaps hunger was making Edith light-headed. "Did you apologize for nearly running me down? For insulting my cloak? For attaching yourself to me without my permission? For accusing me of hatching some scheme to add to your enormous heap of imaginary miseries? For insulting my appearance?"

That last had hurt. Edith had never been pretty, but she'd troubled over her complexion and taken care to always be tidy. If she was looking peaked, that was another step down from the serene pinnacle of feminine grace an earl's daughter should have inhabited.

"Well, you are peaked," Emory observed. "You look like you've lost flesh since leaving my employment."

"Your mother's employment." All of Edith's dresses were looser, as were her boots.

"Are we in a footrace, my lady? I am compelled to say this is not the sort of neighborhood I'd expect you to frequent."

The neighborhood was respectable. Five streets on, it would become shabby. "Nothing compels you to say any such thing, Your Grace. You toss that barb at me out of a mean-spiritedness I do not deserve and would not have attributed to you previously. I know I left your mother's employ—"

"My employ."

"—without much notice, but I had my reasons. If you would please take yourself off, I would be much obliged."

She marched on with as much speed as dignity allowed, though Emory remained at her side. Perhaps that was providential—she was overdue for some kindness from providence—because before she'd gone six steps, her vision wavered, her boot caught on an up-thrust brick, and she was again pitched hard against the duke.

CHAPTER 2

"His Grace lacks the two essential qualities of a gentleman about Town—wit, and a tailor with an imagination."
From *How to Ruin a Duke* by Anonymous

For a woman who could spew three hundred pages of unrelenting calumny, Lady Edith felt like eiderdown in Thaddeus's arms. When he'd first collided with her outside the publisher's offices, she had nearly bounced off of him like one of those lap dogs that doubles its perceived dimensions with an abundance of hair and yapping.

She was too slight for the pink atrocity of a cloak she wore, and she did look pale and tired. Success as a satirist was apparently a taxing business.

"Is this a ploy?" he asked her, a hand under her pointy elbow. "Are you attempting to extort my sympathy by feigning weakness?"

Furious blue eyes glared up at him. "I am not weak, I am famished. I have not eaten since the day before yesterday. I wanted cab fare for my appointment with Mr. Ventnor in case it rained. A woman resembling a drowned rat hardly inspires confidence in a prospective employer."

Not a drowned rat, but a cornered cat. One who hadn't seen regular meals or a warm fireplace in some time. *How to Ruin a Duke* was rumored to be in its fifth printing. Lady Edith's appearance and the success of the book were facts in contradiction.

Thaddeus was constitutionally incapable of ignoring facts in contradiction.

"Perhaps a meal will improve your manners," he said, guiding her several doors down the street. The neighborhood was going seedy about the edges, but the inn looked respectable enough.

"I cannot be seen to sit down to a meal with you in public." The edge of ire had left her speech. She was reciting a rule rather than scolding him.

Her scolds had been impressive, considering she'd presumed to scold a duke who could ruin her.

"You march around London," he said, "like a supervisor of the watch. You neglect adequate nutrition. You insult a peer of the realm without batting an eye. You can share a trencher with me at an obscure establishment such as this. The pubs and inns always have the best food, and as it happens, I am hungry as well."

She closed her eyes, doubtless marshalling some sham of martyrdom.

"My objective was to seek you out today," Thaddeus went on. "I was surprised to find you at Ventnor's, because he is not your publisher. I thought perhaps he could send me in the right direction though. Instead I find my quarry landing almost literally at my feet. This has put me in a better humor."

She opened her eyes. "One shudders to think what your version of a poor humor is. I will eat with you, for two reasons. Firstly, because I need food. Secondly, because I suspect you will not leave me in peace until you've aired whatever daft notions have resulted in your pestering me with your presence."

Clever alliteration had been a signal characteristic of the prose in *How to Ruin a Duke*.

Thaddeus held the door for her. "I will leave you in peace—on this occasion—if you will share a meal with me."

She swept past him, as dignified as the queen mother, into the gloom of the common. Her pink cloak caused some stares, or perhaps Emory's height and attire were gaining the notice of the patrons. The working classes were notably shorter than the aristocracy, and Emory was tall even among his peers.

Lady Edith was tall as well, something he'd liked about her. She wasn't a wilting, vapid, fading little creature who could barely waft through a Beethoven slow movement before drifting to the garden for a nap in a hammock. Mama had been in a much better mood during Lady Edith's tenure as a companion, and the entire ducal staff had been less prone to insurrections and feuds.

"You will have a steak," Thaddeus said, choosing a table well away from the window and from any other patrons. "Steak is the best thing for restoring vigor. You will need your vigor if I'm to ruin you."

She unpinned her bonnet, the millinery adorned with a tired collection of feathers and silk flowers.

"Will this be a literal ruination or figurative? Lord Jeremiah struck me as more the ruining kind. You, on the other hand,"—she perused him in a manner more frank than flattering—"you have the arrogance for true villainy, but your dignity wouldn't allow it. Shrieking virgins, swoons, dramatics, I don't think you have the patience for them."

A serving maid came over to the table, her apron tidy, her cap neat. Thaddeus ordered steak all around, a small pint for Lady Edith and summer ale for himself.

"You condescend to consume ale," Lady Edith said, unbuttoning her cloak. "I, on the other hand, would rather have had a good, restorative pot of China black. Don't worry. The ale will not go to waste, though my goodwill where you are concerned—which used to be substantial—has apparently been squandered."

She drew off her gloves, revealing pale, slender hands with an ink stain near her right wrist.

"I have puzzled over your motive," Thaddeus replied, removing his hat and setting it on the bench beside him. "You left our household of your own volition, and while Her Grace was not pleased with the short notice, she wrote you a decent character. You've apparently spent the entire intervening six months plotting revenge against us for some fictitious slight. I cannot fathom what that slight might be."

He tugged off his gloves, prepared to hear that an underbutler had started a false rumor regarding her ladyship's use of hair coloring —her hair was golden—or a maid had purposely scorched her ladyship's favorite cloak. Any justification was better than believing he himself might have given Lady Edith cause for offense.

"I do not want to ruin you," he said, when the serving maid had bustled off. "But I cannot ignore ongoing literary character assassination."

"Surely it is beneath the consequence of a duke to ruin a mere failed lady's companion."

Her ladyship was either not afraid to be ruined, or she did not take the threat seriously.

"I could do it. All it would take is mention in my club of a rumor or two. A hint, an aside, and you would never be received in polite society again." Thaddeus did not want that outcome on his conscience, but to whom did he owe greater allegiance? A former companion who'd apparently acquired the disposition of a dyspeptic hedgehog or his own family?

How could he have been so wrong about her?

Lady Edith gave the humble inn a slow perusal, then she swiveled her gaze back to Thaddeus. "My father died up to his ears in debt from his gaming and wagering. My step-mother followed him within months. I attribute his demise to an excessive fondness for spirits, while the countess passed away due to a surfeit of mortification.

"Polite society did nothing to aid us," she went on. "Our worldly goods were sold before Papa was cold in the ground, my step-brother's dog led off by a neighbor while the boy cried his heart out all the way down the drive. We were passed from one relative to another, until the last of the aunts died. I pray for her eternal rest every night, because she at least wrote to your mother on my behalf before expiring."

The pink cloak and the worn feathers took on a new significance. "So you hate all who are well to do?" Though again, facts in contradiction caught Thaddeus's notice. A lady fallen on hard times should not have left her post on a whim.

"I loathe hypocrisy, Your Grace, and a society that pretends to be polite while laughing behind their painted fans at anybody who suffers misfortune, a society that blames children for their parents' bad judgment, deserves not only contempt but divine judgment."

The serving maid reappeared with a pint and a small pint on a tray along with half a loaf of sliced bread and a plate of butter pats.

"A pot of China black," Emory said, "with all the trimmings."

The maid put the offerings on the table, bobbed a curtsey, and moved away.

"They'll serve adulterated tea," he said, letting the foam on his ale settle.

"No, they won't. The publican's wife will not allow weak tea to be brought to your table."

"What makes you say that?" The ale was quite good. The bread smelled fresh from the oven.

Lady Edith put a table napkin on her lap and bowed her head. "For what I am about to receive, I am most sincerely grateful. Would that all going without such fare soon have reason to pray similarly. I would also appreciate it if the Architect of All Worldly Affairs could see fit to serve His Grace the truth regarding that awful book. Amen."

Would a woman who gave thanks for bread and butter find it morally acceptable to wreck another's social standing, and then mislead her victim while she said grace?

She took up her knife and spread a liberal portion of butter on a slice of bread. "With regard to the tea, you need have no fear of being cheated. Your boots cost more than most of these people would see in a year. Your sartorial splendor would blind the angels. Your height proclaims your blue blood, and you would send watered down tea back to the kitchen, making more work for any who sought to cheat you."

She was right, also fond of butter, apparently.

Her ladyship took a delicate nibble of her bread. "You won't ruin me, because I don't deserve ruin, though it stares me in the face without your good offices to help it along. I gather you think I wrote *How to Ruin a Duke*."

Her expression as she consumed a humble slice of buttered bread was enraptured. No expensive courtesan had ever gazed upon Thaddeus with that blend of soft focus, quiet joy, and profound appreciation. Thaddeus left off swilling his ale, fascinated by the transformation. Lady Edith, he realized, was not a plain woman, but a woman who'd learned to *appear* plain.

Severe bun, no cosmetics, no jewelry, clothing far from fashionable, nothing flirtatious or engaging about her. She set out to be overlooked, or perhaps that succession of begrudging relatives simply hadn't included anybody who might have shown a young girl how to present herself.

None of which must sway him from his course. "I know you wrote that dratted book. Nobody else could have."

She hadn't set down her bread since taking the first bite, but she did pause in her consumption of it.

"Do you think, if I'd written such a wildly popular novel, I'd be subjecting myself to a meal in the company of a titled buffoon who cannot be bothered to consider facts?"

"I always consider facts."

The food arrived, smelling divine and requiring a hiatus in the skirmishing. Thaddeus's objective mattered to him—he would secure her ladyship's promise to stop publishing satire aimed at him or his family—but good English beef was not to be ignored.

Lady Edith ate sparingly of the meat, and only half of her potato. She added both milk and sugar to her tea and drank two cups in quick succession. When she'd poured her third cup of tea, she sat back. Her cheeks had acquired a bit of color and the battle light was back in her eye.

"We should order a sweet," Thaddeus said, which was inane of him, but he did not care to resume hostilities quite so soon. Lady Edith had suggested a contradiction—literary revenue and straightened circumstances—and she had a point.

Maybe.

"I have eaten all I can manage for now," she replied. "The belly loses the habit of digesting substantial meals."

Two slices of bread, half a potato and a few bites of beef was not a substantial meal. "Then I will order a sweet, because I am an arrogant, ungentlemanly buffoon with the appetite of a mastodon."

"Suit yourself." She gestured with her teaspoon. *As you always do.*

Splendid. She could now insult him without even speaking.

"If you didn't write the blasted, blighted book, who did?" And since when was alliteration contagious?

"Let's see...." She peered into the teapot. "Your butler knows every secret associated with your entire family back for at least five generations and he's nearing retirement. Your mother is at the end of her patience with both of her sons for different reasons, and she's quite well read. Maybe she thought to shame you into holy matrimony. Your cousin Antigone is angry with you because you would not approve her match to that fortune-hunting rake, Sir Prancing Ninny."

Sir Prendergast Nanceforth. "I'd forgotten about that."

"Last year, you were rumored to be considering a marquess's daughter for your duchess, but decided not to offer for her when she turned out to have a fondness for wagering. She might not be your greatest admirer."

"One wagering fool in the family is one too many." Thaddeus had forgotten about the marquess's daughter too.

"You don't want to ruin me. Now you can ruin her instead."

"I don't have time to ruin you for any but the most pressing reasons," Thaddeus said, motioning to the serving maid. He ordered lemon cake with orange glaze and fresh raspberries—two servings.

Lady Edith poured herself the last of the tea, though it had to be cold by now. "I told you I haven't room for any more food."

"Fear not," Thaddeus replied, starting on the lady's pint. "Nothing goes to waste when a mastodon sits down to dine. I not only don't have time to ruin you for my own pleasure, the undertaking would be inefficient."

More milk and sugar went into her ladyship's teacup. "The horror of an inefficient duke boggles and bewilders the imagination."

"The book has been selling for the past month," Thaddeus went on. "The damage has been done. If I were to ruin you now simply for having written the dratted thing, that would be an act of revenge, and revenge on a woman for a jest in poor taste would not reflect well on me." Especially not revenge that sat about for a month re-reading the damned book and pondering options.

"So the ducal arrogance will spare me from ruination. My relief beggars description, especially considering I *did not write that wretched book*. I could not have written it."

The maid brought the dessert to the table, handsome portions liberally topped with fresh fruit and preserves. She set down one bowl before her ladyship, the other before Thaddeus.

"Try a bite," he said. "I'll eat what you don't finish." He expected a lecture about ignoring her wishes and wants.

Instead, the lady picked up her fork and speared a fat red raspberry.

"Why should I eliminate you as a potential author of the book?" he asked.

She put the single berry into her mouth. "I miss fresh fruit. I miss it more than strong tea." She ducked her head and speared another berry.

Her admission was troubling. Irksome. A distraction, possibly. "Why could you not have written *How to Ruin a Duke*? You've a lady's education, you observed my family at close quarters for two years, and likely heard all sorts of tales from the staff. My mother and Lord Jeremiah have also been known to spin the occasional entertaining bit of family lore. Am I to believe ladylike sensibilities alone stopped you from airing my linen in exchange for a small fortune?"

She took a bite of cake this time, dabbing it in the preserves. "Of course not. If I'd been ingenious enough to write such a tale, we'd be having a very different conversation in a very different venue, but I wasn't. To make public what should remain private is an act of desperation and the thought of debtor's prison should make the stoutest soul tremble. I wish I had written that book. If you were foolish enough to race from London to Brighton under a quarter moon, then the world deserves to be entertained by your foolishness."

Nobody had ever referred to Thaddeus as foolish before. He did not care for the term, and yet, that race had been stupid beyond all description, despite the fact that he'd won by a five-minute margin.

And Lady Edith was also correct that debtor's prison was worse than a death sentence. While the debtor slowly rotted from the inevitable ravages of consumption, he or she was charged exorbitant sums for basic necessities. Between disease and despair, a sad end was inevitable.

"You admit to being sufficiently desperate to go after the lure of dangled wealth," Thaddeus said, ignoring his dessert. "So why shouldn't I attribute authorship of that vile book to you?"

"Because," she said. "I have no patience with dangling modifiers, and what ruin isn't visited upon the fictitious Duke of Amorous is inflicted by the author on the English language. If I set out to ruin you, Your Grace, I'd at least do it in the king's proper English."

Verbally brawling with Emory enlightened Edith on one point: She finally understood why young men delighted in pounding each other to flinders in the name of pugilistic science. All of her worry, all of her ire at a fate she and Foster had done nothing to earn, found a target in the person of the duke who was ignoring his sweet while he argued with a lady.

Maybe this was why gentlemen were prohibited from engaging in disputes with women—because the ladies could too easily learn to enjoy winning those arguments. Where would masculine self-regard be then?

"I have silenced you," Edith said, savoring another fat, tart raspberry slathered in sweetened juices. "Have a care when you step out of doors, Your Grace."

"You fear for my welfare. I am touched, Lady Edith. Moved in the tenderest profundities of my heart. What occasions your concern, when my social disrepute does not?"

"Low-flying swine. If ever an omen augured for their appearance, your silence does. You should not waste your sweet."

He moved the bowl of lemon cake closer and made no move to pick up his fork. "You make a jest of me and then scold me, but your point fails to prove that you didn't write *How to Ruin a Duke*. A skilled writer can affect any number of less-skilled mannerisms in her prose."

"I liked you better when you held your tongue. These raspberries are delectable, and one shouldn't spoil good food with harsh words."

The duke gazed across the common, apparently at nothing in particular. An older couple sat at a table by the window sharing a meal in silence while they each read from a newspaper. A trio of young men did justice to a pitcher of ale closer to the door. Two maids were wiping down empty tables, and a boy with a tray collected dirty dishes.

A scene like this would have fascinated a younger Edith for its plebian details. Nobody here carried a parasol, despite the brilliant sunshine outside. Nobody wore silk or lace at this establishment, but for the lace adorning His Grace's cravat.

"Your conclusion," Edith said, "that an author of some skill penned the book, eliminates your cousin Antigone as a suspect. She can barely write her name."

His Grace buttered one of the four remaining slices of bread. "Her gifts lie more in the direction of social discourse and water colors."

Gallant of him, to defend a chatterbox who'd never had a governess worthy of the name. "Antigone knows everybody and is liked by all. She might have collaborated with a co-author."

The duke made two bread and butter sandwiches, using up every last dab of butter. "Now you toy with me. If we bring co-authors and collaborators into the equation, half of Mayfair might have written that infernal tome."

A pot of strong tea and some real victuals had taken the edge off of Edith's foul mood, enough that she could make a dispassionate inspection of the man across the table.

Emory carried a vague air of annoyance with him everywhere, a counterpoint to his luscious scent and fine tailoring. He doubtless had reason to be testy. His mama was a restless and discontented woman by nature, given to meddling and gossip. His younger brother was the typical spare waiting to be deposed by a nephew.

Lord Jeremiah was a fribbling *bon vivant* for whom Edith had no respect, though she'd liked him well enough on first impression. His lordship had the gift of making anybody feel as if they were the sole focus of his attention and always would be. Perhaps fribbles developed that skill early.

His Grace's extended family called upon him mostly when they wanted something—a post for a young fellow completing the university education Emory had paid for, entrée at some fancy dress ball to which Emory would be invited as a matter of course.

Never had Edith seen or heard the duke complain regarding his duties. He groused at length about the king's financial irresponsibility, he lamented without limit the idiocy that passed for Parliament's governance, and he had pointed opinions about women who wore enormous hats.

But on his own behalf, he never complained, and he wasn't complaining for himself now. *How to Ruin a Duke* was affecting his family, and Emory took their welfare very seriously indeed.

"A co-author bears thinking about," Edith said. "Your mother's circle includes the set at Almack's, and they've all but banished Lady Caroline for her literary accomplishments. If Her Grace wrote *How to Ruin a Duke*, she could hide behind the skirts of a collaborator or hack writer."

His Grace next began slicing up the uneaten portion of Edith's steak. Perhaps he was one of those people who had to keep his hands busy, though in two years of sharing meals with him, she'd never noticed that about him.

"Lady Caroline had worn her welcome thin in polite society long before she took up her pen," Emory observed, "and for the viciousness of her satire, she deserved banishment. At least whoever decided to lampoon me left the rest of my friends and family unscathed."

"Which again suggests your mother, a cousin, or a rejected marital prospect. The author's ire is personal to you, Your Grace."

He finished slicing the meat and set down the utensils. "Sir Prendergast made a scene at Tattersalls." This recollection inspired Emory to a slight smile, more a change of the light in his eyes than a curving of his lips. The only time Edith had seen him truly joyous was on the occasion of becoming godfather to some new member of the extended family. No man had ever looked more pleased to have his nose seized in a tiny fist. No baby had ever been more carefully cradled in his godfather's arms.

The ceremony had gone forth, with the duke caught variously by the nose, the chin, or the gloved finger, and Edith feeling oddly enchanted by the sight.

"Perhaps Sir Prendergast is your culprit."

"He found another fortune to marry. Once his bruises healed, I made it a point to introduce him to a few cits who wouldn't mind seeing their daughter on the arm of a gallant knight."

Edith's lemon cake was half gone. She stopped eating, lest she regret over-indulging. "Generous of you."

"Prudent. He dwells in the north now."

"Which does not rule him out as your nemesis."

His Grace raised a hand and the serving maid scampered over. "If you'd be so good as to wrap up the rest of this food, I'd appreciate it."

A common request, but the maid looked as if she'd never been given a greater compliment. "Of course, sir. At once."

"All of it," he said. "Every morsel, and some plum tarts and cheese wouldn't go amiss either. You know how hunger can strike two hours after a decent repast, and good food shouldn't go to waste when a man of my robust proportions is on hand to enjoy it."

"Quite so, sir. Exactly. Waste not, want not. Ma says the same thing at least seventeen times a day. Eighteen, possibly."

The maid gathered up the plates while Edith tried not to watch. This was the best meal she'd eaten in ages, and Emory wasn't having the leftovers boxed up for himself.

"Thank you," she said, when the maid had bustled off to the kitchen.

His Grace looked at Edith directly, something she could not recall happening previously. Emory stalked through life, intent on pressing business. At the ducal residence he'd often been trailed by a secretary, solicitor, footman, steward or butler, all of whom followed him about as he'd lobbed orders in every direction.

At table, Emory tended to focus on the food, the wine, the appointments in the room.

On the dance floor, he was so much taller than most of his partners, he usually stared past their shoulders.

The full brunt of his gaze was unnerving. His eyes were brown, the deep, soft shade of mink in summer. They gave his countenance gravity, and Edith well knew those eyes could narrow on the deserving in preparation for a scathing setdown.

His gaze could also, apparently, be kind.

"Hunger makes me irritable," he said. "I cannot think as clearly, I cannot moderate my words as effectively, and we mastodons require substantial fare on a regular basis. If you've finished, I'll walk you home."

That was as close to an apology as a duke was likely to come, but Edith did not want him to walk her home. Foster might be there, and that would occasion questions such as only a nosy younger sibling could ask. He left the house each day "to look for work," but no work ever found him, and matters were becoming dire.

"That courtesy is not necessary, Your Grace. I appreciate the meal. Have you exonerated me of literary crimes against your person?" Edith never had borne him ill will—just the opposite—and no sane woman wanted a duke taking aim at her.

"If you were clever—and you are—you would toss out other candidates to throw me off the scent."

He stood and offered Edith his hand, still bare because they hadn't yet put their gloves back on. "What would my fate be, if I admitted to authorship of *How to Ruin a Duke?*"

"I'd offer you a substantial sum to return to your needlepoint and gothic novels. We would sign an agreement giving me all right, title, and interest in any further literary works written by you or based on your recollections of my household, and society could move on to its next scandal."

His idea of a substantial sum would doubtless be enough to see Foster commissioned as an officer, but then what? A lady—a woman raised to privilege—had few means of earning any coin at all, and Edith regarded writing as her best option for remaining a lady in any sense.

She took his hand and rose. "I cannot accept that offer, Your Grace. As it happens, I was calling on Mr. Ventnor precisely because I hope to become established as an authority on domestic matters in homes with some means. Signing away my ability to earn a living would not be prudent."

The duke left a pile of coins on the table—a generous sum—and collected a sack from the beaming serving maid.

"You are a shrewd negotiator," he said as he held the door for Edith. "Perhaps you called upon Ventnor because you seek more lucrative terms upon which to write a sequel to the first volume."

"A sequel?" Edith blinked at the bright sunshine and still—still—she had the impulse to open a parasol out of habit. "Somebody is at work on a sequel?"

"You needn't sound so pleased. Why haven't you a parasol?"

The meal had fortified Edith, put her back on her mettle. "I pawned all of my parasols months ago."

"And your good cloak as well, apparently, and yet you disdain to take my coin." The insult to her cloak was half-hearted, and His Grace's pace down the walkway more leisurely.

"Honesty rather than pride prevents me from taking your money, sir. I did not write *How to Ruin a Duke*. You could buy the rights to ten books from me, and I'd still not be able to prevent that sequel from being published."

His Grace fell silent, which was a mercy. The day was too beautiful and the meal had been too lovely to resume bickering. Edith made no further attempts to send Emory on his way, because the truth was, she liked having him at her side.

Even on this pretty day in this mostly decent neighborhood, Emory's escort made her feel safer and a little bit more the respected lady she'd been raised to be.

"Never was a correspondent more conscientious than you, Mama." Jeremiah kissed the duchess's cheek, which affection she pretended to ignore, though he knew she enjoyed the little touches.

The woman should remarry. She had taken good care of her appearance and enjoyed a lavish dower portion, though what mature man of sense would willingly take on a widowed duchess prone to managing and carping?

"A lady does not neglect her letters," the duchess replied, dipping her pen into the ink. "You would do well to stay in touch with some of your university friends, my boy. Life is long and the associations we form in our youth can be some of the dearest we ever know."

What associations had Mama formed in her youth? She longed to become one of the patronesses at Almack's, but Emory had scotched such a notion the few times it had come up. Emory had a positive genius for finding the flaws in other people's plans, though in his defense, becoming further entangled with the pit of vipers at the assembly rooms would have made Mama miserable.

And when Mama was miserable, both of her sons were miserable.

Jeremiah flipped out his tails and took the chair opposite Mama's escritoire. "Most of the fellows I went to university with are either married or have bought their colors. The ranks here in London are thinner by the year."

She put down her pen and sat back. "And does marriage or an officer's uniform turn a man illiterate? Particularly when a fellow is posted far from home, society news can bring great comfort. This business with that nasty book, for example, is just the sort of incident most of your set would find hilarious be they in London, Lower Canada, or India."

Jeremiah found it hilarious, though the book was refusing to die. Five printings already, and Emory looking delectably frustrated for a change.

"His Grace is trying to find the author," Jeremiah said. "I can't tell if he means to sue the fellow or pay him off."

Mama capped her ink and sanded the letter, her movements unhurried and graceful. "What makes you so sure the author is a man?"

"Because the incidents recounted are true, and they mostly happened in male company."

She wrinkled her nose, not as splendid a proboscis as Emory

boasted, but a nose that could charitably be called aristocratic. "Even that bit about the gin? I cannot imagine my firstborn consuming gin, much less wagering on such a feat."

"It's true, all of it," Jeremiah said, "though the author omitted some extenuating circumstances. I don't believe Emory has touched a drop of gin since."

"Then a suit for defamation cannot be brought." Mama seemed relieved about that.

Jeremiah was relieved as well, because litigation could only pour fuel on the flames of gossip. Poking fun at a titled man who enjoyed a reputation for unrelenting seriousness was one thing, miring a family in scandal was quite another.

"Emory is not one to change his mind once he's come to a decision," Jeremiah said. "Why do you say he won't sue?"

"Because truth is a defense to any claim of defamation, young man. To tell lies about a person is to slander him, to share the truth is entertaining. Publishers know that, and while they might push the boundaries of decency, they avoid lawyers at all costs. I see you are dressed for riding. Are you accompanying me to the park today?"

He'd come to beg off actually. A few hands of cards or a visit to Madam Bellassai's establishment always made for a pleasant afternoon.

"Emory pled the press of business. He did not inquire as to whether my own business might also obligate me elsewhere."

"On such a lovely day? Jeremiah, what business could you possibly have to attend to?" Mama smiled at him as if he'd made a jest. "Your cousin Antigone has accepted an invitation to ride with me, and she's bringing that lovely Miss Faraday."

Mama was nothing, if not relentless. "Miss Faraday and I would not suit."

"She's rich, agreeable, pretty, and pragmatic, Jeremiah. You'd suit."

"How will she like a remove to India, Mama? I'm told the heat alone can kill a woman of delicate constitution. They have snakes there longer than the train of the monarch's coronation cloak, and diseases that can debilitate a woman for the rest of her days if they don't steal her life outright."

Mama patted his arm. "Such a flair for drama you have. Until Emory has his heir and spare, you won't be posting to anywhere half so exciting as India, even assuming His Grace does buy you a commission, which we both know he's refused to do."

"He has other heirs," Jeremiah said, not for the first time. "Cousin Eldridge and Cousin Harry."

"They are eight and eleven years old respectively, and a pair of reckless little scamps." Mama poured the sand from her letter into the dust bin beside the escritoire. "Until I can find a match for Emory, he will not be swayed. Trust me on that. Perhaps you might use the time with Miss Faraday to extol your brother's virtues if you can't see fit to impress her with your own."

Emory underestimated Mama, and Jeremiah had the sense she preferred it that way. She had a gift for strategy, and Jeremiah had six married female cousins to show for it.

"I'm to sing Emory's praises? That will be a short chorus, Mama. I love him without limit, but from the perspective of a lady, he's not exactly brilliant company."

Mama folded her letter and dripped claret-colored wax onto the flap. A rosy fragrance filled the air, the sealing wax being scented with her signature perfume.

"Emory is a duke, he need not be charming." She pressed a signet ring into the hot wax and set the letter on a stack of four others. "I suspect he envies you your social skills. You could give him a few pointers."

"One has tried, Mama. As you say, he's a duke. I will sing his praises up one carriageway and down another, but the poor fellow is as dull as last year's bonnet trimmings when in the company of females." And that, very likely, was precisely as Emory intended.

Mama rose on a rustle of velvet. "So it's only in the company of you fellows that he ever cuts loose. A mother does wonder. I don't begrudge either of my boys the occasional lark, but if half of what's in the dratted book is true, then there's a side to Emory I would never have guessed at. I'll meet you out front in twenty minutes."

She patted Jeremiah's cheek and glided away.

He waited until she'd quit the room before he rifled her outgoing correspondence. Every letter was to a male relative or acquaintance of longstanding—three of Jeremiah's uncles, a cousin of Mama's, the bereaved spouse of one of Mama's late friends. Each letter was a single sheet and folded such that no writing was visible on the outside.

Her Grace was up to something. Had Jeremiah more time, he would have broken the seal on one of the letters, read the contents, then resealed the epistle using his own ring. He loved his mother dearly, but he knew better than to trust her.

Time to share a meal tête-à-tête with an uncle or two. Jeremiah replaced the letters in the same order Mama had organized them and went down to the front door to await his penance. He used the time to ponder what he could say to Miss Faraday about his brother that would be honest and cast the duke in a positive light.

"Emory takes the welfare of family seriously," Jeremiah murmured, tapping his top hat onto his head. "He takes everything seriously, including silly little books intended only to entertain and poke fun."

But then, when a book went into five printings, perhaps the book, and its author, should be taken seriously.

CHAPTER 3

"The only good duke is a married duke, and even that kind is prone to wandering."
From *How to Ruin a Duke* by Anonymous

Thaddeus strolled along at Lady Edith's side, while he mentally wrestled with facts in contradiction.

She had quit a lucrative post of her own volition and had done so without first securing another position. Why behave so rashly? Why, with a character from Her Grace of Emory in hand, hadn't Lady Edith found another post of comparable status?

Why reside in this frankly shabby neighborhood if she was the author of the most popular novel since *Waverly*? On the stoops and porches, Thaddeus saw only an occasional pot of struggling heartsease, most of which looked as if a cat had slept curled atop the flowers and weeds. A single crossing sweeper shuffled along the street, doing a desultory job of collecting horse droppings, and a small grubby boy sat cross-legged beneath a street lamp.

Why hadn't Lady Edith applied for support to the present holder of her late father's title? Every man who came into a lofty station did so knowing that dependents and responsibilities went hand-in-glove with his privileges.

Why should Lady Edith have to *ask* for support from the head of her own family?

"Who holds your father's earldom now?" Thaddeus asked as Lady Edith stopped at a side lane.

"A second cousin," she said. "We'd never met prior to Papa's death. You want to know why I'm not kept in a rural hovel like any other poor relation. The answer to that is none of your concern but simple enough: Papa left his heir an enormous pile of debt, a barely habitable country estate, and the bad will of all our neighbors. His lordship had nothing to offer me but the post of housekeeper without pay, and for my brother, perhaps a similarly uncompensated post as undergardener. Working for your mother, I was able to at least save back most of my wages."

"You have a brother?" Had she kept that a secret? Thaddeus took an interest in his employees and should have known this about his mother's companion.

"I do, and I live on this lane, so we've reached our destination."

Lady Edith wasn't looking anywhere in particular. Not at any one of the humble doorways on the narrow lane, not at Thaddeus's face, and certainly not at the sack of food he held in his left hand.

"I'll walk you to your door. Where is your brother now?"

"This isn't necessary, Your Grace. I know how to find my own dwelling."

"What you do not know is how to set aside your pride. If I wanted to find out where you live, I'd simply ask the crossing sweeper and then verify his information with that filthy boy trying to look idle and harmless beneath the street lamp while he doubtless dreams of ill-gotten coin. Tell me more about your brother."

Thaddeus refrained from adding, *I might have work for him.* In the first place, a brother who allowed his sister to come to such a pass as this might be unemployable, and in the second, facts not in contradiction still weighed against Lady Edith's protestations of innocence.

She knew the ducal family's dirty linen. She used language effectively. She grasped how polite society loved to gossip. She desperately needed funds. Very few people fit all of those descriptors. An army of servants might also know family lore, but those servants were either illiterate or not literary. Half of polite society had a gift for tattle, but not a one of them would willingly engage in labor for coin.

Lady Edith led Thaddeus to the fourth door on the left side of the lane. The street ended in a cul-de-sac, with a crumbling, lichen-encrusted fountain in the center of the circle. Once upon a time, this would have been a quaint, tidy address, a place prosperous shop-keepers moved to when their children grew old enough to take over the family business.

Now, these houses were teetering on the edge of neglect. A few had boarded up windows, a sure sign somebody was trying to reduce taxes at the cost of their eyesight. Brick walkways had heaved and buckled under decades of English weather, and a large brindle dog of indeterminant pedigree napped on the sunny side of the decrepit fountain.

"You are not to feed this steak to that wretched canine," Thaddeus said, passing over the sack. "This food is not charity, but rather, a token of appreciation for your insights regarding the mystery before me. I would never have thought to consider Antigone or Mama, or a co-author. You were about to tell me of your brother."

"I was about to wish you good day, and good luck finding the author of your misfortune. My thanks for the food." She tried to hold the sack and open her reticule at the same time.

"Is this brother a wastrel like your father was?"

"No, he is not. Foster is a wastrel of a completely different stripe. He does not drink to excess, he's not prone to wagers, but he had only a gentleman's education." She produced a key, which only made balancing the reticule and the sack of food more complicated.

"Allow me," Thaddeus said, taking both items and leaving her with the key. "If you set that food down, yonder hound will abscond with the lot."

"Galahad is fast asleep."

"Galahad is doubtless fast as a bolting rabbit when it comes to snatching a meal."

The lock squeaked and with some effort, Lady Edith pushed the door open. "I'll take those," she said, holding out her hands.

"This reticule weighs more than some cannonballs. Whatever do you have in here?" Thaddeus grasped the middle of the reticule, a quilted affair slightly worn at the bottom. "Is this a book?"

"*Glenarvon*," she said, "for weight, and to keep the papers I brought with me from being crushed or wrinkled."

"You have a bound copy of *Glenarvon?*" Another fact that weighed against her innocence.

"Half of London has a copy of Lady Caroline's tale and this was a gift from a friend who enjoys a good yarn. My brother was considering turning it into a play at one point. I'll wish you good day, Your Grace." She stood in the doorway, her faded millinery and pink cloak adding a poignant note to the dignity of her bearing.

"Might I come in?"

"That would be most improper."

"No, it would not. I am your former employer, we are well acquainted, I won't tarry long, and if you prefer, we can remain before your front window for all the world to gawk at. That said, I would rather not conclude this conversation where all the world can also hear our every word." All the world being, at the moment, one somnolent dog.

"Then will you go away?"

"Do you know how rarely people tell me to go away?" They might wish him to the Shetland Islands, but they would never say that to his face.

"Not often enough, for you don't appear to grasp the meaning of the words." Lady Edith stepped back and held the door open.

Thaddeus's first impulse was to peer about at the interior, to sniff the air, to generally behave with ill-bred curiosity. Lady Edith would pitch him through the window if he offered her that insult, so he stood just inside the door, where—indeed—he was visible from the street through the window.

"Why would this brother of yours be turning *Glenarvon* into a stage play?"

"Because nobody has yet, and the book was wildly popular." She set her packages on a rickety table with a cracked marble top. "Foster considers himself an amateur thespian and has a gentleman's ability with letters. He abandoned the project because the work is quite long for a staged production. If that's all you needed to—"

"He fancies himself a writer?"

"He's eighteen years old, Your Grace. He fancies himself a writer one day, an explorer the next, a documenter of England's vanishing folklore the day after that."

"Be glad he's not keen to buy an officer's commission and ship out for the jungles of India." Mama had emphatically forbidden Thaddeus to approve that course for Jeremiah, though his lordship longed to buy his colors—or have them purchased for him.

"We cannot afford to buy Foster new boots, much less a commission. When I left my post with your mother, Foster was homeless. He held a job as tutor to a stationer's sons, but the boys accused him of teaching them naughty Latin verses. Foster was turned off without a character and not even given the wages he was owed."

Most boys were born knowing a few naughty Latin verses. Jeremiah had them memorized by the score. "How long ago was this?"

"Six months."

So why would she then also render herself unemployed? "Where is Foster now?"

Her chin came up. "Looking for work."

Perhaps he was, or perhaps he was slumped over a bottle outside the nearest gin shop. A man prone to inebriation could run up all sorts of debts in no time at all, and even an author enjoying lucrative earnings could soon see her wealth dwindle to nothing.

"Your Grace, I do not mean to be rude, but I have been more than patient with your accusations. I did not write that blasted book, and if your interrogation is at an end, then you really should be going."

He should. This was her abode, he was a guest, and he'd overstayed his welcome. He bowed. "Thank you for your time. Good day."

She held the door for him, and then he was back out in the afternoon sunshine, enduring what looked like a pitying gaze from the hound by the fountain.

"Facts in contradiction, dog. They vex me."

A thick tail thumped once, then the beast sighed and went back to napping. Thaddeus tarried in the neighborhood for a few moments, taking stock of Lady Edith's situation and considering possibilities.

For the three minutes he'd been in her house, he'd remained politely in her foyer, if the cramped space near her front door could be called that. A parlor had sat off to the left of the foyer, a worn loveseat, mismatched reading chair, and a desk the sum total of the furnishings therein. The carpet, a faded circle barely six feet across, might have been woven in the days of Good King Hal, and the andirons hadn't been blackened within living memory.

The desk though, had been tidy and ready for use. The blotter had boasted a stack of foolscap, a standish, a bottle of sand, and spare ink as well as a wooden pen tray. Perhaps Lady Edith did have literary aspirations...

Or perhaps her brother, the gentleman of letters without portfolio, had turned the recollections of a duchess's companion into a popular satire regarding her former employer. That theory fit the facts, or most of them, and wanted further study.

Once upon a time, Foster would have occupied the loveseat like a proper young gentleman, eager to slip any commonplace observation into a polite conversation. When he'd come into Edith's life as a shy four-year-old, she—who'd reached the age of fourteen without any siblings—had been enthralled with him. He had been so little, dear, and earnest.

Also lost. A small boy without a father was easily lost, which Papa, to his credit, had tried to rectify. His manner with Foster had been avuncular and affectionate, if somewhat offhand. Then Papa had died without making any provision for his fourteen-year-old step-son, and Foster's earnestness had faded into moodiness and impulsivity.

Now, he lounged on the loveseat, half-reclining, one leg slung over the armrest, morning sun revealing the adult he had become when Edith had been too busy humoring a cranky duchess.

"Breaking bread with a duke," he mused, one stockinged foot swinging. "Any chance of getting your old post back?"

"I would not accept my old post if Emory begged me on bended knee." Though the only time Emory would go down on one knee would be to propose to his duchess. He'd observe all the protocol—flowers, cordial notes, the carriage parade—which only made the tales told about him in *How to Ruin a Duke* more difficult to believe.

"You might have no choice but to apply for your old post," Foster said, "though I could come by some coin by the end of the week. Not a lot, but some, and it could turn into steady work."

His eyes were closed. He'd been out quite late, as was his habit, leaving Edith home alone and fretting.

"You won't tell me the nature of your employment?"

He smiled without opening his eyes. "Not yet. You'll be appalled. Tell me more about Emory's predicament."

Edith drove her needle through the toe of Foster's second pair of white stockings. Darning his stockings had become an almost daily chore, and yet, what sort of work would he find if he couldn't leave the house attired as a gentleman?

"You want to gloat at His Grace's misfortune. He isn't distressed for himself, Foster, he's distressed for his family."

"I'm distressed for my family. Those plum tarts were divine,

Edie. We shouldn't be depending on a duke's charity to keep us in plum tarts."

"I'll pawn my earbobs."

Foster scrubbed his hands over his face and sat up. "You shall not part with your mother's earbobs. You've accepted Emory's charity and that's bad enough."

"Not charity." His Grace had been quite firm on that point. "Appreciation for my insights. The duke prevented a fortune hunter from compromising Miss Antigone Banner and Miss Antigone did not appreciate her cousin's meddling. His Grace had forgotten that. I also pointed out that the duchess might be trying to inspire her son to take a bride, and now that I think on it, the duke also has several boy cousins at university who might consider publishing that book a lark."

"Where are my boots?"

Edith knotted off her thread. "Wherever you left them. I suspect within three yards of your bed." Foster's entire bedroom was barely three yards square.

"Did you mention those boy cousins to the duke?"

"I did not. Emory is loath to think ill of his family." That was not quite true. The duke was loath to admit his family's faults. Not quite the same thing.

"The whole book doesn't make sense to me," Foster said, rising. "You described Emory to me in detail on many occasions. His religious fervor for reform, his disdain for the frequently inebriated, his exasperation with Lord Jeremiah, and yet, the fellow in *How to Ruin a Duke* is a sot who makes foolish wagers and takes even more foolish risks."

An eighteen-year-old might be impulsive and broody, but loyalty to his gender had not yet afflicted him with the blinders he'd acquire later in adulthood.

"You put your finger on a troubling point." Edith snipped the thread right at the knot and rolled the stocking into a cylinder. "The Emory I know never sang other than to move his lips in church to a lot of dusty old hymns. The ruined duke accepted a bet to sing *God Save the King* at midnight outside Almack's."

Foster tugged at his shirt cuffs, which were an inch shorter than fashion required. "And he won the wager. Did Emory imply that the incidents recounted in the book never happened?"

Edith thought back over yesterday's conversation. She'd been so peevish at the time, so out of sorts and mortified, she'd mostly been intent on getting free of Emory's company.

"He never once claimed the book's narrative was untrue, now that you mention it." And the rest of Foster's point—that the ruined duke bore little resemblance to the duke Edith knew—was also puzzling.

Foster used the mantel to balance himself for a series of slow demi-pliés, such as a fencer might make prior to a match.

"You should take pity on a wealthy peer and help Emory solve his mystery, Edie. He'll bumble about like a drunken footman in a china closet, overlooking the obvious, offending the blameless, and getting nowhere."

A slow pirouette followed the pliés, the movement accenting Foster's height and the muscles he'd been developing in recent months. Such grace should have been on display at Almack's, not that Edith had ever applied for vouchers.

"I'm not offended that he'd question me," she said. "I am a logical suspect." Though so too was His Grace's friend and fellow duke, Wrexham, Duke of Elsmore. Elsmore's reputation was one of scrupulous integrity—his family was involved in banking—but then, Emory enjoyed the same reputation.

Or he had, prior to the book's publication. And who knew what constituted a jest among dukes?

"Who else might have written that book, Edie?"

She took up the second stocking and examined it for tears or holes. "Emory has countless opponents in the Lords, which means countless more MPs don't like his politics. His younger cousins at university would know all the family stories, as would any close companion to Lord Jeremiah. Emory went to public school and university with peers and heirs, and many of them might enjoy a joke at His Grace's expense."

Foster swung his leg like a bell-clapper, his bare foot brushing the floor. "Now you think the author is a man?"

"I don't know. All the incidents recounted are the sort of idiocy men get up to when unchaperoned by ladies. Are you training to be a dancer, Foster?" Male dancers were few and usually French.

"I am not, but I do enjoy watching dancers rehearse and perform. Emory should pay you to solve his mystery. Send him a note, tell him you've had a few more ideas. He'll be back on our doorstep like Galahad on the scent of a meat pie."

The last of the cheese and bread would be Edith's fare for the day, unless she walked to market and spent the coins she'd hoarded for coach fare the previous day.

"Mr. Ventnor wants me to send samples of my work." A silver lining, though delivering those samples meant another trek through the London crowds.

"Then send them, you must. Perhaps you could interest him in a sequel to *How to Ruin a Duke*. Surely you know tales regarding Lord Jeremiah or the duchess that the public would enjoy?"

The second stocking was still in good repair, and thank heavens for that, because Edith hadn't much thread left.

"What makes you think of a sequel?"

"*How to Ruin a Duke* is wildly popular, Edie. I wish you *had* written it. You've a way with a pen, you know the material, and polite society hasn't exactly treated you well. I'm just a common orphan, grateful for the charity your family has shown me, but you are a lady in more than name. You ought not to be hoarding cheese to have with your cold potatoes."

Rare temper colored Foster's words, though he switched from the swinging, loose sweeps of his leg to tracing a wide half-circle on the floor with his pointed toe.

For all his sleek muscle, he was skinny, now that Edith took the time to observe him in morning light. "Take the cheese and the last plum tart with you when you go out."

"I'll take some of the cheese, but you shall have the plum tart. You earned it by enduring Emory's company."

"The duke was unfailingly polite." Though unfailingly high-handed too. Edith didn't much mind the highhandedness when the result was good food in the house for the first time in ages. "Foster, you aren't up to anything untoward in your efforts to find employment, are you?"

He sauntered away from the mantel, pushing his hair from his eyes. "If I could find a situation as a cicisbeo, Edie, I'd take it, but English society hasn't the breadth of mind to tolerate such arrangements."

How bitter he sounded for a man of barely eighteen. "Don't compromise your honor for my sake, Foster."

He collected the stockings from her. "I won't if you won't, Edie. If that duke comes sniffing around again, he will mind his manners, I don't care how lofty his title is. Extract some coin from him to solve his mystery, but if he thinks to take advantage of your circumstances, I'll write a theatrical that makes *How to Ruin a Duke* look like a collection of dessert recipes. I'm peddling a script for a play, and so far, the reception has been very positive. Drury Lane promised me a decision by week's end."

"A play?"

"A farce. Something to make people laugh when life doesn't go their way. I'll be out late."

Again. "Best of luck with the play. I'm sure it's brilliant."

He bowed, then left the room with a dramatic flourish, waving the un-darned stocking for comic effect.

Foster had a way with a pen, he'd heard all of Edith's recollections of life in Emory's household, and Foster would know which pubs to frequent to chat up His Grace's footmen and grooms.

Oh, dear. Oh, drat and damnation. Edith put away her sewing, went to the desk, and took out pencil and paper.

"The book should have been a nine days' wonder," Thaddeus said. "A bit of tattle for those moments when Prinny refuses to oblige us with a scandal."

"Which moments are those?" Wrexham, Duke of Elsmore asked, lounging back in the club's well-padded dining chair. "Pass me the wine. It's quite good. I'm sure the author is thrilled to be enjoying weeks rather than days of notoriety."

Thaddeus set the Bordeaux near Elsmore's plate. The wine was good, though too fruity to be an an optimal complement to the *boeuf à la mode*. "That brings us back to the question: Who *is* the author?"

Elsmore topped up both glasses. "You won't let this rest."

"If you were the butt of an ongoing scandal, one that threatened to escalate, would you let it rest?"

"Of course not, but scandal that touches me touches my bank and my darling sisters. You have neither sisters nor a bank, so why not enjoy being perceived as something other than the Duke of Dullards?"

The schoolyard nickname had followed Emory ever since he'd taken successive firsts in Latin. "I have a brother and a mother, and the last thing Jeremiah needs is a reason to dismiss me as a good example. Half the incidents in the dratted book were situations he embroiled me in."

Elsmore held his wineglass up to the candles in the center of the table. "What does he say about possible authors?"

Thaddeus pushed the bowl before him aside. The fare was delicious, but what was Lady Edith dining on this evening?

"Jeremiah is vastly entertained by the whole situation. Maybe an impecunious friend plied him with spirits on occasion simply to hear his lordship expound on matters best kept private. From there to cobbling together a book takes only time and a well stocked desk."

Elsmore took Thaddeus's unfinished portion and poured it into his own bowl. "Lord Jeremiah seems to be friends with half of London. What are you doing with that bread, Emory?"

"I put butter on it."

"And then you made a butter sandwich with another slice. I can say honestly that in all the years I've known you, which are getting to be more than either of us should admit, I've never seen you make a butter sandwich at table."

"I don't know as I've ever made a butter sandwich before." Thaddeus had been thinking of Lady Edith having to choose between hackney fare and a proper meal. "I met with my mother's former companion yesterday. We shared a luncheon."

"Lady Edith?"

"The very one. She might be the author of the damned book." Thaddeus took a bite of his butter sandwich, because he could not very well stuff it into his pocket with Elsmore looking on, nor could he have it sent to her ladyship with compliments from His Grace of Dullards.

"Does her ladyship hate you?" Elsmore asked.

"I don't think so." Thaddeus hoped not, in fact.

"Then she doesn't."

"You're an authority on females now, Elsmore, and you such a legendary bachelor?"

"I am blessed with three sisters, a mama, plus aunties and female cousins without number. I am an authority on *disgruntled* females. Why do you believe Lady Edith wrote the book?"

"After my conversation with her, I'm fairly certain she couldn't have." Bread and butter was good food. Thaddeus had stuffed his maw with it countless times and never appreciated just how good.

"Because she doesn't hate you? You should consider courting her."

Elsmore had been at the wine enthusiastically, but he was a good-sized fellow whom Thaddeus had never seen drunk.

"Court her simply because she doesn't hate me? Town is full of women who don't hate me."

"You hope. Lady Edith could make your dear mama laugh, something I daresay you and Lord Jeremiah don't do often enough. Not a quality to be overlooked by a bachelor duke battling undeserved scandal."

Thaddeus took another bite of his butter sandwich. "Her ladyship carries a copy of *Glenarvon* in her reticule to use as a club." He liked knowing she'd taken that precaution, but he detested that she had to racket about London without so much as a footman to see to her safety.

"Best possible use for that tome. I suppose a lady's companion hears all the family tales belowstairs, doesn't she?"

"Lady Edith is also well read, and more to the point, she hasn't another post. She would need the money such a story should be earning, and if she's not trotting after some crotchety beldame, she'd have the time to do the writing."

Elsmore gestured with his fork. "Maybe she came into an inheritance. Women do."

"She ate as if famished, Elsmore, as we used to eat at public school, watching the food on our plates lest it disappear before we could consume it. I had the kitchen send the leftovers along with us when I walked her ladyship home. That food did not go to waste."

Elsmore set aside his now-empty bowl. "You carried leftovers across London like some ticket porter? That is a fact in contradiction to everything I know of you, my friend. If Lady Edith is truly short of funds, perhaps she'd accept an arrangement that benefits both parties."

Thaddeus's own thoughts had wandered in that direction, late of a solitudinous night. He did not castigate himself for noticing an attractive female, much less one who put him in his place as easily as she dropped a curtsey.

"Her ladyship would fillet me if I even hinted at such a proposition." Which made her refreshingly different from the widows and duchesses-in-waiting who all but sat in Thaddeus's lap to gain his attention. The odd thing was, Lady Edith, in her horrid pink cloak and tired bonnet was more interesting to him than any heiress or courtesan had ever been.

Her ladyship could talk about something other than the weather, fashion, or gossip. She had common sense and a tart tongue, and how had Thaddeus all but failed to notice her for the two years she'd been a member of his household?

But then, he knew how: She'd taken consistent, well thought out measures not to be noticed. A quiet manner, drab attire, unremarkable conversation. Just as she'd weighted her reticule with a hidden means of defense, so too had she avoided catching Thaddeus's eye.

"Not that sort of arrangement," Elsmore said, lowering his voice. "Lady Edith knows your family and your social circle, she would respect your confidences, and you've already explained the problem to her. Offer her something she values in exchange for her assistance tracking down the author of *How to Ruin a Duke*. You could doubtless find her another post, for example."

Thaddeus didn't want to find her another damned post, didn't want her once again consigned to the conundrum of being neither servant nor family, but having the burdens of both statuses.

"I doubt she liked being Mama's companion, but she does fancy herself as an author of domestic advice."

Elsmore finished his wine. "Offer to sponsor those aspirations. Have a word with a publisher on her behalf. You're a duke. The publishers have to be polite to you."

"Lady Edith wasn't polite to me." She'd twitted him, truth be told.

"Then you'd best pay a call on her before she accepts a post in Lesser Road Apple. She's making you smile and inspiring you to fashioning butter sandwiches. She also had you traipsing about London with a sack of comestibles like her personal footman."

"True enough." And—most telling of all—she and her situation had kept Thaddeus awake half the night. "You have a point, Elsmore. That doesn't happen often, so we should remark the rare occasion when it befalls us. You do have a point."

CHAPTER 4

"If the Duke of Amorous asks you to dance, you should smile, curtsey,
and run like the devil."
From *How to Ruin a Duke* by Anonymous

Rainy days were particularly vexing to Edith. Her half-boots did not
keep her feet dry, she had neither umbrella nor parasol, and yet, if she
wanted to procure something to eat, then go out, she must. Foster had
sallied forth to do whatever he did of an early afternoon, while Edith
had put off a trip to the nearest bake shop as long as she could.

"It's not a downpour," she muttered, donning her cloak. "More of
a drizzle. Barely qualifies as rain."

And yet, a London drizzle had a chilly, penetrating quality that
wilted bonnets and spirits alike. She decided against her bonnet and
instead took down the only other choice, a wide-brimmed straw hat
left over from when she'd spent an occasional morning in Her Grace
of Emory's flower garden.

Edith tied the ribbons firmly under her chin—the wind was
gusting most disagreeably—and gathered up her reticule.

"There and home in no time," she said, gloved hand on the door latch.

A stout triple knock had her leaping back. Did bill collectors knock like that? She wasn't behind on anything that she knew of, but Foster's finances were mysterious to her.

Edith cracked the door to find a very wet Duke of Emory standing on her front porch. "Your Grace. Good day."

"Might I come in? This deluge shows no signs of abating and I seem to have misplaced my ark."

Water dripped from his hat brim, and the fragrance of his shaving soap blended with the scent of damp wool and... fresh bread?

"I am home alone," Edith said, stepping aside. "You shouldn't stay long."

The temperature was dropping and the wind picking up. She really could not leave him on the stoop, nor did she want to let the house's meager heat out by standing about with the door open.

"I will stay only long enough to complete my business. I brought food." He held up a sack as Edith closed the door behind him. "You will accept the sustenance. I am hungry, I missed my nuncheon, and you would not be rude to a guest, would you?"

"Not until after we've eaten." Edith took his greatcoat from his shoulders. The garment had three capes and weighed more than her entire wardrobe combined. "I can't even offer you tea to go with the food, though."

"No matter. I brought hot tea as well."

Edith was torn between pleasure at the thought of another meal, dismay that Emory should again have evidence of her straitened circumstances, and—how lowering—pleasure at the simple sight of him. He was a connection to a better time, and as high-handed and imperious as he could be, he was also a gentleman.

He held doors for her.

He escorted her home when he'd no obligation to do so.

He'd thought to bring her food, and he'd arrived on foot—no

carriage, even in the rain, which meant no coachman, grooms, or footmen on hand to speculate about the purpose of the call.

"We can eat at my desk," Edith said. "I don't keep the fire in the kitchen lit, so the front parlor is the warmest room in the house."

His Grace did not peer around, wrinkle his nose, or otherwise indicate that a shabby little sitting room in any way offended his sensibilities. He passed Edith the sack of food, which weighed nearly as much as his coat had.

"I have another suggestion." He lifted the side table, carried it into the parlor, and set it down before the loveseat. "That should suffice."

Edith was too interested in the food to scold him for moving furniture without first asking permission. She withdrew a loaf of bread—still warm—and a crock of butter. A larger crock held beef stew seasoned with basil. The duke had also brought a wedge of cheese, tarts, what looked like a shepherd's pie, and—bless him—a flask of tea.

"The tea has sugar in it," he said. "I hope that will serve?"

"I'll find us some cups." Though all Edith had were mugs and they didn't match.

"No need for that. We'll share. Shall we sit?"

She took one side of the loveseat, he took the other, a cozy arrangement with a man of his proportions. The chop shop, bake shop, or pub where he'd procured this feast had sent along utensils and bowls, and in a few moments, Edith was consuming the best beef stew she'd ever tasted.

"Wherever did you find this? It's delicious."

"I have my sources. Try the tea." He uncorked the flask and passed it to her.

"I'm to drink from the flask?"

"That's the usual approach. Tally ho and all that." He tore a hunk of bread from the loaf, buttered it, and sopped it in his stew.

Edith tipped the flask to her lips, the hot, sweet tea a benediction on such a dreary day. She passed the duke the flask and felt slightly naughty to be sharing it with him. One small step past the bounds of formality reassured her that a few choices yet remained to her, however modest the resulting indulgence.

Emory tossed back some tea as if parlor picnics were a frequent item on his schedule.

"Still hot," he said, buttering another chunk of bread. "I cannot abide tepid tea." He passed Edith the bread reinforcing the sense of casual intimacy.

More than the tea and the food, the duke's unexpected companionability made the meal a pleasure. Nobody warned a lady that poverty was a lonely undertaking. Edith did not call on those who had known her as the duchess's companion. One didn't presume, in the first place, and her wardrobe was no longer up to that challenge in the second.

"I'm told one usually consumes buttered bread," the duke said. "Preferably while the bread is fresh, but save room for a pear tart."

"I adore pear tarts."

"One suspects you have a sweet tooth. Your secret is safe with me. Don't let your soup get cold."

"Not a chance of that happening. Have you discovered who wrote *How to Ruin a Duke*?" And why would a man who could dine at the finest clubs or command his own French chef to prepare him delicacies choose instead to share this meal with Edith?

Now that the worst of her hunger was sated, the odd nature of the call itself troubled her.

"I have not found the author yet, but I might be getting closer. More soup?"

Edith could have consumed the entire crock but that would leave nothing for supper. "A pear tart would serve nicely."

Emory sliced her a wedge of cheese and held out the basket of tarts. "Before we discuss specifics relating to the book, I have a proposition to put to you."

Edith had picked up the flask, the pewter warm against her hand. Her insides, however, went queasy and cold.

"A proposition, Your Grace? A *proposition*? You come here when I am likely to be alone, bringing me much needed sustenance. You pretend to enjoy a meal with me, merely so that you can offer to do more damage to my good standing than any book has done to yours." She shoved the basket back at him. "Please leave."

He took a pear tart and left her holding the basket. "Your imagination has got the better of your common sense, my lady. I can procure the favors of the six most sought-after courtesans in London *at the same time* if I please to. What I seek from you is a rarer skill than what they offer, also of more value to me."

Edith was angry, but also caught in a confusion of contradictory emotions. She had long since noticed Emory's broad shoulders, his sardonic humor, his vigilance where his family's wellbeing was concerned. She knew he genuinely liked Italian opera and also enjoyed a ribald farce. He gave generously to charities and was incensed at the cost royalty inflicted on the national exchequer.

He was, in other words, a good man, if lamentably short of charm. He was also *attractive*. Not in the flirtatious, polished manner of his brother, but in a robust, unapologetically masculine sense. The notion of the duke sharing a bed with a half dozen courtesans put that attractiveness before Edith with startling vividness.

And yet, he was offering her some sort of proposition? "Half a dozen, Your Grace? *At the same time?*"

He took a bite of pear tart. "One doesn't discuss such topics with a lady, but I have it on good authority that more than two at once becomes taxing from an organizational standpoint. Shall we return to the matter at hand?"

The duke's expression was perfectly composed, and yet, his eyes danced.

Edith set aside the basket of pear tarts. "I'm prepared to listen to your proposition, but I will not be insulted in my own home."

"Nor do I offer you any insult. Quite the contrary. Do have a tart. They're quite good."

"Do stop giving me orders, sir."

The smile broke over the rest of his features, from his eyes to his mouth, dimples grooving his cheeks. "Why my mother ever let you go is yet another vexing mystery."

"She had no choice, Your Grace. I was determined to leave. I had had enough of service, and though she offered me an increase in salary, my mind was made up."

The duke wasn't buying that load of wash, but Edith had no intention of providing him a more honest version of the facts. He would not believe her any more than the duchess had.

"A discussion for another time, perhaps," he said, the smile fading. "Her Grace was much happier when you kept her company. We were all much happier, come to that. And now we are *unhappy* in part because of this damned book. You are ideally suited to help me solve the mystery of its authorship."

Edith bit into a pear tart, and oh ye dancing muses of Epicurus, the taste was divine. The crust was a buttery marvel of perfectly cooked pastry, the pears redolent of some elegant vintage sacrificed in the name of a perfect reduction, and the spices both subtle and complex.

"I am in love," she murmured. Perhaps poverty made the palate more discerning, perhaps she had never had a proper pear tart before. "I am in love with this recipe. I'd like to publish it, but first I'd like to eat the rest of that basket of tarts, slowly, one at a time, in complete silence."

Emory regarded her, a half-eaten tart in his hand. "They are good."

"They are incomparably delectable." She took another nibble, and the first was as ambrosial as the second.

The duke watched her enjoying her sweet, his expression thoughtful. "If I promised you an endless supply of these pear tarts would you agree to help me find the author of the dratted book?"

Edith spoke without thinking. "If you agreed to supply me with pear tarts like these, I'd promise you nearly anything."

His smile reignited, blazing from naughty to a degree of wicked merriment that rivaled the pear tart for its scrumptiousness. "You'd promise me *anything*, my lady? Anything at all?"

"I have done something daring," Antigone whispered.

Jeremiah was trapped in the family parlor with the ladies, a penance that had befallen him because of the rain. No riding out this afternoon, no carriage parade, no pleasant stroll over to Mrs. Bellassai's establishment, not that he was welcome there again—yet.

"You have doubtless done something foolish," Jeremiah said. "Tell Cousin Jere your sins, and I'll do what I can to sort them out."

"I made a list," Antigone said, "of every silly prank I ever got up to."

"A long list indeed." Uncle Frederick was at the piano, twiddling away at Mozart. The music provided privacy for Antigone's confidences, and kept Uncle from descending into the usual litany of his own youthful follies.

"My list is interesting, not merely lengthy," Antigone said, scooting closer. "How many young ladies of good breeding have knotted their sheets into a rope and escaped the manor house to dance at midnight under a summer moon?"

In Jeremiah's estimation, that stunt was probably a rite of passage, akin to a youth's first experience of drunkenness. "But did you climb the rope back up to your bedroom undetected?"

Antigone glowered at him over her embroidery hoop. "Of course not. What do you take me for? I came in through the scullery as any sensible woman would."

"And perhaps at some point, you stole a bottle of wine from the pantry of your finishing school, and you and your five closest friends grew tipsy on one glass each?"

The glower became a frown. "We took to stealing a bottle every Saturday night. Cook went into the village to see her sister, and we knew where the pantry keys were. Nobody ever said anything, so we concluded the wine wasn't inventoried."

Jeremiah patted her arm. "The cook tippled, meaning she claimed to use much more of the wine in her recipes than was necessary. Rather than expose her own pilfering, she overlooked yours. At public school, the errand of purloining libation from the wine cellar is assigned to the newest boys. They feel daring and bold and provide a needed service."

He yawned, the weather making him drowsy. Then too, he'd been up late the previous evening.

"Well, I can promise you no public school boy ever stole his papa's cigars and smoked them in the orchard."

"Antigone, dearest, if a boy—any boy, from the royal princes to the drover's pride and joy—has a father who indulges in tobacco, that boy eventually steals from the humidor and coughs himself silly trying to learn to smoke. He ends up light-headed and sick to his stomach, and his dear father ignores the lad's reeking clothing. Some traditions cut across all classes."

Antigone stabbed her needle through the fabric and set aside her hoop. "You are being awful."

"I'm being honest. Why have you prepared this list of follies?"

"So I can attribute each one of them to somebody I dislike and write a wildly popular novel. I will be famous and have lots of money and everybody will wish they'd thought of it first."

Oh, dear. Jeremiah was torn between laughter and terror, for Antigone was stubborn beyond belief. "You do know that Lady Caroline's reputation never recovered from penning *Glenarvon*? She was never allowed back into Almack's, and many fashionable doors remained closed to her. Is that what you want?"

"Nobody ever liked Lady Caroline; besides, I'll write as if I'm a man recounting my sister's mistakes."

An interesting ploy. "And if your identity should be revealed?"

Uncle Frederick thumped away at the pianoforte, taking a repeat that Jeremiah was sure the composer hadn't included in the score.

"Nobody will find out who the author is," Antigone said, leaning near. "Emory has been trying to determine who wrote *How to Ruin a Duke*, and if *he* can't unearth that information, with all his resources, then no anonymous author need worry for her privacy."

Valid point, damn the luck. "How will you manage the vast sums that come pouring into your coffers in exchange for penning this disaster? You aren't yet even permitted your own pin money that I know of."

Antigone turned innocent blue eyes on him. "I was hoping I could count on *you* for that sort of assistance. I know you can be discreet when necessary, and I'd be willing to share a bit of the proceeds with you."

"Do you know what Emory would do to me if I in any way aided you? Do you know what he'd do to you?" Though, thundering choruses on high, what if Antigone enlisted the aid of one of her throng of admirers?

"His Grace can't stop me. Do you know, I'm glad somebody wrote that awful book. Emory is a plague on my freedom. When he's preoccupied with his literary troubles, he hasn't as much time to interfere with my life." She paused to look around the parlor. "I got a letter from Sir Prendergast."

Real alarm replaced Jeremiah's amusement. "I do not want to hear this."

"He's a very resourceful fellow. I'm sure the footmen thought the letter was from a former schoolmate. The penmanship was all flourish-y and the paper was scented with lemon verbena."

Uncle's sonata transitioned into the slow movement, thank the merciful angels.

"Sir Prendergast is a very married fellow, Antigone. He ought not to be sending you anything, ever."

She fluffed her skirts. "He's unhappy. He wrote to apologize to me for all the trouble and disappointment he caused. I thought that quite gallant."

If Jeremiah scolded her, she'd sulk as only Antigone could sulk.

The next time Sir Prancing Ninny wrote to her, she'd tell no one, until some daft elopement was in train—or worse.

"Antigone, do you recall the incident in *How to Ruin a Duke* where His Grace planted some fellow a facer behind Carlton House?"

"Very unsporting of the duke, but who will tell the likes of Emory that brawling nearly on the street isn't the done thing?"

Carlton House's grounds were not 'nearly on the street,' which was beside the point. "Emory drew the other fellow's cork because that man was making ungentlemanly comments about a lady. The lady is of good birth, and this bounder presumed to announce that he could lift her skirts on the way to Gretna Green, and the woman's family would have to accept him as her husband."

"What has that tale to do with me, Jere?" Murmured over the rippling chords of the adagio.

"The idiot announcing his perfidy was Sir Prendergast. Emory could not call him out, because they are of such different stations. I suspect that's all that saved Sir Prendergast's life. Prendergast was boasting about a young woman's ruin, all but on the street, as you say. Now you tell me he's writing to you, probably pilfering his wife's perfume to disguise his letter. Burn that letter, Antigone, and I will inform the gallant knight that you see his wicked lures for the selfish schemes they are."

"You are making this up. Sir Prendergast would never say such things about a proper lady. Maybe she wasn't quite proper. Did you or Emory ever think of that? Not every woman has the scruples I've been raised with."

Stubborn, stubborn, stubborn. "*I was there*, Antigone. Prendergast didn't realize he would be overheard by your cousins. He clearly mentioned the lady's name when he bragged to his cronies."

The sonata shifted into a minor key, appropriate for the rainy day and this hopeless conversation.

"Sir Prendergast was in love with me," Antigone whispered. "I know he was, and maybe he still is. He had to marry that woman, and

I understand that a gentleman needs means. But he would never have run off with some female just to get his hands on her settlements. You don't know anything about love because you're too busy being a... a libertine."

Said as if libertines were so vile as to exceed even the criminals and sinners filling Dante's *Inferno*.

"Antigone, dearest, please believe me when I tell you that it was your name Sir Prendergast bandied about so carelessly. Had anybody other than Emory been present, you would be enjoying a long respite at the family seat under the watchful eye of three aunts, two companions, and a brace of mastiffs. Emory handled the matter quietly for your sake."

Jeremiah braced himself for an explosion, but Antigone instead went still. "*My name?* Sir Prendergast bandied *my name* about in that manner?"

"If you believe nothing else I ever say, please believe I'm being honest with you now. You had a narrow escape."

She was quiet until the slow movement concluded. When Uncle embarked on a lively trio, Antigone took up her hoop again.

"Maybe Sir Prendergast wrote that awful book. He would hate Emory enough to do such a thing." She stabbed the fabric with her needle and pulled the thread taut. "Who else would take an incident like that and turn it into a reproach against our duke?"

"Weren't you just saying Emory was overdue for a set-down?"

"A set-down is one thing, but whoever wrote that book went beyond a set-down. I hope His Grace does find the author and draws his cork too." She paused in her stitching. "There's something else you should know."

"No more secrets, please. I've heard my quota for the year in the past quarter hour." And shared a secret or two as well.

"Well, you can hear one more, because Emory has seen fit to avoid this gathering. I think Her Grace is working on a book. She's been making lists, consulting her spies, and collecting stories. When we drove out the other day in Hyde Park, she was positively glowing over some tidbit she'd gleaned from Lady Westerfield. The scandals that woman has been privy too would probably fill ten books."

Jeremiah experienced a sensation that he associated with the early phases of inebriation when the quality of drink was particularly poor. A sense of events spinning beyond his control while he had neither the means nor the will to prevent a looming disaster.

"You think *the duchess* is working on a book?"

"Who knows. Perhaps she's penning the much-vaunted sequel to *How to Ruin a Duke*. Perhaps this version will include some of your exploits as well, Cousin. Won't that be delightful?"

Lady Edith Charbonneau in the throes of ecstasy, even ecstasy occasioned by one of Cook's pear tarts, distracted Thaddeus from the purpose of his call.

Steady on, old boy. "What would you give me in exchange for a liberal supply of pear tarts?" he asked, taking a bite of his own sweet.

"You are teasing me," she replied. "Besides, woman does not live on pear tarts alone."

"Would you like your previous position back?"

She took up the flask and traced the crest embossed on it. "No, thank you. Two years of being Her Grace's companion taxed my patience to its limits. Your mother enjoys ordering other people around, and I abhor being told what to do."

"As do I. If you do not want your former post back, then what could I offer you in exchange for your assistance finding the author of *How to Ruin a Duke*?"

"You needn't offer me anything." She set down the flask without drinking and took up her tart again. "I'm happy to give you what aid I can out of simple decency, though I am at a loss for what insight you expect me to bring to the task. Nonetheless, I re-read portions of the book last night, and some of the incidents recounted cast you in a very unflattering light. My temper is roused on your behalf, Your Grace."

She sniffed her pear tart, then took a bite from the crust.

Thaddeus rose, because if he remained on the loveseat, he'd be tempted to sniff *her*. Surely his dignity had gone begging along with his reputation.

"I cannot impose on your time without offering you compensation of some sort. I could sponsor subscriptions to your book of advice, for example, or find you another post as a companion with somebody more agreeable than my mother." Nearly anybody would be more agreeable than Mama in a fretful mood.

"I haven't written my advice book yet. I completed an outline and drafted several chapters, but whoever agrees to publish it will doubtless have suggestions regarding the final form of the book."

The desire to craft an exchange of consideration wasn't merely fair dealing from a business perspective. Thaddeus needed to know that Lady Edith had some means, that she was safe from desperate measures and desperate men.

"What about your brother, my lady? Shall I buy him a commission? Lord Jeremiah is certainly eager to embrace an officer's life." Thaddeus understood and respected his brother's desire to make his own way, but Mama did not. Then too, Jeremiah was the spare, and a spare's lot was to wait for an heir of the body to appear.

Lady Edith rose. "No officer's commission, please. Foster is all the family I have left, though we aren't even related. He has never expressed any wish to join the military, and I would rather he not perish in the Canadian wilderness."

"My lady—Edith—I cannot avail myself of your time without—"

She put her hand over his mouth. "Have you never had a friend before, Emory? Friends help each other. I will help you if I can. Come sit with me." She took him by the hand and led him back to the loveseat.

The novelty of being told to hush and then given an order scrambled Thaddeus's wits, for he not only obeyed her and resumed his place on the loveseat like a good duke, he also made no pretense of putting distance between his hip and hers.

And neither did she.

"Finish your tart," he said.

She delivered such a look to him as would have made a lesser man back slowly toward the door.

"I beg your ladyship's pardon. Perhaps you'd consider finishing your tart before we embark on a tedious discussion. I would not want to distract you from your pleasures." Nor could Thaddeus form a proper thought while watching her consume her sweet. Perhaps the infatuations and flirtations that so violently afflicted Antigone, Jeremiah, and other family members were an inherited trait.

The notion was more encouraging than lowering. Thaddeus stuffed another bite of buttered bread into his mouth and fixed his gaze on the pattern of mock orange boughs on the worn carpet before the hearth.

"Where would you like to start?" her ladyship asked, dusting her hands several long moments later.

"With a list of suspects," Thaddeus replied. "Preferably a short list, full of people I don't like and can easily buy off or intimidate."

"You intimidate nearly all who meet you." She wrapped up the bread and put the lid on the butter crock. "I shudder for the young ladies who stand up with you for their first waltz."

"I am competent on the dance floor." In fact, he enjoyed a vigorous set with an enthusiastic partner.

"You are magnificent but your proportions mean most women struggle to keep up with the sweep and scope of your dancing, especially inexperienced women cowed by your glowers and scowls."

Thaddeus tore another pear tart in half and held out the larger portion to Lady Edith. He was torn as well, between pleasure that she had watched his *magnificent* waltzing, and frustration that he'd never asked her to stand up with him.

"I couldn't possibly eat another bite," she said, wrapping up the basket of pear tarts and the cheese in another square of linen.

"Liar." Thaddeus held the tart up to her mouth.

She nibbled, watching him all the while, and his battle against obvious signs of arousal lost ground.

"We will need pencil and paper," she said, patting her mouth with a table napkin.

I will soon need to stand in the cold rain without my coat. "Excellent idea." He retrieved those items from the desk as Lady Edith finished tidying up their meal.

"I will put the leftovers in the pantry," she said, "and you can start on a list of people who have motive to wish you ill, plus literary ability, and enough proximity to you to paint you in a credibly bad light. I'll be right back."

"No hurry," Thaddeus replied. "I fear the list will be quite long."

And she still hadn't told him what he could offer her by way of compensation.

The parlor became smaller than ever with His Grace of Emory on the love seat. When he rose to pace, Edith noticed how low the ceiling was, how worn the carpet, and that the water stain where the walls met was growing. But sharing a parlor picnic with him also gave the room a cozy quality, taking off the chill of a dreary afternoon.

Or the food had done that. Good food that had to have come from the ducal kitchen. She recognized the weave of the table napkins, and the flask was embossed with the family crest. A griffin *segreant,* prepared to do as griffins legendarily did and guard priceless treasures on both land, in the manner of lions, and as the eagles did, from the heavens.

Who guarded Emory's reputation, and who benefitted from tarnishing it?

"Before we make your list," Edith said, resuming her place on the loveseat, "can you tell me a bit more about the famous curricle race?"

"The infamous race. What would you like to know?"

"You are not by nature incautious. What possessed you to bet another peer that you could beat him to Brighton in a vehicle you'd never driven before, much less by moonlight?"

The duke held up the plate with half a pear tart. Edith took a bite because she did not want to seem rude.

"I chose to start at moonrise," he said, "because the roads are less crowded and fewer people would be abroad to witness my folly."

"Why race at all?"

He helped himself to a bite of the tart. "My dear, idiot brother had bet his new curricle that he could travel the distance to Brighton and beat his opponent, if not the Regent's record. He must have been half-seas over to make such an asinine wager. Beating the Regent's time publicly is not the done thing, moreover, Jeremiah had only recently won the curricle in a game of cards. He wasn't experienced enough to handle such an unstable vehicle at speed, much less in a race."

This admission was made grudgingly, though Edith could easily picture Lord Jeremiah making a dangerous boast when among his cronies.

"The book depicts the whole incident much differently." Very differently, with Emory nearly going into the ditch and winning by the slimmest margin. "Did you win?"

"I won the race without besting the Regent's personal record, though it was a near thing. I did not want Jeremiah to lose a prized possession, but neither could I have the Regent taking us into disfavor."

"From whom did Lord Jeremiah win the vehicle?"

Emory took another bite of the tart then passed it to her. "Finish this, please. The curricle had been the property of one of his drinking companions who doubtless goaded him into the wager in hopes of recovering the carriage for himself."

"Do you have a name?"

"Not yet, but I will." He scribbled something on the paper. "Any more questions?"

"What about the drinking wager?"

"I will never touch another drop of gin for so long as I live, that's what about the drinking wager. The very recollection makes my head pound and my gut roil."

"And yet, you won that one too."

His Grace grumbled out an explanation: A friend of Jeremiah's had proposed to drink under the table any man holding his vowels in exchange for a return of the IOU. Losing the bet would ruin the fellow, and yet, he was more of a braggart than a drunkard or a Captain Sharp. Emory had accepted the wager, altering the terms such that if the duke could out-drink the other fellow, the duke came into possession of the debts of honor.

"I am a mastodon," he said, "according to a noted authority, and thus able to hold my liquor. I won the bet and gave the notes of hand to Jeremiah to be collected if and when the fellow could pay."

Again, very different from what the book had portrayed.

"It's almost as if," Edith said, "somebody who had no firsthand knowledge of these incidents colored them all with a fierce resentment for you, and relied on readers also not having any firsthand knowledge to fuel the book's appeal."

Emory ranged an arm along the back of the sofa and crossed his feet at the ankles. "One attempts discretion, especially when indulging in rank folly. Those who were witnesses to the lunacy would be unlikely to gossip beyond the masculine confessional of the gentlemen's club."

And what was said behind the walls of a gentlemen's club was not to be repeated elsewhere.

"So we are likely dealing with a woman," Emory went on. "A woman who hears a lot of male gossip, or can consult with male gossips, but not with the men who were present when I was making such an ass of myself."

Edith liked watching his mind work, she liked that he'd abandon formal manners with her, and she liked very much sitting beside him when he did. She loathed that his basic decency had been misconstrued by some misanthropic female.

"What woman has cause to be angry with you, besides Miss Antigone?"

The duke's expression was bleakly amused. "My mother, but then, she's easily and often vexed. She fits the criteria though: She's quite literary, she has the ear of half the tattlers in the realm, and she might well think a book of this nature would chivvy me into taking a duchess."

"Has it?" That was none of Edith's business, of course, but she wanted Emory to have at least one reliable ally to call his own. When she'd first joined his household, she'd realized that beneath his posturing and consequence, he was a decent fellow.

Even she hadn't understood how decent.

Emory perused the notes he'd made. "Mama's novel hasn't inspired me in the sense she doubtless intended—if she wrote the blasted thing. Who among the young ladies would have taken me into dislike?"

They discussed disappointed hopefuls, matchmakers who might be out of patience with Emory, and wallflowers given to bitterness. That list was troublingly long, though few of the names on it had as much entré among the gentlemen as a well connected duchess would have.

"A widow, I suppose," Emory said, rising and stretching. "I have been avoiding them in recent months, not that I was ever much of a gallant in that regard. The hour grows late, but we have made progress. When might I call upon you again?"

Edith arranged her skirts and found a ducal hand extended in her direction. A gentleman typically did assist a lady to rise.

Well. She took his hand, but with the side table still before the loveseat, the confines were cramped. His shaving soap was still evident this close—a subtle blend of woods and spice. The fragrance graced a rainy, chilly day with a note of elegance, and memories of the ease Edith had enjoyed in the ducal household.

When she wasn't being run off her feet by endless silly demands.

"May I ask you something?" Emory said, peering down at her. The afternoon light was waning, and the rain had slowed to desultory dripping from the eaves.

"You may."

"Slap me if I give offense, but earlier, when you thought I offered you a proposition of an objectionable nature..."

"I was peckish and out of sorts. You would never—"

He touched a finger to her lips. "If I had, if I'd intimated that I sought a discreet, intimate liaison on terms acceptable to you, would your objection have been to the nature of the relationship, or personally, to the other party involved?"

His dignity was on display, so was his willingness to be dealt a blow, not as a duke, but as a man. Edith became acutely aware of the attraction she'd denied since first watching him turn down the room with this or that marquess's daughter.

He was a fine specimen, she'd long known that. Now he was revealing himself to be a fine man, one whom Edith might have flirted with, had their situation been different.

"My objection would not have been personal to the other party involved."

His smile was slight as he bowed over her hand. "I see. Good to know. It's time I was on my way. Let's continue to consider the conundrum before us, shall we?"

Which conundrum was that? Edith helped him into his coat, and while he stood, top hat in hand, she kissed his cheek. A reward for bravery, a gesture of encouragement to a man much besieged with injustice.

"We'll solve the riddle, Your Grace. The problem wants only time and determination."

He tapped his hat onto his head and pulled on his gloves. "My thanks for those sentiments, and keep well until next we meet."

CHAPTER 5

"No good duke goes unpunished."
From *How to Ruin a Duke* by Anonymous

For five days and six nights, Thaddeus debated possibilities. Was Mama writing the blasted sequel? She tended to her correspondence incessantly, with volumes of letters both arriving to and departing from the ducal residence. At the theater, Antigone sent Thaddeus brooding glances, and at the formal balls, every matchmaker and wallflower came under his scrutiny.

And through all the sorting and considering, he was haunted by one fleeting kiss from a woman he'd spent two years assiduously ignoring. He'd ignored the musical lilt in Lady Edith's voice, the warmth in her smile. He'd ignored her humor and her patience. He had rigidly forbidden himself to do more than notice her figure—she'd been a woman in his employment, and thus her figure was *entirely* irrelevant—and yet, she had a fine figure.

"Shall you eat that trifle," Elsmore asked, "or stare the raspberries into submission?"

Lady Edith was fond of raspberries. Was she fond of Thaddeus?

"Help yourself." He passed the bowl across the table. "Does your mama pester you to take a duchess?"

"My mother is a duchess, pestering anybody is beneath her. With so many potential heirs to the title already dangling from the family tree, she doubtless considers getting my sisters fired off a higher priority, and thank heavens for that. What has put you off your feed, my friend?"

Elsmore tucked into the dessert, and Thaddeus battled the absurd urge to snatch the sweet away, because doubtless, Lady Edith had not had trifle in months.

"I am pre-occupied," Thaddeus said, studying the bottle of cordial brought out with the dessert. "I am considering the notion that my own mother also regards pestering beneath her, while embarrassing me into wedlock does fit her character. She thrives on intrigues and petty scandals."

Elsmore paused, a spoonful of cream and fruit halfway to his mouth. "That book transcended petty scandal a month ago. I've heard some of your famous lines quoted over cards, and my valet asked if I'd like my hair styled *a la épave de phaéton.*"

"The vehicle was a curricle, not a phaeton, and I did not wreck it." Though Thaddeus had doubtless finished the race looking as if he'd survived a wreck. The distinction between a curricle and a phaeton was exactly the sort of altered detail a female author would regard as insignificant.

"I heard about the floral society," Elsmore said quietly. "You don't really take their foolishness seriously?"

The Society for the Floral Improvement of the Metropolis was one of a dozen charitable organizations that boasted the Duke of Emory among its honorary directors. That term was a euphemism for financial sponsorship, which Emory had agreed to at the duchess's request.

"Jeremiah didn't grumble all that much," Thaddeus replied. "For him to be the sponsor of record, when he hasn't a groat to spare, amused him enormously. I won't miss two-hour meetings devoted to the benefits of potted salvia over herbaceous borders, but I don't care to be told to stand in the corner by yet another charity."

"How many does that make?"

"Four." In every case, the suggested solution to having a disgraced duke on the board of directors was to quietly request that Lord Jeremiah "serve the cause" for a time instead. Jeremiah was bearing up good-naturedly. Nonetheless, a scolding from the very groups who ought to be trumpeting Thaddeus's generosity was annoying.

"If you'd like to turn one or two charities over to me," Elsmore said, "I can find a cousin or sister to attend most of the meetings in my stead."

"Thank you, but I hope that won't be necessary. Elsmore, would you mind very much if I left you in solitude to finish your dessert? The press of business intrudes on my plans."

Elsmore regarded Thaddeus across the table. "I have never seen you so out of sorts. What could be in that sequel you're so worried about?"

"Lies that reflect poorly not only on me, but also on my brother? Jeremiah is hardly a pattern card of probity, but he is my heir. If both of us are sunk in scandal, where does that leave the succession?"

Elsmore poured a dash of plum cordial over his dessert. "Perhaps that's a fruitful line of inquiry? Have you cousins lurking in the hedges that would like to see you and Lord Jeremiah disgraced past all redemption?"

For a duke and his heir that would take a deal of disgracing. Thaddeus rose, because again, he'd like to have the benefit of Lady Edith's thoughts on this possibility.

"You will excuse me. I apologize for leaving you without a companion, but..." *What to say? I am drawn to the company of a woman who no longer owns even a decent tea service?*

Elsmore took up his spoon. "Away with you. Do you know how rarely I am permitted to enjoy a meal to myself? How unique a pleasure it is for me to be free of the burden of polite conversation when all I want is to partake of my food in peace? You have but the one immediate heir, while I have a dozen first cousins all clamoring for my favor and influence. The aunties and their endless progression of god-daughters line up behind the cousins, until I sometimes feel like a waltzing, bowing, smiling automaton."

For Elsmore, who was at all times gracious, mannerly, and pleasant, that amounted to a tantrum.

"Try a bit of scandal," Thaddeus said. "Clears a man's schedule handily."

"Are you complaining?"

"No, actually." The lunch and dinner invitations had all but stopped, leaving only the courtesy invitations which Thaddeus was free to decline. Jeremiah had been happy to do some of the obligatory socializing, proving that fraternal loyalty was not yet dead in Merry Olde England. "I will wish you the joy of your trifle."

While the day wasn't gorgeous, it was at least dry. Rather than summon his coach, Thaddeus walked the distance to Lady Edith's door, stopping only to procure sustenance at the inn where they'd eaten the previous week.

Will she be home to me?

Did that kiss mean anything to her, and if so, what?

What do I want it to have meant?

Thaddeus's imagination took the answers to that last question to all manner of inappropriate places, such that by the time he arrived at Lady Edith's house, he felt like an adolescent standing up at his first tea dance.

"Your Grace." She curtseyed and stepped back. "Won't you come in?"

Was it progress, that her ladyship wasn't warning him to keep the visit short? If so, progress toward what exactly? And what was wrong with civilization that the daughter of an earl had to answer her own door?

"You will think me presuming in the extreme," he said, passing over his parcel, "but I stopped to enjoy a meal at the establishment down the street, and realized that I need not eat in solitude when excellent company was available not far away." *Forgive me, Elsmore.*

"You are being charitable," she said, gesturing him into her house. "I am just hungry enough to pretend I'm delighted to be the object of your kindness."

"My kindness is being held in low regard these days. I have been sent to Coventry by several of the charities to which I've been a staunch contributor." Lady Edith took his coat and hung it on a peg, then accepted his hat and walking stick. She smoothed the wool of his coat, so the sleeves hung straight, a gesture Thaddeus found... *wifely.*

She turned a curious gaze on him. "Why would any charity...? Oh. They don't want to be tainted by your notoriety?"

"They aren't that honest. The hypocrites want proximity to the ducal purse and the family name, but not to the Flying Demon of the Brighton Road."

"He is a rather colorful fellow," Lady Edith said. "Let's eat on the back terrace, shall we?"

The back terrace was a euphemism for an uneven patch of slates at the rear of the house. Grass intruded between the stones, and the garden walls were encrusted with lichens, but irises apparently found the space congenial. A bed of purple flowers along each side wall was just beginning to bloom. Two venerable maples cast the little yard in dappled shade, which also meant that Lady Edith would have privacy when she sat out here.

The wrought iron chairs were sturdy, if ancient, and Thaddeus had no sooner unwrapped his sandwich than an impertinent pigeon came around begging for crumbs. Lady Edith tossed the bird a crust, so of course three more of the damned beggars appeared, strutting about and making pigeon noises.

"How are you?" Thaddeus asked, when the lady had consumed half a sandwich.

"I am well, and you?"

She was not well. She was quiet and troubled, even more than she'd been the last time he'd imposed his company on her.

"I am vexed past all bearing by this damnable book, and I've had a few ideas I'd like to put before you. First, though, might you kiss me again?"

Shortly after putting off mourning, Edith had begun keeping company with a local squire who had owned a patch of property near her aunt's cottage. They'd walked out together, and matters had progressed along the predictable lines of a rural courtship.

Within weeks, she'd developed an understanding with her swain, and her prospective groom had developed the ability to charm his way under her skirts, as often happened with engaged couples. When it became apparent that he'd had a fine time with the vicar's daughter as well, and that the vicar was soon to become a grandpapa, Edith had joined the household of a relative in the next county. She did not want a husband she couldn't trust, no matter how skilled he was in the hay mow.

And the gardener's shed.

And the saddle room.

For several years thereafter, she'd told herself that she'd had a near miss, and in exchange for bruised pride, she'd had a precious and rare education. That education had stood her in good stead when she'd become a duchess's paid companion, and rakes and roués had besieged her even under her employer's roof.

Nothing had prepared her for the Duke of Emory bearing sandwiches though.

Edith took up an orange, one of four the duke had brought along with sandwiches, lemonade, meat pastries, and shortbread. His generosity meant she needn't pawn her earbobs today, but that day would soon arrive. She rolled the orange between her palms, enjoying the texture and scent of fresh critus, a pleasure she'd too long taken for granted.

From most men, a request for a kiss would have been easily

brushed aside, but Emory needn't ask anybody for anything. He was a duke, a wealthy, powerful man who had better things to do than share a porch picnic with an impoverished spinster. And memories of him—lounging on the loveseat, pacing the parlor, standing in the rain on her front stoop—had kept her awake late at night.

"You'd like me to kiss you again?" Edith would enjoy kissing him, of that she had no doubt.

"I would, or I could kiss you. The point is,"—he tossed the last of his sandwich crust to the cooing pigeons—"your kiss has been on my mind."

"You have been on my mind too. You and your situation."

He plucked the orange from her grasp and tore off a strip of the rind. "My damned situation seems to be growing worse by the week. I receive only the courtesy invitations these days, and when Mama drags me to Almack's, I'm the only wallflower ever to sport a ducal title."

Watching him peel an orange ought not to have been an erotic experience, but such was the attraction of Emory's hands—strong, competent, masculine—that Edith let herself gawk.

"Even the patronesses *at Almack's* are turning up their noses at you?"

"Not explicitly, but those women excel at innuendo, and there was that business about singing *God Save the King* on the steps of the assembly rooms."

He popped a bit of orange rind into his mouth and shredded another piece to scatter on the paving stones. The birds leapt upon those offerings, nimble little sparrows joining the pigeons.

"According to the book, you sang after midnight, when the doors were already closed." Edith would have liked to have heard him, and liked to have seen the looks on the faces of his audience when he'd held forth.

"I timed my aria for when the orchestra was blasting away on some waltz or other, so I know I wasn't heard inside, but still... Not well done of me."

"Why did you do it?"

He spread out a table napkin and separated the orange into sections. "One of Jeremiah's more foolish friends dared him to serenade Almack's with a drinking song, at midnight, in full voice. Other fellows joined in the nonsense and soon bets were flying in all directions. Had Jeremiah stepped up to the challenge—and you know how little regard my brother has for rules—he might well have been barred from the dances for the rest of the Season. Mama would have been wroth, a petty war would have begun... but my folly was sure to be overlooked, or so I thought."

"Because you are a duke."

"Because I am a duke, and because, until recently, nobody would have believed me capable of such nonsense. Besides, *God Save the King* is regularly sung in every pub and tavern in the realm, and who could object to that song at any hour in any location?"

"Nobody should object, but placed side by side with a half dozen other incidents, even *God Save the King* becomes suspect." Edith sensed a pattern to the tales told about Emory, a consistency regarding the direction in which each vignette was slanted to show him in disrepute, but she could not focus her thoughts on that puzzle.

Not when Emory held out the table napkin, the glistening pieces of orange offered like a bouquet.

"I want to kiss you," Edith said, taking three succulent sections, "and indulge in rather more than that, but I am not interested in anything tawdry."

Emory chose three pieces for himself and set the rest on the table. "You echo my own sentiments. My esteem for you is genuine, but also the esteem of a man who appreciates a woman's intimate company. I am not in the habit of... that is to say... I respect you, and I flatter myself that you respect me as well, thus creating a foundation for rare and lasting goodwill. Jeopardizing your opinion of me is the opposite of my aim. The *very* opposite, if you take my meaning."

If His Grace had ever kept a mistress, he'd done so discreetly enough that even the duchess, *even Lord Jeremiah*, hadn't remarked it. His lordship would have mentioned such a topic purely for the pleasure of testing Edith's composure.

The rotter. Edith nibbled a section of orange, enjoying everything from the juicy texture, to the sweet, sunny flavor, to the tart burst of citrus on her tongue.

"I am not without experience, Your Grace."

"Neither am I, though my recollections of intimate congress are growing dim."

This amused him, and it pleased Edith. "None of the scandals laid at your feet in *How to Ruin a Duke* relate to women." Was that a coincidence or a clue?

"Another factor that leads me to believe the author is female."

"Possibly." She finished her part of the orange and wiped her fingers on the linen Emory had brought along. If she accepted Emory's overture, she'd be embarking on an affair the duchess would have called a friendly liaison. Nothing legal or lasting, and nothing sordid either. No money changing hands, which in Edith's circumstances was an upside-down comfort.

A year ago, even a month ago, she would have been dismayed to be the object of Emory's intimate interest. A lady was virtuous, a duke was a gentleman. The very society that spelled out in detail what a lady must do to maintain her respectability offered not one useful suggestion about how that lady was to keep body and soul together when cast on her own resources.

Hypocrites, the lot of them, whereas Emory offered companionship, pleasure, comfort, and a respite from all woes. Better still, if Edith found she did not enjoy his attentions, she could simply say so without risking judgment from matchmakers and wallflowers.

Perhaps being a lady was over-rated, at least being a relentlessly proper lady.

"Our discussion adds more urgency to my desire to sort out that ruddy book," Emory said, wrapping up the uneaten food. "One cannot go forward in a public sense—for a duke there is always the public sense to be considered—with such a cloud ever present over one's head. Elsmore has suggested I look to the spares for someone with a motivation to ruin me and Jeremiah."

"Lord Jeremiah is hardly ruined by this book, Emory."

"Might you on occasion—when the moment is comfortable—call me Thaddeus? I have asked you to consider sharing personal intimacies with me, after all, and one hopes the undertaking will be accompanied by a certain informality when private." He wrapped up the orange sections in tidy folds of linen, though Edith had the sense his request was anything but casual.

She did very much enjoy watching his hands. "Yes, when the moment feels comfortable." He'd offered to become her lover, after all. The gift of his name was a privilege he'd granted to very few. That gesture suggested a friendly liaison with Emory could be enjoyable in a more than physical sense.

Edith craved the emotional surcease that intimate pleasures could provide, and quite selfishly, she wanted the fortification Emory's regard gave her. Not a perspective she would have understood a year ago, but then, a year ago, she'd been a paid companion.

A post she'd neither wanted nor enjoyed. "Your spare is a second cousin, as I recall."

"A pleasant enough fellow tending his acres in East Anglia. We have him to dinner when he comes up to Town, and he notifies me when his wife presents him with another child so Mama can send along a basket of comestibles and spirits. His idea of literature is an agricultural pamphlet read of a Sunday evening. I can't see him conceiving of, much less writing, an entire book."

"What of your uncles?"

"My uncles?"

"But for you, wouldn't one of them have inherited the title? I'm looking for a motive, Your Grace, for a reason why somebody would cast you in such an unflattering light." *And I am watching your hands and your mouth, and the way the breeze riffles your hair.* Concentrating on the book was becoming nearly impossible.

Emory leaned closer. "I appreciate your diligence more than you know, but at this very moment, at this very special moment, I am looking for a private place to take you in my arms and indulge in pleasures that make *How to Ruin a Duke* read like an etiquette manual, assuming those pleasures interest you."

His inflection was polite, his tone merely conversational. He rose and the birds fluttered into the boughs, much like Edith's sense of composure had flitted off to who knew where.

She had nothing to lose. He'd be discreet, considerate, and gentlemanly. "I am interested."

"You're certain this is what you want?" Emory asked. "That I am who you want? I haven't gone about the business in the manner you're entitled to expect, but I am very sure of my choice. I make this overture to you in good faith, knowing we still have much to discuss."

He was paying her a compliment—several compliments. Giving her the latitude to change her mind, apologizing for a blunt approach to a topic most people handled delicately, and assuring her of her desirability in his eyes.

"I am certain of my decision too, Your Grace. We have the house to ourselves for the afternoon. Let's go inside." She led the way. Emory gathered up the food and followed.

Edith had never envisioned that she might one day indulge in a friendly tryst with Emory. On the one hand, she was closer to destitution than she'd ever been. On the other, having been entirely forgotten by polite society, she had enormous freedom. She could think of no one with whom she'd rather share that freedom than her almost-ruined duke.

Whoever wrote the dratted book would be furious to know that its publication had resulted in Thaddeus happening across—for the second time—the woman ideally suited to be his companion in life. Lady Edith had duchess written all over her, in her poise, her dignity, her patience, her sense of humor, her honesty, and her common sense. She even got along with Thaddeus's mother, for heaven's sake.

Thaddeus had kept a distance when Edith had been his mother's companion, but thank benevolent Providence he could make a different choice now.

That he'd embark on an engagement with Lady Edith so precipitously, without the expected folderol, and then consummate the understanding immediately suggested the fictional duke and the real man had a few characteristics in common.

Boldness in the face of a challenge.

A fine appreciation for physical pleasure.

Indifference to convention when convention stood between him and somebody he cared for.

Thaddeus had no sooner set down the parcels of food than Lady Edith stepped near. "My circumstances are humble, Your Grace."

"What do I care for circumstances when I'm about to kiss you?"

This earned him a smack on the lips. "I care. I'd like for this encounter to be the stuff of fairytales and pleasant memories." That admission caused her to blush.

So would I. "Very well, fairytales and memories it shall be. I am duly challenged." Though this was only the first of many encounters, most of which would happen beneath the velvet canopies covering his various ducal beds. "I will be content if you enjoy yourself enough to invite me to another such encounter."

She slipped away and headed for the steps that led from the foyer. "Are you coming? My bedroom is upstairs."

He trundled along after her, up the narrow steps, down a short, dim corridor that nonetheless hadn't a single cobweb.

Her bedroom, like the rest of the house, had seen better days, and yet, she'd made this space her own. The quilt was a bright patchwork of green, lavender, and cream squares. The floor polished enough to reflect the afternoon sunlight onto a tarnished mirror hung over a walnut washstand that, given a good oiling, would have been attractive. A sliver of hard-milled soap sat on a folded flannel, and a bound copy of *How to Ruin a Duke* sat by the lamp on her bedside table.

The rug was thick, though the pattern had faded, and the colors might once have complimented the hues in the quilt. A few dresses hung on the line of pegs along the wall, a worn pair of boots arranged beneath them.

What cheered Thaddeus most was a bouquet of half-bloomed irises in a green glass jar sitting on the windowsill. Lady Edith had gathered into the place where she dreamed what comfort and cheer she could find, and now she was to gather Thaddeus near as well.

"I can hardly believe my good fortune," he said. "I awakened focused on that blasted book, but also knowing I had dreamed of you. Again. Lovely dreams they were too. Shall I undo your hooks?"

She gave the irises a drink from the pitcher on the washstand. "We're to undress?"

"One often does, in the circumstances." Though Thaddeus had nothing against the occasional hasty coupling against a wall. The moment didn't seem appropriate to air that bit of broadmindedness.

"Then yes," Edith said, "I would like you to undo my hooks." She set the pitcher on the washstand. "Please." She turned her back to him, posture as stiff as if she were bracing for a scold.

Thaddeus began by kissing her nape, where a faint scent of roses lingered. She was to be his intimate companion in every sense, and only a fool would rush what should be savored.

"You do that well," she said, when Thaddeus had managed to undo all of three hooks.

"My lady is entitled to fairytales." Three more hooks, and he could brush his lips along the top of her shoulder. Such soft skin she had, and how still she stood, like a cat reposing in a shaft of spring sunshine.

Three more hooks and she turned to face him. "Are you entitled to fairytales too, Emory?" She followed her question with a kiss, this one a lingering press of her lips to the corner of his mouth. The off-center starting point left him wild to taste her, but he made himself wait.

To *be* savored was lovely and precious, and a perfect beginning to all that he hoped would follow.

"Shall I undress you?" she asked, slipping the pin from his cravat.

Her décolletage gapped, revealing the top of her chemise and a hint of cleavage. Thaddeus had to focus his mental faculties to comprehend her question. Something about tearing off his clothes...

"Assistance disrobing would be appreciated."

She smiled the smile of a woman who knew her lover to be more nervous than the Flying Demon of Lady Edith's Boudoir ought to be.

Thaddeus's sexual education had begun the week he'd arrived at university, and he'd applied himself diligently to that course of study. Today the curriculum had shifted, from the pleasurable and fascinating business of erotic skill, to the rare privilege of being Lady Edith's intimate and devoted companion. To excel at that scholarship, Thaddeus needed to learn *her*.

She drew off his cravat and draped it over the washstand. His coat came next, and she hung that over one of her dresses.

"I like that," he said, holding out his wrist for her to remove his sleeve buttons. "My morning coat sharing a peg with your frock. It's... friendly." The first word to come to his mind had been *domestic*, but for his prospective duchess, domesticity would mean greater comfort than these surrounds had to offer.

Edith removed his second sleeve button and set both on the bedside table. "Shall you remove your boots?"

He put his everyday handkerchief on the table beside his sleeve buttons. The only place to sit was on the bed, which took up nearly half the room. Lady Edith's chamber must have been the master bedroom at one time, for in all the house, no other piece of furniture was half so imposing.

He sat on the bed and tugged off the first boot. "Are you nervous, my lady?"

"Yes, also... determined."

"Determined? If you think I'll climb out the window to elude your charms, you are very much mistaken." He set his boots beside her bed and stood before her. "Determined on what, exactly?"

"I'm not sure." She stared hard at his chest. "And I can't seem to get my mind to focus on the question when you're about to remove your shirt."

He bent near. "Actually, I'm about to remove your slippers, if you'll permit me that privilege?"

Determination was an interesting quality to bring to the start of relationship, or the start of a new phase of a relationship.

"I am determined as well," Thaddeus said, going down on one knee. "I am determined that you will enjoy yourself, that you will never have cause to regret joining me in these intimacies."

He untied her slippers, which were so worn at the heel as to barely qualify as shoes. Her stockings were neatly mended, her garters plain. With each article of stitched, faded, and worn clothing, Thaddeus's respect for Edith grew.

She was allowing him to see her reality, to see the evidence of her poverty, and her dignity in the face of adversity. That trust, given to a man whom half of London now regarded as beyond the pale, laid him bare as a lack of clothing never would.

He rested his forehead against her knee. "I want to buy you every frilly garter and silk stocking in London, every..." Everything. The world. Whatever her heart desired. Her trousseau would be the delight of every modiste and milliner in Mayfair.

She ruffled his hair. "You will buy me nothing. I've been hard at work on a new literary project, and I have high hopes for its success. I'd very much like your opinion on the whole undertaking, but we can discuss that *later*."

Thaddeus rose. "Once my breeches come off, you won't get a sensible word out of me."

She undid the first button of his falls. "A duke rendered speechless. How often does that happen?"

More buttons came undone. "My guess is, it will happen

frequently when I'm private with you." What a revelation that was. For so long, Thaddeus had regarded his duty to marry as only that—an obligation hovering near the top of his long list of obligations, but never quite ascending to the highest position. He had an heir and a spare, and while marriage might entail some pleasant aspects, as a dinner obligation might include a good selection of wines, he'd never imagined himself in a match that involved passion, much less...

Lady Edith stepped back, having undone the falls of Thaddeus's breeches.

"Your dress next?" he asked.

She nodded and reached for her hem, but Thaddeus stopped her. "Allow me."

He drew the dress up slowly, careful not to catch any hooks or buttons on her hair. Her chemise was worn to a whisper, remnants of white work embroidery still visible about the hem. She'd tied off her stays in front, which made untying them simple.

"That moment when a woman is freed of her corsetry has to count among the most pleasurable of her whole day," Edith said, folding her stays and laying them on the shelf of the washstand. "You mustn't tell anybody I said that."

"Your secret is safe with me. I feel the same way about shedding evening attire." They shared the sort of smile lovers often exchanged, not erotic, but pleased and trusting. "Shall we to bed, my lady?"

He longed to remove her wrinkled shift and behold the naked whole of her, but that decision was hers.

"Bed in the middle of the day seems so decadent," she said, climbing onto the mattress. "But it's not as if we're to indulge in the nap, is it?"

"A nap would be more indulgent than lovemaking?" Thaddeus pulled his shirt over his head and draped it over another one of her dresses.

"In some regards, yes. Napping is the ultimate indulgence. I've been tempted to climb under the covers and not wake up until..." She scooted beneath the quilt. "My brother has a play under consideration. The theater told him they'd make a decision last week, but they've put him off again."

Thaddeus wanted to offer her reassurances. His wealth was considerable. He could buy her brother a theater, guarantee her the right to nap all day when she pleased to, and promise her a world where waking up would be, if not a joy, at least not a sorrow.

The lady was all but naked amid the pillows. She did not need fine speeches from him now—more fine speeches.

Instead, he peeled out of his breeches and linen and stood naked beside the bed. "Are we agreed, that if I doze off after our exertions, you will do me the great honor of joining me in slumber?"

Her smile was sweet, naughty, and wistful. "We are agreed. Naps all around in the middle of the afternoon. Won't you please come to bed, Your Grace?"

Thaddeus stroked the erection already at full salute. "Perhaps now would be a good time to abandon proper address?"

She patted the bed. "You may call me Edie. Come to bed, Thaddeus."

He came to bed.

CHAPTER 6

"Some scandals are infinitely more diverting than others."
From *How to Ruin a Duke* by Anonymous

"Mama, your lap desk has become an appendage of late." Jeremiah took the wing chair facing Her Grace's loveseat. "Don't you collect enough gossip during the Season to sustain you?"

She did not so much as look up from her scribbling. "If you were more attentive to correspondence, you might have a diplomatic post by now. One never knows when an old school chum or his papa might hear of a vacancy."

"Preserve me from a post where I must eavesdrop over cheap wine at some pumpernickel court, or worse, perish of lung fever in St. Petersburg."

The duchess dipped her quill. "And yet you long to perish of malaria in the jungles of India. How like a male to bring not a jot of logic to his own situation. Emory could likely get you a position in France or Belgium. Possibly Italy. Even the Germans have excellent wine, if that's the criteria by which you evaluate an opportunity."

She was in a mood, as only Mama could be in a mood. "Why

hasn't Emory hired you a new companion? It's been what, three months, since Lady Edith quit the field?"

Now Mama looked up, her gaze suggesting Jeremiah had told a ribald joke at a formal dinner party, a transgression he hadn't committed for three dreary, well-behaved years.

"Her ladyship left this household six months ago, sir. She refused to remain even when I offered to increase her salary by half. Perhaps you know why that might be?"

"Haven't a clue. Women are fickle. Witness, nobody was willing to marry the old dear, were they?" He'd stretched the facts a bit with that remark. Lady Edith wasn't old, wasn't even close to old, more's the pity.

"And nobody is clamoring to marry you either, my boy. They aren't even clamoring to marry your brother these days, and that is a problem I had not foreseen."

The afternoon was taking a tedious turn. "Angels defend us, when a duke has to work at winning a woman's favor. He should be able to simply wave his... *hand,* and line up potential duchesses for parade inspection, is that it? A title acquits a man of all faults, from lack of humor to lack of humility and everything in between. Emory doesn't even trouble over his wardrobe overmuch, and yet, you claim he's to have any duchess he pleases at the snap of his fingers."

Mama went back to her writing. "Jealousy is such an unbecoming trait in a man who wants for nothing and never has."

"Spite is no more attractive in a woman who has everything she desires and more. And as for my wants, what would you know of them? You are too busy summoning your coven to choose the next hapless bachelor and giggling demoiselle to consign to wedlock. I want more than dancing slippers and good wine for my lot, Mama. A man can make his fortune in India, he can escape the thankless tedium of perpetual heir-dom. He can live his own life."

"I have given birth to two idiots, though you, as the better looking and more charming of the two give me the greater sorrow. Marry an heiress if you don't care for heir-dom. Stop whining about India, where you can be felled by fever within a week of strutting off the boat. Emory will stand firm against buying you your colors until his own nursery is in hand. If you haven't the patience to serve out that sentence, then do something productive."

Perhaps only an idiot could give birth to idiots. Jeremiah ought not to hold such sentiments toward his only surviving parent, but Mama ought not to be such a shrew.

"I am now responsible for serving in Emory's stead on no less than four charitable boards."

"And you find," Mama said, setting aside her letter, "that what you thought would be great fun—impersonating the duke—is so much tedium. Why do you think I did not offer to serve in his stead?"

Mama was at her most vexing, which was very vexatious indeed, when she was right. "You declined the honor of supporting charitable causes because you're too busy running the realm from your lap desk."

She also hadn't a companion to drag along with her to the meetings, and doubtless, Lady Edith had done any real work associated with those gatherings. A twinge of guilt had Jeremiah on his feet.

"Off to mind the press of business?" Mama asked. "Or the press of Mrs. Bellassai's person to your own?"

"For your information," Jeremiah said, making a decorous progress toward the door, "I haven't frequented her establishment for some weeks. My family is already battling enough scandal that I needn't stir that pot." Besides, the lady had made it plain he wasn't welcome, of all the nerve.

Mama took out another sheet of paper. "Jeremiah, I despair of you. I truly do. It's a wonder you weren't the subject of some scandalous book: *How to Waste Good Tailoring and a Generous Allowance.* Find a decent woman with adequate settlements who'll have you, and perhaps Emory will follow your example. Lord knows you seem unable to follow his."

India was not far enough away from such maternal devotion. The Antipodes were not far enough away.

"Would you have me follow him onto the pages of the tattlers, Mama? Though I do believe his reputation is improved by the mischief recounted in that book."

"You think so because, as noted, you haven't an ounce of sense. That book went too far, Jeremiah, and I'm learning that many of the incidents recounted weren't half so madcap as they've been portrayed."

This appeared to worry the duchess. Well, good. Without a companion to vent her spleen upon, Her Grace was clearly in need of something to occupy her. Fretting over Emory would serve nicely.

"I'm going out," Jeremiah said. "Maybe I'll run into an heiress who has a use for a man who's charming, witty, intelligent, handsome, kind to children and animals, and,"—he opened the door—"patient with the elderly."

He closed the door just as a soft thud sounded against the other side, proving he was not a useless cipher after all. If Mama was back to throwing her slippers—a behavior she'd eschewed under Lady Edith's watch—then Jeremiah had at least cheered up his mother.

Though if she were to hire another pretty, soft-spoken, endlessly agreeable companion, that would cheer Jeremiah up a bit too.

Edith's afternoon had taken on the quality of a fairytale. She beheld an entirely naked, very well made lover in a frankly aroused state, and that lover was climbing into bed with her. While the part of her brought up to be a pattern card of feminine decorum admitted to a touch of consternation—His Grace of Emory could rebuke the sovereign with little more than a raised eyebrow—the rest of Edith rejoiced.

Poverty was lonely and uncomfortable. A lady fallen on hard times became invisible to those who could help her, and all too obvious to those who'd mock her. Thaddeus offered a respite, a place and time set apart from life's frustrations, and he offered her the pleasure of his intimate company.

"Come here," he said, settling on his back and raising an arm. "We must deal with the bow and curtsey."

Edith snuggled against his side. "I beg your pardon?"

"The part where I admit I don't know everything about pleasing a lady, though I have, through diligent study, learned that if a woman is asked, she will often tell me when I'm on the right path—and when I'm not. In the latter event, or even in the former, please don't wait to be asked."

If this bow and curtsey was part of intimate protocol, then Edith's education in frolicking had heretofore been neglected. Her previous experiences hadn't included much in the way of such consideration other than, "Hold still," "Hush, for the love of God," and, "Thanks, pet. Hope you don't mind that I nodded off for a bit."

"You are on the right path," she said, tracing the muscles of Emory's chest. "If I'm not batting at your hands, yanking on your hair, or telling you to for pity's sake give me room to breathe, you're on the right path."

He drew a pin from her hair. "Somebody has not acquitted himself according to the standard to which you, or any female, is entitled." More pins followed the first, forming a pile on the bedside table, until Edith's braid came loose. "I have a theory," Emory went on, "that decent women are kept in sexual ignorance so men might wallow in blissful selfishness, but my theory does not comport with available observations."

Such talk—full of long, prosy sentences, and long, impressive words—inspired Edith to wrap her hand around another long, impressive display.

"What observations are those?" she asked.

"A moment, if you please. My speaking powers are overwhelmed by my gratitude. Do that again."

She stroked him with a slow, loose grip. "About your observations?"

"I haven't any, other than to observe that your touch is divine."

"Focus, Emory. You believe a woman's sexual ignorance allows men to be selfish, but something contradicts your theory." What a delight, to talk in bed and tease a lover.

"If all I wanted was to spend," he said, moving his hips in counterpoint to her hand, "I could and do afford myself that pleasure regularly. If what I want is more than simple animal gratification, then pleasing my lover can only... increase.... my own... satisfaction."

In the next instant, Edith was on her back, a naked duke draped over her.

"Allow me to demonstrate." His kisses began softly, a buss to her check, a ticklish nuzzle along her jaw. The Duke of Emory had a playful streak—and so did Edith. She kissed him back, until flirtatious fencing became dueling in earnest.

When he broke the kiss, they were both panting. "Edith, at the risk of being precipitous..."

She wrapped her hand around him again. "Now would be wonderful. Right here,"—she scooted her hips—"and right *this very moment.*"

Silence spread, the quiet all the more profound for the banter and wrestling that had preceded it. Emory moved slowly as he joined himself to her, his rhythm perfectly designed to shift the mood from lusty to intimately precious.

A thread of sadness wove its way past Edith's growing desire. This interlude was stolen against loneliness, worry, and despair, and Edith would not have traded it for all the creature comforts in the world. Still, she could long for more. Emory spoke of being welcome in her bed again, but Edith could not afford to develop expectations where he was concerned.

"Why the sigh?" he whispered, pausing to kiss her brow.

"I'm happy." Part of the truth.

"Let's see if we can make you happier."

He did, oh, he did. The diabolical wretch inspired such an explosion of pleasure that she cried out, clinging to him and wringing the last drop of satisfaction from him, only to lie spent as he withdrew and finished on her belly.

The bliss of gratification was all encompassing, chasing away every regret and doubt Edith had ever claimed. If she'd kept her post as a companion, she could not have had this moment, Emory drowsing in her arms while she sketched the petals of an iris on his back. If she had remained in his mother's employ, the distance between her and Emory would have been unbridgeable, the swift currents of propriety and differing stations ever separating them.

"Being a well mannered mastodon," Emory said, "I will make use of that handkerchief, if you'll pass it to me."

Edith obliged, resenting the intrusion of practicality even as she appreciated Emory's lack of pretension. He was brisk and thorough about the tidying up, and when she expected him to be just as brisk about donning his clothing, he instead pitched the linen in the direction of his boots and rolled to his side.

"Let's move on to the truly decadent portion of the program," he said, pulling Edith into the curve of his body. "Let's have a nap, shall we?"

He had the knack of cuddling without smothering, of being warm but not hot, of keeping a moment light without shading into frivolity. He was, in short, the fairytale lover of Edith's dreams, and she was going to miss him for the rest of her life.

Thaddeus drifted off on a rose-scented breeze. For the rest of his life, the simple, profound, mysterious delight of making love with Edith Charbonneau, soon to be Edith, Her Grace of Emory, was to be his. That great gift made up for all the slanderous books anybody could ever write about him or his progeny.

Edith was a passionate, inventive, demanding lover, and Thaddeus was honestly, blissfully worn out. Withdrawing had been a habit, and thank God for that. If Edith wanted a lengthy engagement,

Thaddeus would oblige with good grace, provided the engagement wasn't celibate.

His nap was short and deep, as if his soul knew he'd at last found his way into the right bed. Edith, by contrast, slumbered on, allowing him the smug pleasure of concluding he'd loved her to exhaustion.

And, true to mastodon form, he was hungry again. They'd shared one meal on the back porch and another in the parlor. Why not bring his lady a snack in bed?

Thaddeus eased from the covers and donned shirt and breeches in silence. Edith stirred sleepily, a fetching picture amid the pillows. Her braid had come loose, a golden skein curling past her shoulder, and one rosy breast peeking from beneath the quilt.

"Food," he muttered. "Sustenance. Allow the lady to keep up her strength. We aren't all mastodons."

The notion of rearing a herd of little mastodons and mastodonesses with Edith cheered him as he made his way to the kitchen and retrieved a glass of lemonade, an orange, and two pieces of shortbread. He passed Edith's desk, where her work in progress had clearly occupied her prior to his arrival.

He didn't think to peek, though she'd mentioned discussing the project with him. His intent was to leave her a note, a small expression of fondness for her to find after he'd left, though fondness was putting the situation mildly. Thaddeus finally understood all the friends who'd become distracted, smiling, oddly quiet creatures upon the occasion of taking a spouse.

"They are happy, those fellows. I suspect their wives are too." He set the food on the edge of the desk and took the chair. He was so far gone on newfound dreams of connubial joy that he was even pleased to be sitting in the very chair where Edith sat.

"Daft," he said, taking a bite of a shortbread. "But happy. A fair trade."

He reached for a sheet of foolscap, though Edith's manuscript sat just to his left. Her penmanship was all that a lady's should be, graceful, legible, and without a blot or correction.

He didn't mean to peek, truly he didn't, and yet...

Dear reader, if you assume the escapades of the Duke of Amorous were sufficient to fill only one volume, I must respectfully inform you that you are in error. His Grace's peccadillos are more interesting and numerous than you have been led to believe. That revelation astounds the imagination, I know, but read on and be amazed....

The shortbread turned to ashes in Thaddeus's mouth. He absolutely *was* astounded, at his own stupidity. His own gullibility. His own...

"The mastodon became extinct, probably because he was no smarter than I have been."

Thaddeus could not bring himself to read on, and before he could retrieve the rest of his clothes from the bedroom he needed time to marshal his wits. He rose from the chair, feeling unclean, furious, and...

Determined, by God. The word took on new meaning, in fact. Perhaps Lady Edith had been determined to extract the last ounce of revenge upon his family for some slight from Mama, perhaps her ladyship was angry at all of polite society. Not by word or deed would Thaddeus gratify her petty maneuvers with an opportunity to fling her excuses in his face.

He forced himself to breathe slowly and evenly, to set aside hurt feelings and shame. He returned the rest of the food to the kitchen for his appetite had been replaced by nausea. Logic came to his aid, and a plan began to take shape. If Lady Edith thought she could destroy the reputation of a duke, well, she'd tilted at that windmill, and Thaddeus was still standing. She'd failed to account for the fact that, much more easily than a duke could be brought low by undeserved defamation, he could push an impoverished schemer into utter ruin merely by airing the truth.

First, he would depart the premises without disclosing what he'd learned.

Second, he would have a word with Mama, and through her vast network of gossips, he'd put the truth of Lady Edith's perfidy before all of polite society.

Third, he'd offer her ladyship a small sum in exchange for the rights to her scribblings and a promise that she'd quit the metropolis, never to return.

Fourth, he'd get quietly drunk and try to forgive himself for having trusted her.

When he returned to the bedroom, he found the author of his troubles still asleep, the picture of feminine innocence. He tucked the covers up around her, because the sight of her dreaming so peacefully exacerbated his temper.

How dare she? He dressed quickly and quietly, seething all the while. He'd provided her a home and a livelihood for months, and she'd thanked him by turning her back on his family, then penning a pack of misrepresentations and exaggerations. The nerve, the unmitigated hubris, the sheer, unpardonable...

He'd just finished tying his cravat when he realized Edith watched him from the bed.

"Must you go?" she asked, sitting up. "I know better than to ask that. You're a busy man, but I wish you could tarry longer."

So she could snack on the remnants of his dignity? Thaddeus pulled the knot in his linen snug and smiled at her over his shoulder.

"Alas, I must leave, my lady. I wish I had no cause to abandon you, but I am compelled by the duties of my station to quit the premises. You needn't see me out." He didn't want her hands on him, didn't want to see her unclothed, didn't want to acknowledge what a great, pathetic fool he'd been.

She fished her chemise from beneath the covers and slipped it over her head. Thaddeus fiddled with his sleeve buttons rather than gawk at what he should never have seen.

"I'll at least kiss you farewell," she said. "This interlude was an unexpected pleasure. I hope you have no regrets?"

Oh, he had regrets. He regretted not trusting his first instincts where she was concerned, he regretted that she was so much that he could esteem and everything he abhorred. He regretted ever welcoming her into his household.

"Regrets are so tedious," he said, consulting his watch. "If you have regrets, I hope they won't trouble you for long." Three or four eternities should be sufficient, provided they were spent in a purgatory of unrelenting opprobrium.

She left the bed and drew on a dressing gown that had been draped over the footboard. "I have no regrets. None at all."

She snuggled up against him, and he nearly embraced her out of... what? Stupidity? Reflex?

"I really must be going," he said. "Duty calls and all that." He sounded like Jeremiah, sidling away from responsibility while pretending to move briskly toward it, though getting free of Lady Edith's company had become imperative. She wasn't acting guilty, she wasn't acting smug.

She seemed sad to him, but that had to be more of her deceptive nature on display.

"Then be off," she said, smiling up at him. "I have work to do, and I'm sure you have appointments to keep."

He braced himself to endure a kiss on the mouth, but she instead kissed his cheek and lingered near for a moment, then stepped back. His escape was apparently to be successful, no shouting, no accusations, no disclosing his intentions where she was concerned, no... anything.

"Good-bye," she said, gathering the dressing gown around herself.

The bed was rumpled behind her, her feet were bare, and her braid was coming undone. Nonetheless, her bearing was dignified, and that—the quality of her silence, the calm in her gaze—vexed Thaddeus into nearly blurting out what he'd found.

He bowed without taking her hand. "Good-bye." By sheer force of will, he made his way down the steps and out the front door, pausing only to collect his hat, gloves, and walking stick. He kept marching, no looking back, no last glance over his shoulder to see if the lady watched him depart.

He'd been a fool. Women had been making fools of men since the dawn of history. Perhaps somebody should write a book about that, about all the times men had been led astray by...

His steps slowed as he approached the corner. He did steal a glance at the tired, humble dwelling where he'd left a piece of his heart and all of his delusions. Lady Edith stood in the window of the upper story, a pale figure who didn't look to be gloating. She dabbed at her cheek with the edge of a shawl, the quality of the gesture suggesting that Thaddeus had, in fact, left her in tears.

She moved away from the window, and he stepped off the walk-way, nearly getting himself run over by a stylish phaeton pulled by matching bays.

"I have the best news, Edie!" Foster took her by the hand and waltzed with her around the parlor before he'd even removed his top hat. "The very, very best. Behold,"—he stopped mid-twirl and swooped a graceful bow—"the next playwright-in-residence at the Maloney Lane Theater."

Joy made a good effort to push aside Edith's sorrow. "Playwright-in-residence? They will produce your work?"

"My works—plural." Foster doffed his hat and caught it on the handle of his walking stick. "Three plays a year for the next two years. I am to contribute farces and interludes for other major productions, and I have a say on what those productions might be. My duties will be endless. I'm to assist with casting, find sponsors, monitor the directors, consult on the costumes..." He executed a double pirouette and then dipped another bow.

"I have work for you, Edie. Stitching costumes, assisting with stage direction, choosing the props, writing the playbills. I told the committee that my sister is my muse, and I must have your inspiration to call upon. They were shocked, you being a lady and all, but that bunch enjoys shaking things up. Witness,"—more twirling ending in a leap—"they hired me."

He landed in a kneeling position as lightly as a breeze-borne leaf in the center of the hearthrug. "Say you're pleased, dearest Edie. I know the theater isn't quite proper, and you'd rather I become a famous author, but my heart's with the stage."

He rose and dusted himself off, as Edith must dust herself off.

"I am so pleased, and so proud of you, Foster. I don't know what to say. You have accomplished the impossible with nothing to aid you but determination and providence."

"Not so." He tossed his hat through the doorway, so his millinery came to rest on the sideboard. "I had your faith in me, I had your careful eye reading all of my rough drafts. I had you to cheer me on when the larger houses turned up their noses and told me my work was hopeless. I had the knowledge that you were proud of me simply because I'm too stubborn to give up. All those years of bouncing through the homes of cousins and aunties, you took up for me. You refused to be separated from me and I am gloriously happy to be able to repay a small portion of your loyalty now."

He looked gloriously happy, and well he should.

"I knew that if you knocked on the right doors with the right material, your talent would win the day. I am beyond elated for you." Though the prospect of working in a theater... that was another step away from the expectations of a lady.

More like a grand leap in the opposite direction, but not necessarily in the wrong direction. A woman had to eat, though she did not live by bread alone.

"There's more, Edie. I haven't occupied myself entirely with peddling my plays, you know."

If he announced that he was taking a wife, she would... be happy for him, right after she ran back upstairs and indulged in another bout of useless tears.

"Don't keep me in suspense, Foster."

"I've been looking at houses. We can afford to move, Edie. I've found a place I'd like to show you—now, this instant. It's not far, and it's on a little private square. We'll have real grass off the back terrace, nearly three square yards of weeds, so you can take some irises to plant there if you're of a mind to. Say you'll look at it with me, please?"

Edith didn't want to go anywhere. She wanted to crawl back to bed and contemplate the great folly of having shared that bed with His Grace of Emory. He'd been a tender, considerate, passionate lover, both sweetly affectionate and diabolically skilled.

The moments of drifting off to sleep in his arms had been a greater gift even than the erotic glories. For a short while, Edith had felt cherished and sheltered, all the cares and worries held at bay by a lover's embrace.

She'd woken to find a distracted duke rather than an indulgent lover in her bedroom. Emory had dressed quickly, apparently intent on stealing away without bidding her farewell, and that had been a blow to her heart. No coin had changed hands—Edith would have flung it in his handsome face—but his haste had turned a stolen pleasure into something less. His manner, so brisk and casual, had confirmed that tawdry needn't always involve malicious gossip or monetary arrangements.

She'd lied to him, of course, for when she'd seen him consult his watch in her very bedroom, she did regret yielding to temptation with him. She'd liked him better when she'd known him less intimately, but then, he'd given her exactly what she'd asked for, hadn't he? A stolen moment, a time apart, no expectations on either side.

Foster set his hands on her shoulders. "I've sprung my good news on you all of a sudden, and I haven't once asked about your book. How comes the new project?"

"I made a good start, and I have the sense progress will be swift. I know what story I want to tell."

"Always a plus, when the tale reveals itself at the outset. Will you come see this house with me? It's a lovely day for a walk, and I can't wait to get you away from this dreary little street."

A notion worth supporting. "We must not trade on your expectations, Foster. The theater committee can change their minds."

He took her by the wrist and led her to the front door. "Indeed, they can, in which case, they have to buy out the balance of my contract. I haven't watched you haggle with everybody from the coal man to the fishmonger for no purpose, Edie. They are stuck with me, and I have so many ideas for new productions that tossing three at the Maloney each year will be the work of a few afternoons."

Edith donned her pink cloak, though the garment was on the heavy side for the day's weather.

"You need a new bonnet. Let's start there, shall we?" Foster plunked her hat onto her head. "Let me buy you a new bonnet, at least, to celebrate the great day."

"How about a new cloak instead?" Edith said. "We can stop by the milliners and find some new flowers for this bonnet, but a new cloak would be much appreciated."

"You wear blue quite well, though lavender is also quite pretty on you." He opened the door and bowed her through, the gesture automatic with him.

Edith stopped on the threshold and wrapped him in a hug, and bedamned to any neighbor shocked by such a display of sibling affection. "I do love you, Foster. You are the best of brothers, and I am so proud of you I could take out a notice in the *Times*."

"That tears it," he said, giving her a squeeze. "We look at this new house, buy you a new cloak, and then we stop for ices at Gunter's."

Inspired by his great good spirits, Edith found a smile. "Never let it be said I declined an invitation to Gunter's, much less a new cloak."

They moved down the steps arm in arm, though even the afternoon sunshine was an affront to Edith's mood. Why had Emory

turned up so distant on her, and if he ever did come around again—
bearing sandwiches and professing to want her opinion on his troubles—would she even open the door to him?

"What color cloak would you like?" Foster asked. "Perhaps we
should buy you two, or better still, two cloaks and a new shawl or
three."

What a dear, darling brother he was. "One cloak, and any color so
long as it isn't pink."

"What the hell is wrong with me, that I can miss a woman who'd
betray my trust and the trust of my family to such an execrable
degree?" Thaddeus asked, while in the square around him, children
threw sticks for gamboling puppies and couples flirted on benches.

Why must London in springtime be so dreadfully jolly?

Thaddeus had parted from Lady Edith a week ago, and with each
passing day, he told himself to have a blunt discussion with his
mother, and then an even more direct conversation with her ladyship.
And yet, day followed day, and Thaddeus's mood grew only more
bleak as he did exactly nothing about a most bothersome situation.

"Maybe nothing's wrong with you," Elsmore said, tipping his hat
to a nursery maid pushing a perambulator. "Maybe your conclusions
are what's in error."

Thaddeus had kept to himself the intimate details of his last
encounter with Lady Edith, but he'd told Elsmore the rest of the tale:
Her ladyship was writing the sequel to *How to Ruin a Duke*, which
all but proved she'd written the first volume.

Or did it?

"I know what I saw, Elsmore. I saw yet another manuscript
bruiting about the follies and foibles of the Duke of Amorous, and
written in her hand. She wrote enough letters and invitations for
Mama that I recognized her penmanship."

And heaven help him, that was another fact that weighed in favor of the lady's guilt: Every jot and tittle of gossip that Mama had been privy to by virtue of correspondence had doubtless passed before Lady Edith's eyes.

"You don't want her to be the guilty party," Elsmore said, touching his hat brim to a pair of giggling shop girls. "You are an eminently logical man. Some evidence must be contradicting your own conclusion."

"Must you flirt with every female and infant you pass, Elsmore?"

"I enjoy the company of females and infants. Right now, I don't much enjoy your company, old man. Here's a suggestion: Knock on Lady Edith's door. Rap, rap." He gestured in the air with a gloved fist. "Put the question to her: Are you writing the next installment of my ruin, or did I misconstrue the situation when I ever-so-rudely read your work without your permission?"

"She left it in plain sight."

"And....?"

"And that is not the behavior of a guilty woman." That conclusion bothered Thaddeus, because it gave him hope. He did not want to have hope, he wanted to have the whole situation behind him.

Mostly. "She also said she wanted to discuss the project with me. She was doubtless dissembling."

"You saw evidence of three other projects in progress? Some poetry scribbled in draft? An epistolary adventure featuring a plucky governess, a leering viscount, and a runaway carriage or two? Maybe she's working on a biography of King George?"

"I saw only the one work, but I didn't exactly rifle her drawers."

Elsmore twirled his walking stick. "Because I am your friend, and because the current arrangement of my features has become dear to my mother and sisters, I will not comment on that statement."

"Lady Edith didn't act guilty, and she didn't display the sort of means that a popular book should have generated."

"Oh dear." Elsmore kicked a ball back to a knot of little boys across the square. "Facts in contradiction to your assumption. Whatever shall you do, Your Grace? Shall you fume and fret for another week? I think so. I think you don't know what to do for once. Some-body should write a book about that. The Duke of Emory has been felled by Cupid's arrow. His legendary sense has deserted him, and I, for one, am delighted."

"You, for one, are obnoxious. What the hell am I do to? I can't trust the woman and I can't seem to find the resolve to threaten her with ruin." Unless Thaddeus wanted to risk writing to her ladyship, threatening her with ruin would mean seeing her again, and that...

He wanted to see her again, wanted her to protest her innocence, and he wanted to dunk his head in the nearest horse trough until his common sense returned. He also wanted to know that Edith was well, that she hadn't been evicted from the drab little house on the tired little street.

"Emory, I have known you since you were a prosy little prig taking firsts in Latin without trying. What are you always telling me when I face a difficult choice?"

Thaddeus answered without thinking. "Good decisions are made based on good information." Which pronouncement was no damned perishing help whatsoever.

"So consult with your Mama, chat up your uncles and aunties, have a word with your cousin Antigone, and a blunt talk with Lord Jeremiah. I find the elders and infantry are often more observant than I am, and they all know Lady Edith. They've all read the book, they all know you. Ask for their perspective, and you might learn some-thing useful."

Elsmore was awash in family, and he seemed to delight in the role of benevolent patriarch. He could kick a ball straight across the square because at family picnics, he doubtless played with his neph-ews. He made shop girls smile because his legion of lady cousins all relied on him to partner them on their expeditions to the milliner's, and he had perfected the roles of favorite nephew and devoted cousin.

The varlet. "I suppose even your perspective might occasionally bear a passing resemblance to useful."

"Talk to your mother, Emory. Don't lecture her, humor her, or interrupt her. Talk to her."

Must I? But yes, he must. A woman in a pink cloak hurried down the street at the side of the square, and Thaddeus nearly sprinted after her. The shade wasn't quite ugly enough to be Lady Edith's cloak, but London held a plethora of pink cloaks when a man never wanted to see one again.

Or when he dreamed about them every night.

"If you'll excuse me," Thaddeus said, "on the off chance that your suggestion has a scintilla of merit, I must consult with my mother."

He would have parted from Elsmore on that note, but Elsmore's hand on his arm stopped him. "If it's any consolation, my mother and sisters adored Lady Edith. She's either the best confidence trickster in Mayfair, or the instincts that prod you to exonerate her are to be trusted. I liked her, and while I am uniformly pleasant to all in my ambit, I don't permit myself to actually *like* too many of the unattached ladies."

Because a duke's liking was easily misconstrued, and yet, Thaddeus liked Lady Edith too—or had liked her, and then much more than liked her.

"My thanks for your sage advice," Thaddeus said. "Regards to your family."

"Likewise." Elsmore strode off in the direction of the squabbling boys, whom he would all doubtless treat to an ice. The damned man was a curious sort of duke, but he was a more than dear friend.

Thaddeus quit the square at a fast march, before another pink cloak or outlandish bonnet could distract him from his next challenge.

CHAPTER 7

"A titled fool is Cupid's favorite target."
From *How to Ruin a Duke* by Anonymous

"Mama, might I have a few minutes of your time?"

The duchess slowly put down her book as if a distant strain of music had caught her ear. "A moment, please." She rose from her chaise and went to the window. "I see neither a falling sky nor winged swine, and yet, a miracle has occurred. His Grace of Emory is asking *me* for a moment of *my* time rather than the converse."

She crossed the room to take Thaddeus's hand and place it on her brow. "Am I feverish? Perhaps dementia is to strike me down at a tragically young age. Or maybe my hearing is failing. Tell me the truth, Emory. Did you or did you not just ask for a few minutes of my time?"

"I did, and the matter is of some import."

She returned to her chaise and took up her book. "All of your matters are of some import—to you. If you're thinking of offering for that hopeless Blessington girl, please spare me the discussion. She'll make you miserable, and the only person in this household permitted to dabble in misery is myself."

Thaddeus sat on the end of her couch. "*Are* you miserable?" He'd recently realized that one could be miserable amid abundance or one could be content with little. A few irises in a jar brought just as much joy as the two dozen roses purchased to bloom on Mama's writing desk. The trick was to notice both, to appreciate them.

"No, I am not miserable," Mama replied, smiling faintly. "Emory, are you well? This business with that dreadful book has affected your humors."

"I am in good health, but troubled. Did you write *How to Ruin a Duke*, Mama?"

She turned a page. "I am in good health as well, thank you very much." She kept up the pretense of reading for another half a minute. "No, I did not write that book. As far as I can tell, none of your uncles or aunts did either. Antigone hasn't the self-discipline to write a whole volume, and Cousin Anstruther hasn't the wit."

"You've been trying to discover the author?"

A basilisk stare greeted the inquiry. "No, Thaddeus. I've been trying on bonnets all day while rumors abound that a sequel is to be published. When I tire of admiring my reflection, I ring for confits and tea to restore my strength. Self-absorption can be so taxing, don't you think? You would know, after all."

"I thought perhaps you wrote *How to Ruin a Duke*." She had the self-discipline, the free time, and the acerbic wit.

She set her book aside again. "You think that I...? I don't know whether to be flattered or insulted. The person who *should* have written that book is your late father. He meant well, but his notions of how to bring up his son and heir were sadly lacking. Do you know, I wish at least some of the incidents in that blasted book were true."

"They were all true, up to a point, and then the author took liberties with the facts."

"Doom to any who take liberties with the facts, of course, which suggests the author knew you well enough to know how intolerable you find even everyday falsehoods. Whom do you suspect, Thaddeus?"

She almost never used his given name, but then, they almost never talked. They chatted, they quarreled, they exchanged a few comments over breakfast, and yet clearly, Mama was—in her way—an ally.

Good to know.

"I suspect everybody and nobody in particular, but I have wondered if Lady Edith Charbonneau would have a reason to wish me ill."

Mama drew her feet up and wrapped her arms about her knees. "Lady Edith? I cannot think her capable of such malice. She is a truly kind woman. I should know for I tried her patience to the utmost. If she were to write a book excoriating any member of this family, she would go after Jeremiah."

To Thaddeus's consternation, Mama was in complete earnest. "Jeremiah? He's the only member of the family to claim a surfcit of charm." Thaddeus tried to dredge up any mentions made of Jeremiah in his discussions with Lady Edith, and... nothing of any substance came to mind. They'd talked of Mama, Antigone, Cousin Anstruther, but—significantly—not about Jeremiah except in passing.

"Jeremiah exerts himself to be charming when he wants something, Emory. Have you ever noticed that he offers to take me driving toward the end of the fortnight even when it's not his turn? He uses the public outing to press me for advances on his allowance. He knows I will not quarrel with him in the middle of the carriage parade, just as I know he will never pay me back."

Thaddeus got up to pace. "He could not have borrowed money from Lady Edith. She hasn't any, and her wages weren't that generous." Though if Jeremiah had borrowed money from her and not paid the loan back, would that justify a grudge serious enough to result in a slanderous book?

Mama watched him, her expression putting Thaddeus in mind of a cat about to swipe a paw across the nose of an annoying puppy. "Do you truly believe I have employed three different companions in the past five years because my sour nature alone defeats them?"

Thaddeus had thought that very thing. "Lady Edith, at least, left without having another post to go to. Something or somebody made the situation here intolerable, and thus I've speculated that she has a motive to write a nasty book."

Mama swung her legs over the side of the chaise and slipped her feet into a pair of embroidered house mules. "I wasn't aware that Lady Edith hadn't located another post."

"Not as of last week. She's attempting to make a living writing domestic advice, but I gather she hasn't found a publisher yet."

Mama stared at her slippers. "I have wondered whether you were aware of the problem Jeremiah poses. I am finally ready to let you send him to India, Emory. He should have known better than to bother Edith. She is a true lady, and if she'd condemned him publicly, she would have been believed."

Thaddeus felt again the queasy, disoriented dread he'd experienced in Lady Edith's parlor. "You are saying that Jeremiah—*my brother*—bothered a woman in the family's employ? He pressed his attentions upon her ladyship uninvited?"

"He's not you, Thaddeus, to observe all the courtesies and protocols. I fear the boy takes after me rather too much."

"You would never inveigle a footman into improprieties, Mama. You are sure Jeremiah forgot himself with Lady Edith?" Thaddeus wanted this flight to be one of Mama's attempts at humor, a mistake, anything but the truth. And yet... the facts, the damnable, inescapable facts, supported Mama's conclusion.

"Edith left to avoid Jeremiah's advances." Mama rose. "She did not come right out and say that. She hinted, I ignored her hints. The previous two companions had come to me with similar tales. I thought one or two women misconstruing Jeremiah's friendliness was possible, but when Edith... She didn't want more money, she didn't want to become the object of unkind talk, she didn't want anything but the wages due her and a decent character. I gave her both."

"Three women, Mama? He's behaved abominably with *three* women and I'm only learning of it now? Are the maids safe?"

"The housekeeper knows to assign them in pairs. They are safe. It's as if Jeremiah is jealous of my companions because I have a play-mate and he does not. He also thought strutting around in your shoes with those damned charities would be a great lark, but he's learned otherwise. No organization is more inefficient or pompous than an eleemosynary guild devoted to flowers, unless it's the Charitable Committee for the—"

Thaddeus held up a hand. "Please do not attempt to change the subject. I can barely credit that my brother has betrayed the one iron-clad rule of gentlemanly deportment and imposed his attentions on women drawing wages under this very roof."

Mama set her book on the mantel. "He's a spoiled brat, Emory. I know because I am too. You have escaped our fate, which makes me wroth that you have been the butt of that awful book. You have given no one cause to treat you thus—and certainly Lady Edith would not have done so—but then, London is full of spoiled brats, isn't it?"

Thaddeus was torn between the compulsion to find Lady Edith and apologize to her on bended knee—on his damned hands and knees if necessary—and the urgent need to beat Jeremiah senseless.

"You're truly willing to let me buy Jeremiah a commission?" Thaddeus asked.

"I had hoped to keep him safe, but when it comes down to it, my companions aren't safe when he's underfoot. He runs with a naughty crowd, his gambling debts have to be considerable, and he's not maturing as he should."

Jeremiah had gambling debts—substantial gambling debts—and proceeds from the sales of a popular book would help pay them off.

Jeremiah ran with a crowd of inebriated idlers who challenged each other with the most ridiculous and dangerous wagers.

"Jeremiah was involved in every embarrassing, inane incident portrayed in *How to Ruin a Duke*, Mama. Most of them I undertook to spare him a lost wager, a dangerous prank, or a stupid duel. I suspect my own brother is literally the author of my present difficulties."

"Don't kill him," Mama said. "If anybody is to wring his wretched neck it should be me, but Thaddeus?"

He stopped halfway to the door. "I'll do better, Mama. I will take you driving when you don't ask it of me, I will inquire after your health. I will find you another companion who—"

She patted his chest. "Stop. If you turn up doting on me now, I will disown you. About Lady Edith?"

The Lady Edith who was entirely innocent of wrongdoing? "Yes?"

"She fancied you. She was discreet about it, she never said a word, but she knew when you'd come home at night from the way the front door closed. She learned how you take your tea. She knows you cannot be trusted around Italian cream cake."

"Neither can she."

"Well there you have it. You'd never want for something to bicker over if you married her."

"Married her?"

"She's an earl's daughter, you fancied her too, and Jeremiah will have to remain in the army for at least several years before he can sell his commission. Now go pummel your brother."

She kissed his cheek and shoved him on the arm.

"Mama, I can for once promise that your wish will be my command." He stalked from the room, though—drat the damned luck —the butler reported that Jeremiah was out, and had not said when to expect him home.

"Edie, why didn't you tell me you'd gone to the agencies again?" Foster's question was more hurt than chiding, though he'd waited until the maid of all work had withdrawn from the breakfast parlor to pose it.

"Because I've been to the agencies many times. I did not expect a post to become available." Except that this time, Edith had told the sniffy little clerk that she was willing to accept a position anywhere in Britain except London. She'd had three choices within a matter of days.

"You'll come back to see my opening night won't you?" Foster asked, setting the teapot near her elbow.

"I made that a condition of accepting the offer. Manchester isn't so very far away."

"Manchester is 200 miles away over bad roads, Edie. You couldn't find anything closer?"

Both of the other positions had been closer. "The household in Manchester will suit me. I won't have to face polite society again, and you can't know what a relief that will be."

Every tall man striding along the walk in a top hat and morning attire gave Edith a start, and she'd bid Emory farewell nearly ten days ago.

Foster poured her a third cup of tea—luxury upon luxury—and sat back. "You don't have to face polite society here either. I only mentioned working at the theater because I love being there, and I thought you liked having your own money. You could do more writing, which you seem to delight in, and I wouldn't have to fret that you're perishing of cold and overwork in the north."

"I won't perish." If watching Emory march away, and not hearing from him at all, not even the obligatory anonymous bouquet, hadn't felled her, nothing would.

"You won't flourish either. Anybody who can sit at that writing desk for more than a week straight, scribbling away hour after hour, has a vocation not to be ignored. Your book is quite witty and deserves to be published."

How many times in recent months had Edith longed for even a second cup of tea? She was on her third of the morning, and it did nothing to comfort the hollow ache she'd carried for days.

"If the book has promise, that's because I had months to study my subject." And she'd have the rest of her life to wonder what had sent him out the door in such an odd mood. "Emory is the soul of decency, of that I have no doubt." Perhaps he'd had bad experiences with women before, women who clung and tried to extort promises from him.

No matter. He was gone and he wasn't coming back.

"But you aren't even attempting to find a publisher," Foster said. "The past six months have taken a toll on you. The Edie who all but raised me would be waving that manuscript under the noses of every publisher in Town, and why you won't allow me to make inquiries on your behalf utterly defeats my—"

"Please, Foster. You'll be late for rehearsal." She'd written that manuscript out of a need to exorcise a broken heart, or perhaps to justify her decision to become intimate with Emory. He was a good man, a bit stern, a bit imposing, but good. The way he'd left her, nary a word of explanation, wasn't in keeping with his character.

The other duke, the *How to Ruin a Duke* fellow, *he* would have availed himself of a lady's favors and then dodged off to his clubs to brag of his exploits.

"I'm away then," Foster said, rising. "I wish you'd reconsider leaving London—and me. I will miss you desperately." He kissed her cheek and bustled off to a job that was making him happier by the day.

"You will miss me for about twenty minutes," Edith said to the empty room.

This house was in a much nicer neighborhood than the last, and while it was tiny, it was also sturdy, spotless, and situated on a quiet street. The back garden was half in sun and half in shade, but nobody had thought to plant flowers there.

Edith finished her tea and retrieved her new cloak—dark blue—then went around to the mews in the alley and borrowed a bucket and trowel. As she traveled the several streets to her previous abode, she realized that walking unaccompanied no longer bothered her. To go back to the polite fiction that a lady needed an escort at all times would be like donning a corset that laced too snugly, and she wasn't looking forward to it.

Perhaps Manchester would be different. For a certainty, it was rumored to be dirtier than London, which did not seem possible. Edith turned onto her former street and fished in her pocket for a coin. James, the lad who aspired to become a crossing sweeper, was idling as usual beneath a lamp post.

"How fare you today, young James?"

"Miss Edith! I thought you'd piked off."

She dropped the coin into his grimy little mitt. "My brother and I have moved. I'm back to dig up some of the irises so he'll have a few flowers at the new house. When I'm through, you should pick a bouquet to sell to passersby."

The coin disappeared into a pocket. "I can sell your flowers?"

"You'll likely have more luck if you offer them at a spot with plenty of foot traffic. Oxford Road, for example. Pick a bunch and sell them, then pick another bunch tomorrow. Offer them to people dressed well enough to spare a coin for a flower." To devise that scheme would have been beyond her six months ago.

"I like flowers," James said, falling in step beside her. "They smell pretty, like you."

"Flatterer. Bring a few to your mother too. The flowers should not go to waste, and they only bloom for a short time. The new tenant won't move in until the end of the month, and by then the irises will be fading."

James skipped along at her side and chattered about everything from the Mad King to his friend Cora the mud lark. In no time, Edith had a bucketful of muddy roots and green foliage.

"If I sell all of these, I'll be rich!" James said, burying his nose amid his bouquet.

"You will have a few coppers," Edith replied. "Save them for when your mama has nothing to spend at market, and she will thank you for it."

He accompanied her halfway back to her new abode, choosing a busy intersection for his commercial venture.

"Thanks, Miss Edith. Mama will thank you too."

Miss Edith. Being Miss Edith as opposed to Lady Edith wasn't so bad. Lady Edith could not have set this boy on the path to earning money. She would not have carried a muddy bucket down a London street just to ensure her brother had something to remember her by.

And—this thought pounced, like an unseen cat springing from the undergrowth—*Miss Edith* would not have surrendered her post because a philandering numbskull of a courtesy lord had caught her on the backstairs.

James separated a half dozen stems from the armful he'd been carrying. "You should have these, Miss."

"That is very kind of you, James." Edith took two flowers and added them to her bucket. "Good luck with your venture."

"That fancy cove came back around, you know. The tall gent with the fancy walking stick." James had the grace to say this quietly.

"I beg your pardon?"

"The man with the expensive coat." James took a half dozen steps along the walkway at a purposeful march, shoulders angled slightly forward. "All business, that one. He paid a call or two on you before you moved. He came around yesterday and the day before and fair pounded the door down. I told him you'd moved. He gave me tuppence and told me to take a bath. Be he daft?"

"My caller came by again?"

"Twice. He's not friendly. I still have the tuppence and I don't have to take a bath until Saturday."

All manner of emotions welled at James's news. Pleasure, consternation, curiosity, and not a little anger. What sort of lover waits more than a week to stroll by again? Why not send a note? A letter, a bouquet? A little farewell message? *Anything?*

"Thank you for telling me this, James. It matters." Though just how it mattered, Edith did not know.

"If he comes around again, do I give him your direction?"

A young fellow walking a large dog hovered nearby, apparently intent on purchasing flowers.

"No need for that, James. I'm off to Manchester in a few days. I believe your first customer awaits."

She left James transacting business with all the aplomb of London's premier flower nabob, and was soon in her new back yard, tucking iris roots into rich, warm soil. She watered the plants sparingly—irises could rot if overcome with damp—and considered the rest of her day.

She knew now how Emory had felt about discovering the author of *How to Ruin a Duke*. He'd been beyond curious, he'd *had* to know exactly who and what had brought him low. Finding that answer had become a quest for him.

Edith had spent more than a week focusing on memories of her time with the ducal family. She'd gone through the nasty book page by page—thank heavens a friend had been able to borrow the bound version for her from the lending library—she'd considered each incident in detail. She had a very good idea exactly who had penned those lies, and before she left London, she would share her suspicions with Emory.

And then—after conveying to His Perishing Grace a few other sentiments—she would get an explanation from him as to why he'd come back to call on her, and why he'd been least-in-sight for more than a week before he'd done so.

Jeremiah, with suspiciously convenient timing, had chosen to drop out of sight for a few days just when Thaddeus urgently needed to pummel him. His lordship occasionally did this, sometimes to indulge in a marathon card game, sometimes to make a madcap dash to Brighton with friends.

Thaddeus suspected Jeremiah also disappeared periodically to provoke Mama to worrying and to avoid creditors.

Thaddeus's temper had not cooled in the *slightest* during Jeremiah's absence, but he had put the time to good use nonetheless.

"You will excuse us," Thaddeus said to Jeremiah's valet, as his lordship snored away the morning, naked to the knees amid snowy sheets and satin pillows.

"Of course, Your Grace. Found Himself on the stairs at cockcrow. He's likely to wake with a devil of a head."

And that will be the least of his worries. "Splendid. As of next week, his lordship will no longer need your services. Your wages will continue until we can find you a new post. You will have a glowing character and some severance as well."

The man wrinkled his nose. "You needn't pay me severance, Your Grace. I was preparing to give notice. I know the young gents are full of high spirits, but that one..." The valet shook his head. "I'll not speak ill of my betters. You need not worry on that score." He picked up the muddy boots at the foot of Jeremiah's bed and departed.

Thaddeus's gaze landed on a razor strop hanging on a paneled privacy screen in the corner of the room. He opened the bedroom curtains wide, took up the strop and delivered a glancing blow to his lordship's backside.

"A valet has more honor than my heir."

Jeremiah stirred. "Go away, darling. I'm not in the mood to play anymore."

Thaddeus brought the razor strop down again, not as gently. "Get out of that bed. *Now.*"

Jeremiah rolled over and propped himself on his elbows. "What the devil? Emory, what on earth are you about?"

"Why did you do it, Jeremiah?"

Jeremiah eyed the strop. He sat up and scratched his chest, his hair a greasy mess, his eyes rimmed with shadows. "Had a bit of an orgy as best I recall. If you'll send my valet—"

Thaddeus flung a dressing gown at him. "I asked you a question, and unless you want a private reading of *How to Beat the Hell Out of a Courtesy Lord*, you will answer honestly."

Jeremiah shrugged into the dressing gown and rose to belt it around his middle. "Why'd I dash off that bit of tattle everybody finds so amusing?" His air was defiant, though he was keeping an eye on the length of leather in Thaddeus's hands.

"Why did you try to disgrace a brother who's never been anything but decent to you?"

His traitor-ship yawned and stretched, not a care in the world. "One of the fellows said it couldn't be done. Said nobody could tarnish the reputation of His Grace of Emory, and I took the bet."

"Why?"

"Because I am bloody bored waiting for you to find a duchess? Because I could? Because I didn't want to beg you for more coin or scarper on my debts of honor?"

Thaddeus hung the strop back on its hook, lest he lay into his brother for the sin of sheer stupidity. "Instead you pester Mama for coin, just as you pestered her companions for favors. Not the done thing, Jeremiah."

Jeremiah poured himself a glass of brandy from a decanter on his clothes press. "A little harmless flirtation never hurt anybody. You might know that if you'd ever given it a try."

Thaddeus threw a heeled dancing slipper at him, which caused the brandy to slosh over Jeremiah's chest.

"I well know," Thaddeus said, "the difference between private dealings undertaken by consenting adults, and the unwelcome advances you visited upon those women."

Jeremiah tossed back half of his drink—on an empty stomach at mid-day. "If it's any consolation, the average companion apparently knows how to use her knee to excellent advantage. Lady Edith damned near gave me a shiner to go with my bruised jewels. With respect to the book, you needn't cut up so. I hadn't planned on writing more than the one volume, but needs must when a fellow likes the occasional wager. The second book—"

"Was tossed on the fire in the library two days ago because your arrogant lordship left the manuscript sitting in plain sight on your desk. You face a choice. Slink out the back door of this house with the clothes on your back after you've apologized to Mama, or report to Horse Guards three days from now, which three days you will spend selling your worldly goods to pay any debts you still owe.

"If you choose the military," Thaddeus went on, "you will have a commission as a lieutenant in the infantry, and you will take ship for India or Canada, I care not which. You are unwelcome in this house until you prove you deserve the honor of association with your own family."

Jeremiah set down his drink and scrubbed a hand through this hair. "A lieutenancy? I should be at least a major."

"Keep talking, and you will be a vagrant. What's it to be? The dubious charity of your drinking companions or that life of adventure you always claimed you wanted, no protections, no social consequence, nothing between you and misfortune but blind luck and the kindness of strangers. Surely that will make an exciting tale—assuming you survive the living of it."

Jeremiah had gone even paler than he'd been upon climbing from the bed. "Mama won't like this, Emory. You don't want her misery on your conscience. Allow me to spare you that fate. I'll spend the rest of the year at the family seat, no bother to anybody. I can even pen a retraction of the more creative incidents conveyed in *How to Ruin a Duke*. Every peer will commiserate with you, and all will come right. I'll get to work on it straightaway, and you can print my letter of apology in the *Times*."

Jeremiah's smile was the terrified parody offered by a boy who realizes his fate has been sealed.

"Either leave this house within the hour or prepare to take up your commission." Thaddeus had pondered how to set up the choice so it *was* a choice, but not a decision even Jeremiah could bungle. He let a silence build, though Jeremiah looked near to tears.

"The infantry has some lovely uniforms." Jeremiah's hand shook as he picked up his drink. "Three days, you say? Don't suppose a week—?"

"Seventy-two hours, if I have to drag you to Horse Guards myself. You will also write a letter of apology to each of the ladies whom you insulted, starting with Lady Edith."

Jeremiah stared into his drink and nodded. "Not well done of me, I do see that."

Perhaps the remorse was real, perhaps it was for show. Thaddeus didn't particularly care. His next priority was to find Lady Edith Charbonneau and pray she was in a forgiving mood. He was thwarted from pursuing that goal by the footman who informed him a guest was waiting in the blue parlor. The caller sought a brief audience with His Grace if the duke was at home.

The footman held up a silver tray bearing a single card: J. Ventnor, Publisher.

Bloody hell. "I'll see him, but no damned tea tray, if you please. He won't be staying long."

~

Edith donned her new bonnet, took up her blue parasol, left the top button of her new cloak unfastened, and gathered her reticule.

"And His Grace had better be home to me," she muttered. The walk to Emory's doorstep took a quarter hour, and if anybody in his fine neighborhood thought a lady traveling alone on foot was unusual, Edith *did not care.* A woman who could write a first draft of a book—a good book, though not overly long—in less than two weeks need not quibble over niceties.

She rapped the knocker against the door twice and it opened almost immediately.

"Lady Edith! Do come in, my lady." The butler stepped back, his characteristic reserve replaced with a smile. "What a pleasure to see you, ma'am, and on such a fine day. Shall I take your bonnet and cloak and see if Her Grace is at home?"

Edith passed over her hat. "I'm actually here to see His Grace, and my call is not entirely social."

White brows drew up. "Between us, my lady, His Grace's mood of late hasn't been entirely social either. Perhaps you'd like to wait in the blue parlor? That was always your favorite as I recall."

The blue parlor was the everyday guest parlor, not as formal as the gilded wonder where Her Grace received company during her at homes, not as comfy as the family parlor.

"The blue parlor will do. I can see myself down the corridor."

The butler hesitated. "Might I tell the staff you're keeping well? We've missed you and wondered how you're faring."

"I've missed you too. Please thank everybody for their concern. I have a new post, and my brother has become playwright-in-residence at the Maloney."

"Oh, that is excellent news, ma'am. Excellent news." He bustled off, doubtless to spread that excellent news belowstairs.

Edith *had* missed the staff here, but she would eventually make new friends in Manchester. She let herself into the blue parlor expecting to have a few moments of solitude to compose her thoughts.

"Your Grace, Mr. Ventnor. Excuse me. I did not know the room was occupied." Both men were on their feet, suggesting the discussion had been something less than cordial.

Ventnor aimed a puzzled smile at the duke. "I thought you said her ladyship's whereabouts were unknown, Your Grace?"

Emory looked tired and a bit grim, but otherwise hale. "Had I known Lady Edith would do me the very great honor of calling upon me, I would have sent you packing ten minutes ago, Ventnor. My lady, do come in. Please come in, rather. Mr. Ventnor was just leaving."

Ventnor passed Edith a card. "I read your samples. You have quite a gift, my lady. Domestic advice doesn't do justice to your voice, and I would very much like an opportunity to discuss other projects with you."

"On your way, Ventnor," Emory said, jabbing a finger in the direction of the door. "Now."

Ventnor offered Edith an unhurried bow, came up smiling, nodded to the duke, and left.

"The damned man tried to contact you at your previous address," Emory said, closing the door behind the departed publisher. "He recalled that you'd been employed as Mama's companion and stopped by to ask if I knew of your present direction."

"What did you tell him?"

Emory stood before her, his gaze troubled. "I've missed you. I didn't tell him that. I've been an idiot. I didn't mention that either. I've been dreaming of pink cloaks.... How are you?"

What mood was this? "I am well, thank you. And you?"

"Jeremiah wrote that blasted book. I'm buying him a commission and he will be gone from London directly. I owe you an apology."

An encouraging start. A *very* encouraging start. "Shall we be seated, Your Grace? Lord Jeremiah's authorship of *How to Ruin a Duke* doesn't surprise me."

"Figured it out, did you? Well, I hadn't." He took Edith by the hand, then let her go. "Apologies. I did not mean to presume. Jeremiah presumed, didn't he?"

"He tried to," Edith said, taking a place on the sofa. "Just the once, but clearly, I made an enemy of him when I refused to oblige him. Quitting my post was the better part of discretion."

"I made an enemy of him when I expected him to manage on a merely generous allowance. Might I sit with you?"

Where was the harm in that? "You may. I brought you something, a parting gift."

He came down beside her. "Parting, my lady?"

Oh, the scent of him, the sound of his voice... Only a ninny-hammer let trivialities like that pluck at her heartstrings.

"I've accepted a post in the north. My brother has a position with the Maloney Theater, and he doesn't need me hovering about while he embarks on gainful employment."

"I see." Emory studied the carpet for a moment. "I do not see, rather. Not at all. I have a confession."

"I'm not sure I want to hear it." Not if he was about to tell her he was engaged or nearly so to some heiress. That would explain his behavior, though Edith couldn't believe he'd hop into bed with one woman while being in expectation of marriage to another.

Other men would, not Emory.

"This confession does not flatter me," he said. "You had mentioned to me that you were working on another writing project. I happened to see the first few lines when I last called upon you."

"My book," she said, assaying a smile. "I've finished the first draft, and I rather like it."

"Jeremiah had written a complete draft as well, another compendium of half-truths, exaggerations, and complete fictions."

Edith put a hand on Emory's arm. "I'm sorry. That had to have been a blow." Once a rotter, always a rotter. She ought to have suspected Lord Jeremiah much sooner.

The duke took her hand in his. "I thought *you* were penning the sequel. I had convinced myself that you hadn't written the first volume, but then I came across those pages, which promised more of the same drivel. I did not know what to think, and I left without giving you a chance to explain."

Edith had puzzled over the manuscript's opening lines for hours. She'd puzzled over Emory's abrupt departure for days, and she'd never connected the two.

"The first few pages were to lead the reader astray," she said, "to make them think more foolishness and slander would follow. That's not what I did with the story. See what you think."

She withdrew a sheaf of papers from her reticule and untied the string that bound them. "This is my farewell gift. You may do with it as you please, and I will sign all the rights over to you or to the charity of your choice."

He took the papers and began reading, sparing her only one curious glance. Edith rose to pace, very unladylike of her, but she could not sit still while he was so silent.

A few moments later he made a snort-ish sound. "By God, you have Mama to the life."

"You're at the part about the mouse?"

"The dread, fiendish rodent as you term it. Poor little fellow was terrified."

Emory had caught the mouse in his bare hands and carried it to the garden, while Her Grace had stood on the piano bench bellowing for the footmen to bring her a brace of loaded pistols.

"Mama does not care for mice, but you make me out to be some sort of paragon." He set the papers down. "Is the rest of the book like that?"

"Do you like it?"

"No," he said. "No, I do not like it. I *adore* it. I *love* it. I wish... I am enthralled, and you cannot possibly give this to me when Ventnor was willing to breach the ducal citadel in hopes of convincing you to work for him."

"I cannot work for Mr. Ventnor if I'm moving to Manchester. You truly think my prose is acceptable?"

Emory rose but remained by the sofa. "My lady—Edith—did you hear what I said? I read the opening lines of this masterpiece and jumped to the worst possible conclusion. Then I took my leave of you, convinced you meant me ill. Had I not confronted my mother with my suspicions, I might have started untoward talk about you. Revenge should be beneath every sensible man, but I had a plan, you see. I am mortified to add that becoming inebriated figured prominently in this plan."

"I would have liked to have seen that."

His smile was crooked and dear. "Do you forgive me?"

"For what? You entertained an erroneous theory, Your Grace, but you assembled all the relevant facts before taking action. I admit I was puzzled by your silence, but then, I did not—I *do not*, that is to say—have any expectations where you are concerned." His explanation made sense and allowed Edith to part from him on friendly terms.

So why was she blushing and all but stammering?

"I have expectations of myself," he said, coming near and possessing himself of her hand again. "When I leap into bed with a woman, and she with me, and we are compatible in every detail of our natures, right down to both of us being untrustworthy in the presence of Italian cream cake, then I expect myself to offer for that woman. I would not have risked intimacies with you otherwise, my lady. The consequences are too momentous. Not to put too fine a point on the matter, I will follow you to Manchester and sing maudlin ballads beneath your window—at midnight—if that will win your favor."

Edith forced herself to hold his hand lightly. "You erred in assuming I would write a slanderous book about you. I erred in allowing you to leave without establishing how things stood between us. I told myself I wanted only an interlude, a memory, but I was not honest."

He covered her hand with his. "Is that still all you want?"

What did she want? A month ago, the answer was simple: A decent post for herself, a future for Foster.

Now? She wanted much, much more. "I want to sit beside you in your curricle the next time you race to Brighton, I want *God Save the King* at midnight, I want,"—she kissed him—"more of that, and the pleasures that follow."

"And if I sing *God Save the King* at midnight only for the woman wearing the Emory tiara, are you still interested?"

That question occasioned more kissing. When Edith recalled that the drapes were open, and the parlor was visible to anybody peering over the garden wall, she drew back enough to rest against Emory.

"Yes, Your Grace, I am still interested."

"Yes, you will be my duchess? What about the blandishments of Manchester?"

"Who will rescue me from dread, fiendish rodents in Manchester? Who will arm-wrestle me for the last piece of cream cake in Manchester? Who will help me polish my next book in Manchester?"

Emory tucked an arm around her waist and walked her to the sofa. "Have you a title for that book, the one that paints me in such a flattering light?"

"Not a flattering light, sir. An accurate light. I thought I might call it, *How to Rescue a Duke.*"

Rather than assist Edith to take a seat, Emory settled in the corner and pulled her into his lap. "I think we should begin your research on the third volume in the trilogy."

Sitting in his lap was a novel and cozy experience. Edith scooted about until she found a pillow to wedge against the armrest. "A *third* volume? Have you more interesting incidents to regale me with, Your Grace? Whatever would the title of this third volume be?"

Emory waited for her to settle. "The third volume will be for private reading only, and will outshine the other two for its wit, passion, and sheer cleverness. That tome will be titled, *How to Ravish a Duke.* Perhaps you'd like to explore the topic with me now?"

"Such a topic will require much study, Your Grace."

"Then we'd best get started, my love."

And so they did.

A KISS BY THE SEA

(Originally published
in the Bluestocking Belles anthology,
Storm and Shelter)

TITLE PAGE AND DEDICATION

A Kiss by the Sea,
by Grace Burrowes

This story originally appeared in the novella anthology *Storm and Shelter*, published in 2021

Dedicated to all the summer loves

CHAPTER ONE

A blacksmith's job was mostly solving problems for mute beasts. The squire's morning gelding was shying at stiles. Miss Fifi's stoat of a pony was three-legged lame. Because the animals could not convey the details of their difficulties, an astute blacksmith learned to notice what was otherwise ignored.

For Thaddeus Pennrith—Thad Penn to his neighbors in Fenwick on Sea—ignoring the lady in the elegant coach would have been impossible. Her coachy, groom, and footmen had the martyred air of London servants forbidden to wear fancy livery, while the team in the traces—matched chestnuts, white stockings on all sixteen glossy legs—fairly shouted a Mayfair provenance.

When a lady's relief teams were London-fancy this far from Town, the lady herself was bound to be fancy as well.

She did not disappoint, though she did intrigue. Even climbing down from a conveyance into the muck of Fenwick's thoroughly soaked high street, she had the sort of grace that comes from years of deportment instruction. The boot that first appeared on the iron step was doubtless Hoby, and polished to a high shine. The lace peeking out from the hem of the woman's carriage dress was as frothy as summer white caps on the North Sea, and her bonnet gave the rest of the game away.

The bonnet was nearly plain, but for the green satin ribbons adorning the brim and tied under a chin charitably described as firm. A young woman chose such millinery when she wanted to go about in society without calling attention to herself. That her entire ensemble otherwise revealed her to be wealthy, pampered, and far from home had apparently escaped her notice.

Alas, great wealth and great intelligence were not always found in the same person. The lady's expression was obscured by the brim of her bonnet, but she used that firm chin to point in Thad's direction.

"Mr. MacAdams," she said, hand on the footman's arm, "please explain our situation to yonder blacksmith."

The voice was so euphonious as to make a command into a gentle request. Thad had fled the siren call of such voices five years ago, and yet, that sheer gracious warmth blended with a just a hint of wrought iron still affected him.

When he should have turned his back on the fine lady and her sniffy servants, he instead waited for the coachman's approach. The fellow was older, and like many a coachman, moved gingerly as he climbed down from the box. Years of battling the elements, head-strong teams, and what passed for English roads took a heavy toll on a man's body.

"Good sir," the coachman called, splashing across the muck. "A word. Can you refashion a spring for a vehicle designed with a post undercarriage?"

An undercarriage such as the post coaches and public stages favored was unusual on a private conveyance. The design was intended to smooth out the ride on heavily laden vehicles, and unnecessarily complicated for most personal travel.

"To whom do I have the pleasure of speaking?" Thad asked.

"John MacAdams, coachman to—"

"John." The lady's quiet tone had taken on more of that wrought iron quality.

"Mrs. Winston, late of Surrey," the coachman said, drawing himself up as if that would better disguise his mendacity. "Time is of the essence and my mistress will compensate you handsomely."

Truly, the lot of them were wanting in the brainbox. "The coach road has been washed out by the storm," Thad said, not unkindly. "If the queen of the fairies magically repaired your coach by sunset, you'd still have nowhere to go."

John looked askance at Mrs. Never-in-a-century-was-she-a-Winston.

She turned to regard Thad, and while he had expected her to be pretty, he had not expected her to be stunning.

Her eyes were the same green as her bonnet ribbons, a luminous, grassy hue offset by auburn hair. The combination was unusual in the English aristocracy, and given her slightly too-wide mouth, and ever so gently aquiline nose, she would never be called pretty, but neither would a man easily forget the sight of her.

And she would never be mistaken for plain Mrs. Winston of Surrey, either.

Thaddeus bowed, not to the depth a London gentleman would offer a lady of high degree, but rather, as a yeoman would bob deferentially at gentry. He remained silent, for no introductions had been made, and even a bumpkin knew not to assume uninvited familiarity with the Quality.

"We are cut off from the main roads?" she asked.

The question was put directly to Thad, so he answered. "The Great Flood would have done less damage than the storm that just came through here. If you look to the water, you'll see the ocean is still showing the effects." Even Granny McClintock couldn't recall such swells in her nearly ninety years of earthly toil.

Mrs. Winston dropped the footman's arm and approached Thad. He resorted to gentlemanly euphemisms out of old habit: The lady was *well formed*, her three-quarter-length spencer showing off an abundance of curves. She was of middle height, which put the top of her head in the vicinity of Thad's shoulder.

She would be, to use less genteel parlance, a lovely armful. Not that her kind ever enjoyed *armful* status, which was a grand shame and a poor reflection on the Creator Himself.

"I grasp that inclement weather has made the roads impassable for a time," the lady said. "But I must be in a position to resume my travels at the earliest opportunity. I can pay you to make my coach repairs a priority."

"No, madam, you cannot. You are in a hurry to meet some bounder hiding from his creditors in Great Yarmouth," Thaddeus said, "but my neighbors are in a hurry to plough up destroyed fields in the hopes of replanting so we don't starve come winter. When I am the only fellow who can repair their ploughs, your naughty little tryst is of no moment. Every cart horse and cob in the village will pull a shoe in the muck this storm has left, and those animals are the difference between a midwife attending a difficult birthing or a mother suffering in agony with none to aid her. I'll have a look at your coach, but I can make no promises."

The longer he'd spoken, the more unreadable Mrs. Winston's expression had become, until her physiognomy resembled the blank face of an Elgin marble.

Then her gaze narrowed as the wind whipped the green satin ribbons against her chin. "You are not from around here." She visually inventoried him with all the dispassion of a bidder at Tatt's eyeing up a new hack. "You are public-school educated. Your proportions suggest generations of good nutrition added to Viking ancestry, and you are rude. How long ago did you leave London, and why shouldn't I alert the authorities to your whereabouts?"

Thad managed not to smile, barely. "The only authority concerned about my whereabouts is my grandmother, and I write to her each fortnight lest she have me taken up by her minions. If you can lower the tip of your nose even an inch, the innkeeper at The

Queen's Barque might find a room for you while your coach awaits repairs."

She raised the tip of her nose, of course. "I can pay you."

"So you've said, but unless you can deliver a baby, provide medical care to the sick, plough under a lost crop, or otherwise do more than beautify the landscape, your coach will have to wait."

She glanced at her coachman, who was admiring the humble storm-washed prospect of a Suffolk village's high street. The Queen's Barque coaching inn was the central edifice in the hamlet, bringing the occasional eccentric traveler, news of the greater world, and the promise of escape to those longing for life beyond rural obscurity.

Thad, to his surprise, was no longer in that latter group.

"Excuse me," Thad said, honestly forgetting to bow. "Fifi, hold up a moment." He ambled across the smithy's humble forecourt, the cobbles still slick with rain and brine.

A small, muddy person whom Thad knew to be of the female persuasion glowered up at him from Mrs. Peabody's side yard.

"I can catch him, Mr. Penn. I always do."

Fifi never caught her mount. Thelwell, named for a vicar since gone to his reward, simply grazed his fill and—being the laziest equine ever to dump child into mudpuddle—caught forty winks until Fifi led him home.

She advanced upon her shaggy steed with all the subtlety of a game beater in high brush. Thelwell flicked a hairy ear but did not cease his efforts to trim Mrs. Peabody's yard.

"Wellie, come," Fifi crooned. "I've got a bit of carrot for you."

Wellie disdained to heed her summons. His reins trailed in the grass, and because he was hatched from the union of a demon and a unicorn, he would surely tromp upon those reins to break them when it suited his purposes.

"Wel-lie dearest, wouldn't you like some nice scratchies?" Fifi asked, inching closer.

Thelwell sighed and toddled six feet down the hedge.

This went on for another five minutes, and all the while Mrs.

Winston held her peace.

"Won't you help the child?" she said at length. "That dratted pony will founder on spring grass before she catches him."

Perhaps Mrs. Winston had ventured beyond the confines of Mayfair in her childhood.

"Fifi," Thad called. "Hold your ground. I'll have a go from the other side." He rounded the far end of the hedge and advanced on the pony.

Thelwell, having lost several arguments with Thad at the forge, snatched a few more mouthful of grass and went to his fate with the dignity of an affronted elder. His put-upon air said that the child had come out of the saddle through no fault of her long-suffering pony, and all this grass was going to waste and looking so untidy, and truly, one grew vexed with the tedium of human incompetence.

Grandmother had the same ability to pack an entire lecture into a single sigh.

Thad tightened the girth, earning a glower from the pony, and used his handkerchief to swipe a streak of mud from Fifi's cheek.

"Don't gallop," he said, depositing the child into the saddle. FiFi was young enough to ride astride, though that would change all too soon. "The footing is rotten, and Wellie has a full tummy. You may trot, you may not canter. Do you understand me, Fiona Sweeney?"

She gathered up the reins. "Yes, sir, Mr. Penn, and thank you. Wellie says thank you, too. He really is a sweet boy." She patted the useless beast on the shoulder.

Thad took Wellie's reins close to the bit. "You've had your fun, you equine market hog. Behave on the way home or you'll wish you had. I'll toss you into the sea and let the mermaids snack on you."

Wellie turned an innocent eye on him, and—possibly—on Mrs. Winston. Fiona trotted off, bouncing gamely in rhythm with the pony's choppy gait.

"I had a whole string of Wellie's," Mrs. Winston said. "They taught me what the better schooled mounts could not."

"What was that?"

"How to deal with temperamental creatures much larger than I."

Grandmother didn't like anybody, but she would *approve* of Mrs. Winston. "I will have a look at your carriage this afternoon. I have some shoes to reset, and as the storm damage becomes more apparent, my dance card will doubtless fill up. If the road is to become passable again, that will involve picks, shovels, and any number of tools inclined to break when they are most needed."

"I understand," she said. "I am a supplicant at the mercy of your availability. I will be at the posting inn should you need me."

Her air of utter self-possession goaded Thad into doing what he never did—explaining himself. "Storms bring on babies," he said, a truth doubtless unknown to every other earl's heir in the whole of England. "Our midwife is getting on. Mrs. Gatesby needs reliable transportation, but her gelding's right-front shoe sounded clinchy to me when she came by to visit Mrs. Peabody yesterday morning. I will stop by Mrs. Gatesby's cottage and have a look, and that means having a cup of tea... and my time is not my own."

Mrs. Winston signaled to her footman. "You are right, Mr. Penn. My concerns are trivial compared to those of others in this village. I will bide at the inn." She surveyed the high street, some emotion brewing in her emerald gaze. "If I cannot leave this place, then others cannot find me here. Enjoy your cup of tea with Mrs. Gatesby."

She strode off, as self-possessed as Boudicea on the morning of battle. And yet, as Thad gathered up his tools and made his way to Mrs. Gatesby's cottage, he was uneasy. A woman as well-heeled as Mrs. Winston ought to be traveling the major thoroughfares, not the coastal track winding through Fenwick.

She ought to have a sniffy companion and an even sniffier lady's maid traveling with her.

Her coachy, grooms, and footman should have been in livery.

And she should not have been gazing upon the lowly main thoroughfare of Fenwick with fear in her eyes.

∾

Storms bring on babies.

Of all the lessons Lady Sarah Weatherby had learned on this ill-fated journey—and she had learned many—that was the most surprising. As she sat in her coach, waiting for MacAdams to parlay with the innkeeper, she mentally listed others.

Comfortable shoes were a greater necessity than a matching reticule and parasol. Thank God and blind chance, she'd worn her older pair of half-boots when she'd left Town.

Another lesson: Whatever she was paying MacAdams and his fellows, it wasn't enough. Sarah did not know how to raise this topic with her coachman, which reflected badly on her education. Uncle Burton claimed to have hired her the best governesses, tutors, and companions, but after five London Seasons, Sarah still had no idea what it cost to run her own household.

She had learned that Anglia was beautiful, though its roads were for the most part terrible.

She had also become aware that she should not have packed carriage dresses that fairly screamed of London's finest modistes, nor should she have brought a London coachman—dear though he was—who'd got turned around seventeen miles back, and not realized his error until the sea was before their very eyes.

But then, all of Sarah's dresses were of excellent quality, and her only other option would have been to steal from Miss Framington's wardrobe. The idea of wearing a turncoat's clothing was too repugnant to be borne.

MacAdams stalked out of the inn, his homely features set in a scowl as he approached the coach window. "No room, my—I mean Mrs. Winston. The innkeep is happy to put up the horses, and the lads and I are welcome to sleep in the stable, but for a proper lady, he has nothing to offer."

"Should we turn around?" Sarah asked.

MacAdams shook his head. "The storm has wreaked havoc all along the coast, and many of the roads are low-lying for a good distance inland. Innkeep says we are likely to find a lot of flooding and destruction and not much in the way of accommodations."

An apt metaphor for the state of her life generally.

Another lesson Sarah had learned was to make the best of bad situations. If she was stranded and without accommodations, the not-very-honorable Matthew Tewksbury likely was as well. He'd hate that, though this whole venture could be laid at his handsome, booted feet.

"I can bide in the common, I suppose."

"My la—Mrs. Winston, you cannot. The inn is a madhouse, full of all manner of folk. The innkeeper suggested we inquire at Mrs. Peabody's, for she occasionally has rooms to let."

Sarah considered the two-story Tudor cottage with the lush yard and cheerful pots of heartsease by the door. The place looked inviting, for all it sat next to the smithy. But that was the nature of an English village, with everybody living cheek by jowl, and shop-keepers dwelling above their business establishments.

"Please inquire of Mrs. Peabody, Mr. MacAdams, and you have my thanks."

Not by word or expression did MacAdams indicate that Sarah's thanks had become cold consolation, but after driving for hours through bad weather, her stalwart Scot was looking much the worse for wear.

He was nonetheless wreathed in smiles when he returned from the cottage. "Mrs. Peabody will be happy to let you a room to yourself, and that includes breakfast and dinner. Her establishment, if I might say so, is clean enough to make my sainted granny smile. I'll have the lads unload your valise, and you'll be enjoying a cup of hot tea in no time."

"Thank you, Mr. MacAdams."

And if anybody inquired for Sarah at the inn, the innkeeper could honestly say no fine London ladies answering to her description bided at his establishment.

She climbed down from the coach and took Thomas's arm to

cross to the cottage. She was admitted by a cheerful maid in a clean apron and tidy white cap. The girl looked to be about fourteen, while the appreciative eye she ran over Thomas's broad shoulders was that of a grown woman.

"I'll send Mrs. P to you directly, ma'am," the girl said, when Thomas had returned to the coach, and Sarah had been shown to a parlor awash in cabbage roses and sunshine.

Whereas a London home of modest means might have adorned its guest parlor with framed cutwork or embroidered samplers done by the ladies of the house, Mrs. Peabody's parlor was dominated by a sunny landscape of a long, sandy beach, imposing headlands, and a pair of sailboats running close to the wind on a white-capped sea.

Racing, perhaps. Or perhaps the lead boat was piloted by a lady trying to outrun a devious and importunate suitor in the second vessel.

The mantel sported a collection of curiosities, including a nearly intact crab shell, some fearsome looking gray objects that vaguely resembled small caltrops, a tiny starfish with five delicate arms, various intricately spiraled whelks, and smooth lumps of cloudy green and blue glass.

"My nieces and nephews collect that lot from the beach," said a blond, softly rounded lady in a lacy mobcap and lavender day dress. "They love the fresh air and sunshine, and the ocean breeze is good for us, I say. You must be Mrs. Winston. I'm Penelope Peabody."

Of course, nobody was on hand to make introductions. Most of the world apparently gave that great awkwardness no thought whatsoever.

Sarah curtseyed. "Mrs. Peabody, a pleasure. You have a lovely home." And that was the truth rather than a polite fiction.

Mrs. Peabody reviewed the terms of room rental with brisk good cheer, even to naming the sum owed per night or per week. "Let me show you to your room, and then I'll send along a tea tray and some hot water for washing." She bustled from the parlor, leaving Sarah to follow in her wake.

"We have dinner at seven, though with the days getting longer, I'll soon be moving that back. I lock the door at ten of the clock, and I daresay, if you are abroad after that hour in Fenwick, you must be involved in the coastal trade or a darts tournament at The Queen's Barque. Neither pastime speaks well for your judgment."

She offered that conclusion with a friendly smile and a wink, suggesting the coastal trade—and the darts tournament—were in fact regarded locally with some affection.

Mrs. Peabody continued up a set of steps, the bannister of polished oak, the walls papered in green silk.

"If you are inclined to practice arias or that sort of thing, Mrs. Winston, please do so during daylight hours. Some of my tenants work long hours, and need their rest. Breakfast is on the buffet by 7 am, though we can put something together earlier if you've a mind to march out at dawn."

She took a key from her pocket and opened the door to a corner room. The space was dominated by a large, uncanopied bed set against the inside wall. The fireplace was full-sized and laid with coal, though bricks of peat were stacked in a brass bucket on the hearth. A privacy screen shielded a wash stand and mirror from the door, and a writing desk sat near the windows.

"I have a balcony?" Sarah said, peering out the French door.

"What's the use of having a view of the sea if nobody can admire it? You share a balcony with the next room, though you'll probably have it to yourself. Those of us who live here tend to take a less romantic view of the ocean. We respect it, but we know it can bring storms as well as pretty shells to our beaches."

The balcony also had a view of the smithy's yard next door. As Sarah watched, the blacksmith, Mr. Penn, strode across the cobbles with a tool box in his hand. He'd put on a coat and something resembling a neckcloth. His hat was a battered straw affair that clearly had more to do with protecting his eyes from the sun's glare than impressing anybody with his turnout.

He'd meant what he'd said, then, about tending to the midwife's gelding's loose shoe. *My time is not my own.*

His magnificent body was most assuredly his own. He strode along with a confidence that said he belonged here, and he took seriously the welfare of everybody in Fenwick from little Fifi to the aging Mrs. Gatesby and even the unborn children and their gravid mothers.

Sarah had never met such a large man, not only tall but bristling with muscle. She ought to have been intimidated, but something about Mr. Penn's demeanor spoke of a benevolent outlook on life, despite his unruly dark hair and dark eyes. He would be happy at his forge, a merry Hephaestus cheerfully fashioning Cupid's arrow and Athena's shield, and not much missing the blandishments of Olympus.

"I'll leave you now," Mrs. Peabody said, "but don't fall asleep just yet. You'll want to enjoy your tea hot."

"I am a bit fatigued," Sarah said, an understatement.

"You are fair exhausted, Mrs. Winston. Running off from Town is hard on a lady's nerves, and more than a bit tiring. If your jilted groom should come calling, what shall I tell him?"

Drat the luck. "That you never saw me."

"Precisely. I never saw you. If he's bungled matters so badly that you've fled his loving embrace, he can work a bit to win you over. Be warned though, we're not as isolated from London society as you might think. Even the maids at the Queen's Barque send and receive regular correspondence from Town, some of them nigh daily."

Mrs. Peabody pulled the door closed, leaving Sarah in blessed solitude. Matthew Tewksbury could labor until Judgement Day and Sarah would not willingly return to his far-from-loving embrace.

She returned to the French door and watched Mr. Penn's progress as he jaunted down the high street. He greeted everybody, doffed his hat to the ladies, and knelt to speak to small children. The sheer friendliness exchanged among the townsfolk made her homesick, but not for her groom's loving embrace.

Never that. Never, ever that.

CHAPTER TWO

Like the flotsam and jetsam washed up on its beaches, Fenwick's citizenry tended to include curiosities among its number. Thad felt at home among them, never having dreamed that an earl's wayward heir could find welcome in an obscure coastal town. He had happy memories of boyhood summers at Grandmother's cottage, though, so to the coast he had fled.

The neighbors doubtless speculated about who or what had sent him pelting from London in high dudgeon five years ago, but they did not pry. Some of them had doubtless put the pieces together. Mrs. Peabody read two different London papers every evening, and the staff at The Queen's Barque heard all the Town gossip courtesy of the coachies and tinkers passing through.

Fenwick was obscure, but—barring roads washed out by monstrous storms—not isolated.

He tipped his hat to Millicent Whyard, who was towing six-year-old Tommy by the hand. "Off to the beach?" Thad asked. Half the village was out on the sands, picking over storm-tide's offerings.

"Thomas thought to investigate by himself," Millicent said, glowering at the boy. "I woke up to find his bed empty. I never had such a fright in my life, with the roads washed out, the marshes flooded, and my only son nowhere to be found."

She sounded furious, but Fenwick knew—the whole village knew—that Thomas was the only child to survive infancy out of three babies born to the Whyard family. Thomas was as reckless a little fellow as ever kicked off his shoes and went barreling into the surf.

Thad knelt, the better to see into the soul of a lad intent on staring at the ground. "You wanted to see what the storm had tossed up, didn't you, young Thomas?"

He nodded, lower lip stuck out in a pout.

"And now you'll be among the last to have a good look, because you were forgetful."

Tommy peered at him. "What did I forget?"

"To ask mum's permission."

"Mum weren't even awake yet."

"Do you suppose, if some considerate lad had brought mum some jam and bread to start her day, she would have minded a wee tap on her door on such a glorious morning?"

"Jam and bread? With butter too?"

"Most ladies enjoy a dollop of butter with their jam and bread, but it's too late for that, lad. You must do as honor compels now."

Tommy assayed a dubious a glance at his mother. "'Pologize?"

"Afraid so, my boy, but take the time to get the words right. Don't fling a few sorries at your poor mum right here on the street. You were thoughtless, but you can make it right by apologizing and doing better."

Tommy nodded, and Thad stood up.

"Has the captain's boat come in yet?" Thad asked.

Martha shook her head. "He said he'd put in at Great Yarmouth, if the weather turned foul. There's talk of shipwrecks, though, and in such a gale who could see the lighthouses?"

"If anybody could, it's Tom Whyard. He's been fishing these waters man and boy, and so has his crew. He would not be careless for the sake of one more catch. He has two very good reasons to be cautious."

Martha smoothed a hand over the boy's fair hair. "He would not let Tommy go with him yesterday."

And Tommy doubtless knew his father hadn't come home last night, and had run down to the sea searching for Papa's boat.

"Perhaps some jam and bread all around is a good idea. The road is washed out, so word from Great Yarmouth will take some time to get through, and tacking south against this wind won't be easy either."

Martha nodded tersely, then surprised Thad by wrapping him in a quick one-armed hug. "Thank you, Mr. Penn." She hurried off, the boy's hand still clutched in her firm grip.

Thad was still pre-occupied with the encounter when he knocked on Birdy Gatesby's door.

"You came," Birdy said, beaming up at him. She was graying, diminutive, and wore a pair of spectacles that gave her the inquisitive air of a wren on the kitchen windowsill. Thad would have been surprised if anybody in Fenwick knew her true given name.

"I said I would, and the day is too fair to spend entirely at the forge." He leaned down to accept a peck on the cheek.

"Bless you, my boy. I do fear you must hurry, for Socrates and I will doubtless be making calls. That was a birthing storm, mark my words."

"I can manage if you haven't finished your breakfast," Thad said. "Socrates isn't the fidgety sort." A midwife's cart horse learned patience and fortitude, like the midwife her self.

"Breakfast was hours ago, young man. Has Captain Whyard's boat put in yet?" Birdy asked, escorting Thad to the outbuilding that served as Socrates' stable. The gelding shared his quarters with a chicken coop, garden shed, hog wallow and goat pen, all neatly organized and as spotless as such a place could be.

"Not yet," Thad said, scratching behind Socrates's hairy ear. "Whyard promised the missus he'd put in at Great Yarmouth."

Birdy passed him a headstall with lead rope attached. "And you promised your grandmama you'd only bide with us for a year or two."

He'd told her that on the occasion of having been stranded at a birthing out on the marshes. Socrates had come up lame, and Birdy had prevailed upon Thad to drive her to a remote, tumbledown farm. Weather had closed in, and he'd sat the vigil out with the farmer, though Birdy had pressed the husband into service in the birthing room as well.

The experience had provoked confidences from Thad that he'd long since regretted, though Birdy had at least kept his disclosures to herself.

"Do you know," Thad said, opening the half door, and slipping the headstall onto the gelding, "my own grandmother reminds me by post, every two weeks without fail, that I was to have abandoned my life here long since. I'm to return to wenching, wagering, and waltzing, according to her, because that is my solemn duty."

He led Socrates out onto the little cobbled yard and passed Birdy the lead rope.

"Wagering," she said, "is admittedly so much nonsense, but what about the wenching and waltzing did you find so burdensome?"

Between Birdy Gatesby and Pen Peabody, Thad felt as if he had both a great-auntie and an older sister intent on stirring the cauldron of his guilt.

"The wagers came to include my bachelorhood, Miss Birdy, and I am not a horse to be auctioned off by the Mayfair hostesses. Socrates, my lad, you will need new front boots if you're to traverse the muddy roads."

Thad managed with a reset of the front shoes and did a quick trim on the hind feet for good measure.

"Keep his feet picked out," Thad said, dropping his tools back in their box. "The wet ground makes for soft soles, and that is never good for the foot." He took the lead from Birdy, though the horse had not moved other than to lift or put down a hoof at Thad's request.

"How old is he?" Thad asked, scratching Socrates about the withers.

"He's a mere lad of twelve. In a few years, he might even have some common sense. You cannot stay here forever, Thaddeus. Arbuckle's eldest is almost old enough to take over the smithy, and your granny has been patient long enough."

"I like Fenwick," Thad said, leading the horse back to his stall. "I am useful here, and Arbuckle's eldest should not have to take on the support of his entire family just because my grandmother wants to see me leg-shackled."

"Arbuckle would help the boy."

"Arbuckle would shout at the lad the live-long day, until young Arnold hopped on the London stagecoach and was never seen again. Give Arnie another few years to pop into Norwich for a spot of carousing while he finishes learning the trade."

"Your grandmother won't live forever," Birdy said, as Thad shrugged back into his jacket. "And neither will you. There are worse things than taking a wife and starting a family, Thaddeus Pennrith. You have the means."

"Starting a family takes more than means, Miss Birdy."

"I daresay you have the necessary equipment and the ability to use it too. Come in for a cup of tea."

Birdy did not invite, she commanded. Grandmother would either get into rousing battles with her or join ranks with her—if she hadn't already.

"A cup of tea sounds—"

One of the Pallant boys trotted into Birdy's stable yard. The entire family had bright red hair and prominent teeth, and each child's name began with a P. Peter, Patrick, Patricia, Posie... Thad lost track of them after that.

"Ma said to fetch ye," the boy panted. "Baby's coming. Pa said please come quick."

"I'll hitch up the horse," Thaddeus said. "Miss Birdy, you find your cloak and bag." Birdy hustled off to her cottage at a sprightly pace. "Patrick, if Miss Birdy isn't back home by suppertime, you come pen the chickens, milk the nanny goat, and feed and water the hogs. Same thing in the morning, even if she's driving back by then."

"Aye, Mr. Penn." Patrick scrubbed a hand over his face. "Petey's tending to the livestock at home. Pa were walking with Ma. Ma said it helps the pangs."

"Maybe it does, and walking also helps your father not worry so much, but don't tell him I said that."

By the time Thad had the horse hitched to the dogcart, Birdy was back, wearing her cloak and bonnet and carrying a valise that was part overnight bag and part medical kit. She popped onto the bench, took up the reins, and clattered out of the yard, Patrick up beside her.

Grandmother wanted Thad to leave this—people who cared for one another, children who were loved by their parents, work that mattered—to resume life as Mayfair's largest fribble.

Soon, he would have to, but not yet. Not quite yet.

He ambled back to the smithy saying a silent prayer for Mrs. Pallant, and for all the Pallants. For good measure, he asked the Almighty to send word that Tom Whyard and his crew were sitting safe and snug in a Great Yarmouth tavern.

A line had formed outside the smithy, three men holding horses, two more sitting in wagons that held some piece of large, damaged equipment.

"What have you brought me, Oxborrow?" Thad asked the man in the closest wagon.

"Archimedes screw needs mendin'," Oxborrow replied. "Whole damned marsh pasture is turned into a broad."

Broads were unique to Anglia, a cross between rivers and flat, shallow lakes. The old folks said they were ancient peat cuts submerged by rising estuary levels, the young folks said they were God's gift to the mosquito population.

Without an irrigation pump to drain his marshes, Oxborrow could lose all of his spring pasture. "I'll get to it today," Thad said, "and you can pick it up tomorrow. Leave the screw with young Arnie. Spall, is that a plough bottom, I see?"

He moved down the line, mentally organizing the rest of his day, which would be quite long. More customers came, mostly with sprung and pulled horseshoes, and Arnie worked with him tirelessly to see every one of them tended to.

When the last customer had been sent on his way, his gelding wearing four brand new shoes, Thad smacked Arnie on the shoulder, then pressed a coin into his hand.

"Go have a pint at the Barque," he said, gathering up his shirt, neckcloth, and waistcoat. "Catch up on all the news. Your parents will want to know, and inquire particularly after Tom Whyard's boat."

"He made port," Arnie said, grinning. "No significant damage. Word came when Mrs. P sent over your supper."

Thad was abruptly famished. "I trust my supper did not go to waste?"

Arnie thumped his skinny belly. "You were willin' to let it get cold. Mrs. P's shepherd's pie deserved appreciatin'."

"You deserve a knock on the head. Be off with you."

Arnie trotted across the street, his energy making Thad feel elderly. Birdy was right that the lad would soon be in a position to take over his father's smithy, provided he had some help. He was only a few inches shorter than Thad, and year by year, he was growing into the muscle needed to tend a forge.

Thad went around to the side of the smithy, draped his shirt and waistcoat on hooks set into the side of the building, and worked the handle of the pump that filled the horse trough. He used his neck-cloth to wash himself thoroughly, everywhere above the waist. Summer was coming, but the evening air was bracing particularly when driven by a brisk sea breeze.

Thad used his shirt as a towel and spared a thought for his supper. Pen Peabody made a delicious shepherd's pie, alas. He was scrubbing his hands through his damp hair when he happened to look up and catch sight of somebody in a long, pale dress—or night robe?—on the balcony along the back of the Peabody cottage.

A female, watching him at his ablutions. A slim, petite female, standing absolutely still in the evening shadows. If Pen Peabody were to watch him, as she often had, she'd make some bawdy remark about his physique, or wishing she were younger, though she might be all of ten years Thad's senior.

He did not know who watched him—Pen occasionally took in the overflow from the Barque, and with the storm, she'd doubtless have filled every room in the cottage.

The lady remained on the balcony, suggesting she liked what she saw. Thad had brought his height and a Corinthian's appetite for sport with him from London, but the forge had put muscle on him beyond what any London dandy could claim. The lady remained watchful on her balcony, probably never having seen a blacksmith without his shirt.

Thad smiled and waved, then went back to drying off, while two admissions claimed his attention. First, Arnie would indeed soon be ready to take over his father's business. He was old enough to enjoy a pint at the Barque with the menfolk, and skilled enough to handle all of the farriery if not all of the smithing.

Second, Thad did have the equipment necessary to start a family, *and* the ability to use it. For too long, though, he hadn't had the *opportunity* to use that equipment. That thought had him working the pump handle, and sticking his head right back under the cascade of brutally frigid water.

Village life was a revelation to Sarah—the life of this village, anyway. People in Fenwick on Sea greeted one another by name, stopped and chatted, laughed, and—this fascinated her—they touched one another.

Children were the recipients of universal affection, from a chuck under the chin to ruffling of their hair. Women touched each other's arms, men slapped one another on the back or shook hands. Sarah had even seen a pair of women hug—right on the street—and nobody passing by had thought anything of it.

She had seen the blacksmith, Mr. Penn, gently cuff the gangly young man on the shoulder, which had the young man grinning and scampering off in the direction of the posting inn. The exchange was easy, friendly, and to Sarah, utterly novel.

The sight of Mr. Penn without his shirt so far surpassed novelty that Sarah had been unable to look away. A proper young woman would have withdrawn the instant it became obvious she was about to see a man tending to his ablutions.

But then, proper young women did not bolt from London, no lady's maid, no companion, not even a handy cousin or uncle to serve as escort.

Mr. Penn's physique was *excessively* impressive. He would have made two of Matthew Tewksbury, and Matthew considered himself a fine figure of a man. She was intrigued with Mr. Penn's sheer abundance of muscle, and even more so by the easy grace with which he moved. He'd stripped off his shirt with no hint of self-consciousness. When he'd waved to Sarah, the gesture had been purely friendly—no swagger, flirtation, or arrogance about it.

He was honestly unconcerned about being seen half-naked.

Rather than gawk at him as he resumed washing, Sarah stepped back into her room to retrieve a shawl. The sunset over the water had been amazing, but the sea air was brisk, and night coming on quickly.

When Sarah returned to her balcony, Mr. Penn was nowhere to be seen, and that was for the best. She needed time to think, to plan next steps, and to simply enjoy the rare thrill of solitude. In London, her lady's maid had slept in her dressing closet, and Sarah had often awakened to a chambermaid tending to the hearth or her lady's maid laying out the first outfit of the day.

No solitude and no privacy—except for when Matthew Tewksbury had sought privacy with her.

Sarah sank into the chair on the balcony, wrapping herself in her shawl. The last indigo streaks of the sunset painted the clouds over the horizon, and fatigue dragged at her. Still she did not want this vexing, intriguing, day to end.

A door latch clicked several yards down the balcony, and a very large shape emerged into the gloom.

"You're still here." The voice was masculine, deep, and amused.

Sarah would recognize it anywhere. "Mr. Penn, good evening."

"Mrs. Winston, greetings. Do you mind if I join you?"

He wore no jacket, only a billowing white shirt and darker waist-coat. His casual dishabille aside, for a man and a woman without a family connection to tarry in the dark alone was so far beyond the bounds of propriety as to exceed the imagination.

But not quite as far as running from a wealthy, handsome, and exceeding well placed fiancé.

"The balcony is a shared treasure," Sarah said, "based on what Mrs. Peabody said. Please do have a seat." The gathering darkness was fortunate, for Sarah blushed to offer that invitation.

Mr. Penn pulled a heavy wooden chair over—one handed—and set it a few feet away. He lowered himself with a grand sigh, stretched out his legs, and crossed his feet at the ankles.

"Storms are great for bringing coin and custom to the smithy, but they play merry hell on a man's back. I should be able to get to your coach tomorrow, though that's not a promise, and besides, the road is still washed out."

In London, one did not discuss commerce. In London, one did not use profanity before a lady. In London, one did not delight when a man broke both rules in one sentence.

Thank the merciful powers, Sarah was no longer in London. "I have enjoyed my day in Fenwick on Sea, Mr. Penn. I suspect I will find another such day equally pleasant. You need not turn aside other business to tend to my coach."

He sank lower in his chair. "Have you truly enjoyed your day in Fenwick?"

"I had never seen the ocean before, and I find it... any words I could use to describe the sea would not do it justice, like talking about God. The ocean provokes me to silence, as if I have come upon an enormous, ancient cathedral and have all to myself."

"You don't mind the sand getting everywhere?"

"I did not venture onto the beach, so no, I did not notice the sand." Sarah promised herself that tomorrow, she would start her day on the beach, and maybe even—the idea itself gave her a thrill—let the surf touch her bare toes.

"What else did you notice about our fair village?" Mr. Penn asked.

This was not small talk, or maybe it was small talk between strangers in a small village. Sarah had no way of knowing.

"I noticed that no footmen or maids trailed behind their employers, eavesdropping and looking impatient. Children were not harried by nannies and governesses, and come to that, I found it odd that children were even allowed out of their school rooms, much less permitted to go barefoot on the beach. Where was Fifi's groom? Why was the child permitted off the lead line if she can't control her pony? People shout here—raise their voices to bellow at one another across the high street. I never knew small villages made so much noise.

"And the *air*," she went on. "The air is magical. Never have I seen such clear air, almost as if the air itself embraces the sunlight. The sun on the water is nearly too bright to behold and the sunset over the marshes was proof everlasting of benevolent almighty powers."

Don't prattle, Sarah Louise. She sank back, though was it prattling to admire the Creator's handiwork?

"You are wiser than I," Mr. Penn said. "When I arrived here, on a horse going lame I might add, all I noticed was that the local speech is nigh unintelligible. The letter R runs amok in these surrounds, disappearing from its proper locations and popping up where it has no business. *Oi fell orf me hoss and hit me head s' hawd.*"

"And g's at the end of the words are a rarity," Sarah added. "*The sun is shinin' this mornin'.* I find that charming."

"I found it incomprehensible. I thought the ocean stank, the marshes reeked, and the salt air would ruin my boots. I was right about that part. Sea air will rust a pair of horseshoes almost as fast as I can reset them."

He propped his feet on the balustrade, casual as you please.

"Did you come here to ply your trade?" Sarah asked, though he was certainly well spoken for a man involved in commerce.

"I did not." He crossed his feet at the ankle, taking a moment either to get comfortable or to choose his words. "I arrived in Fenwick for a repairing lease, I suppose you might say. My horse came up lame, the farrier had nobody to hold the beast while he pulled the shoes. My gelding needed some time to recover from a stone bruise, and I had nothing better to do than make a nuisance of myself at the smithy. When an unruly mare tromped on Henry Arbuckle's foot, I became a kind of apprentice, and now here I am."

"How long ago did your horse turn up lame?"

"Five years, give or take." He said this softly, perhaps sadly. "They have been good years, too. What of you? What brings you to Fenwick on Sea?"

Over supper, Sarah had been asked the same question. She'd responded that she was on her way to visit relatives in the area, which was only a slight embellishment on the truth. A lady did not propound falsehoods, except in service to kindness or tact.

"I need a repairing lease too," she said. "I found myself engaged to marry a party who turned out to be unsuitable, and those around me were not inclined to listen when I said so. I learned that my intended was about to abduct me for an unscheduled journey north." Sarah kept the worst of it to herself: Uncle had not only approved Matthew's scheme, he'd all but authored it.

"You don't strike me as being very abduct-able."

"Is that a compliment or an insult?"

White teeth gleamed in the darkness. "Given that you are here, and your intended is not, that's a statement of the truth. I can understand why your fiancé would wish to make off with you, but what sort of man can only procure a wife by stealth and force?"

"A determined one. The gentleman is quite smitten with my settlements."

"Then he's not a gentleman. Is he an honorable?"

In for a penny... "Yes."

"They are the worst. Just enough consequence to be arrogant, not enough responsibility to grow up. Congratulations on a narrow escape." Mr. Penn spoke as if he too had had a narrow escape.

"I suspect my former intended will attempt to persuade me to resume our engagement, if he can find me. I have caused a very great scandal. No one else will have me."

Uncle had flung that observation at her with particular frequency and force. Used goods, soiled goods, a jilt... And the accusations, thanks to Matthew's charm and Sarah's stupidity, were true.

Come, Sarah. What's the point of getting engaged if you won't let me under your skirts?

Very well, but don't muss my hair.

On the half-dozen occasions when Matthew had been *under her skirts*, he'd accomplished his aims without mussing her hair. Those experiences had left Sarah increasingly unwilling to speak her vows.

"I very much doubt that no one else will have you," Mr. Penn mused. "But if so, you are free, and to be envied that rare and blessed state. Be warned though, the longer you tarry in Fenwick, the more it begins to feel like home, and that becomes a powerful anchor."

He fell silent, and Sarah found she had no need to chatter. A glow on the horizon of the vast silvery sea to the east presaged an imminent moonrise.

The conversation with Mr. Penn had been extraordinary. No talk of the weather. No malicious gossip about other women. No speculation about who would offer for whom. The whole day, from Mrs. Peabody's odd friendliness and scrumptious shepherds' pie, to the hum and bustle of the village, to the sight of Mr. Penn without his shirt, had been a revelation.

Proof that life—and good life—existed outside of Mayfair, beyond Uncle's lectures, out past Miss Framington's hypocritical sermons. People lived and loved without consulting DeBrett's or etiquette manuals. They had things to do besides fittings, at homes, and calls. They cared for one another without a thought for who had large settlements or a large bosom.

The relief—the vindication—Fenwick on Sea had provided in the space of a day was as immense as the ocean.

And Mr. Penn was part of that vindication. He'd been naked before her from the waist up, and hadn't turned the moment scandalous. He was sitting alone with her in the dark, and his hands weren't wandering. He had *commended* her on breaking her engagement, and he had done her the precious courtesy of listening to her.

The first sliver of golden light broke the horizon gilding the waves and whitecaps.

"I have not watched a moonrise in too long," Mr. Penn said, "much less in such congenial company. I hope you'll tarry a while in Fenwick, Mrs. Winston."

"My maternal grandmother was Mrs. Winston. My given name is Sarah, and I am nobody's missus, thank heavens."

Another slight pause followed. Perhaps Mr. Penn was allowing Sarah a moment to give him the rest of her name, or perhaps she had shocked him.

"The locals know me as Thaddeus Penn, but my full name is Thaddeus Pennrith—at your service." He added that last with an ironic smile.

She did not say, *Your secret is safe* with me, because he had to know that, just as she knew he would not spread her confidences in the high street. His name sounded vaguely familiar—Sarah had studied Debrett's thoroughly before making her come-out—but the details refused to come to her.

The moon drifted higher until it cleared the horizon, casting silver beams on the flooded marshes as well as the endless sea. Night birds sang, and in the distance, the roar and retreat of the surf confirmed—as if the whole day had not—that Sarah was blessedly far from London.

"If I don't seek my bed now," Mr. Penn said—Mr. Pennrith, "I will fall asleep out here. Tomorrow promises to be hectic, so I'll bid you good night."

He rose and stretched, a great beast of a man with more manners and consideration than all the honorables in Mayfair combined.

"Sleep well, Mr. Pennrith."

He remained at the balustrade, the moonshine putting highlights in his dark hair. "Thaddeus."

"Sleep well, Thaddeus."

He turned to regard her. "Are you glad you left London?"

"I am now. Talking to you helped me sort that out. The night air is a bit cool, isn't it?" She made to rise and found his hand extended to her. Because the chair was low and she needed to keep her shawl about her, she accepted his assistance.

He kept her hand in his. "I am glad you've found your way here, and welcome to Fenwick, Sarah."

She realized he was asking some sort of permission or offering an invitation. Whatever he was about, it had nothing to do with getting under her skirts and everything to do with genuine welcome.

"Sweet dreams," she said, going up on her toes to brush a kiss to his cheek. "And thank you for the moonrise."

CHAPTER THREE

Thad should have been asleep before his head hit the pillow. He lay on his bed, his whole body aching with fatigue and the knowledge that tomorrow would be even busier. Road repair was hard on tools, sodden ground was hard on farm equipment, and mud was pure misery on shod hooves.

He would be swamped with work for at least a week, and spring was a busy time of year to begin with. Henry Arbuckle would have to be temporarily coaxed out of his advisory role if customers weren't to grumble.

Sleep eluded Thad, despite his exhaustion. He revisited his conversation with Sarah, and revisited his decision not to tell her that he too was a refugee from Mayfair's marriage madness. She'd had nothing good to say about a mere honorable, and for Thaddeus to mention his title had seemed ill-advised.

Though he really should find a way to tell her the truth before allowing any more kisses to his cheek. Rather than ponder how he'd convey his particulars, he instead imagined Sarah preparing to retire, taking down her hair, slipping out of her night robe, and climbing onto the big bed in the room next door. Thad had taken that room for his first few months in Fenwick, until this one—with a higher ceiling —had become available.

Sarah's hair was an unfashionable auburn, and for all she wore it captured in a tidy chignon, she brought to mind the old horseman's adage, "Chestnut mare, better beware." She had apparently kicked over the traces and bolted from a proper match, and as many weary travelers bearing strange tales had, she'd washed up on Fenwick's shores.

He liked hearing her voice, particularly in the dark. Every word was a grace note, every thought dipped in ladylike elocution. She was no snob—he'd been wrong about that—and she was already ensnared in Fenwick's charm.

He had noticed her charms too. She was womanly rather than girlish, with a well-rounded fundament and generous breasts. A gentleman could note those blessings without gawking, and when she'd kissed him goodnight, she'd briefly pressed all that luscious softness close to him.

He had friends in Fenwick, true neighbors, people with whom he could share a tankard of ale and depend on to jolly him out of a passing low mood. Fenwick's denizens were good folk, the salt of the earth, and he loved them as he'd never loved the posturing dandies at his London clubs.

But Thad had to acknowledge that he was nonetheless lonely in Fenwick. He occasionally made the trip into Norwich to pass the time with a discreet and friendly widow, and that eased the ache in his body.

It did not ease the ache in his heart. He was Thad Penn, the blacksmith with a past. Nobody here had seen him fencing at Angelo's, or accompanying some soprano as she warbled of true love and blushes at a Mayfair musicale.

Once upon a time, he'd had gentlemanly accomplishments. Once upon a time, he'd danced with the wallflowers and claimed some charm.

He did not miss the wallflowers, but did miss being known for who he truly was. Missed hearing his family name, missed—a little—the speculation in the eyes of the matchmakers. Yes, he was a big brute, but he had the title, thirty thousand acres, and an old fortune. Even if the ladies hadn't coveted his kisses, and frankly shuddered to consider the wedding night, they'd coveted the wealth and standing he could bring to a marriage.

His hand drifted down over his belly, and lower, to grasp his half-aroused manhood. He let his imagination wander idly, to questions with no answers. Just what had Sarah's fiancé done, that a genteel young lady took her chances on the King's highway? How long was her unbound hair? Would she ever hike her skirts enough to wade at low tide and allow a fellow a glimpse of trim ankles and sturdy calves?

Did she kiss on the mouth as sweetly as she pressed her lips to a man's cheek?

Desire welled from a combination of hopeless longing and hoarded joy. *She* had kissed *him*. Brought him the scent of roses. She'd laid her hand on his chest and brushed her lips over his cheek, as if he were not a prodigal heir who'd never meet proper society's standards for lordly refinement, but as if he were someone special and precious.

Thank you for the moonrise. Whoever her dimwitted *former* fiancé was, he deserved to lose her if he couldn't be bothered to share the occasional moonrise with his intended.

Satisfaction, when it came, brought a hint of joy to go with the pleasure. Had Thad met Sarah in Mayfair, he would have been properly introduced by a mutual acquaintance. He would have asked her for the honor of a quadrille or a waltz. They would have minced around a crowded dance floor together, and he would have bowed politely over her hand before leading her to her next partner.

They would not have spoken of failed engagements or repairing leases, she would never have kissed his cheek or sat conversing with him in the dark. Soon, he'd have to leave Fenwick and bow to Grandmother's increasingly querulous demands, but not quite yet.

Sarah had decided the repairs to her coach were not urgent, and that was fortunate. Maybe before Thad sent her on her way, he and she could make a few more sweet memories here in Fenwick on Sea.

Sarah could not leave common sense so far behind that she eschewed headwear altogether, but she did accept the wide-brimmed floppy straw hat Mrs. Peabody offered rather than any of the millinery packed from London.

Beneath the late morning sun, the ocean was too bright to stare at directly, and on such a day, it was nearly impossible to believe that a hundred miles to the east lay the coast of the Netherlands, and beyond that, France. The Corsican had escaped his island prison, the French Army was all but declaring for him, and everybody spoke of war.

Here in Fenwick, such thoughts seemed obscene.

Sarah had broken her fast in Mrs. Peabody's sunny dining parlor, equally relieved and disappointed that Mr. Pennrith did not join the other guests for his first meal of the day. She'd eaten a prodigious amount of buttered toast, eggs, and apple tart, and consumed three cups of stout black tea. Miss Framingham would be scandalized at such an appetite, but then, Miss Framingham had much to answer for.

Sarah had written a letter to Great-Aunt Fletcher explaining her situation and location, but because the road was washed away, she'd had to inquire at The Queen's Barque for a special courier willing to carry her missive the more than forty miles to Cromer.

The sun was directly overhead by the time she found her way to Fenwick's gleaming sandy beach. She quickly realized that trudging through the deep sand was much more work than walking closer to the water, where the tide packed the sand close. Her destination was an outcropping of rocks a hundred yards or so distant. The rocks weren't visible from the village, being partly around a bend in the shoreline.

She would sit upon those rocks, and turn her focus to the scandal she'd created, just as soon as she could pry that focus loose from the more interesting subject of Thaddeus Pennrith's hands. His hands were enormous, like the rest of him, and they were warm.

What had made Sarah aware of the chilly night air was the contrast between the brisk breeze and the enveloping warmth of Mr. Pennrith's grip around her fingers. His touch had been delicate and gentlemanly, but also strange for being without gloves, and for the abundance of his calluses.

Calluses between a men's third and fourth finger were the natural result of hours on horseback, even wearing gloves. Mr. Pennrith had calluses everywhere—fingertips, palms, the heel of his thumb. And yet, Sarah suspected his touch on a lady's person would be gentle and cherishing.

He would not bend his intended over a handy chair, ruck up her skirts, and tell her to hold still as he thumped away and the lady mentally composed a menu for her uncle's next formal dinner.

Sarah reached her destination, delighted to find that the rocks sheltered substantial depressions that were filled with sea water. Little worlds existed in the resulting tidal pools, full of strange brown and the green plant life, tiny scuttling crabs, and clusters of blue-black mussels.

She perched above one particularly clear pool, fascinated with the variety of life within.

"It's a miniature world," said a deep and familiar male voice. "They have everything they need in there, and the whole vast sea remains unknown to them, like an isolated village."

Mr. Pennrith carried his boots, and sizeable boots they were too. He'd turned up the cuffs of his trousers, and his toes were covered with sand.

"I was thinking of Mayfair," Sarah said, sitting back. "Of how insular and self-absorbed most people I know are—how insular I am. Will you join me?"

He settled beside her on her rocky perch, his coat over his arm. "Do you miss it?"

"No. I ought to. It's all I know, save for a few summers spent with my great aunt, but I dread to return. I thought you were expecting a great lot of business today."

"I have been at the forge since before dawn. We are awash in sprung horseshoes, broken pickaxes, and bent blades. The work is too demanding to be done on an empty stomach for long." He held up a cloth sack that his coat had hidden. "Will you join me?"

"A picnic by the sea?" What a marvelous idea.

"More of a sandwich in the middle of the day." He opened his sack and passed her a parcel wrapped in paper. "Must you return to London?"

"Eventually. I have to live somewhere, and my uncle's home is the one available to me. Aunt Fletcher can host me for a visit, but Uncle is my trustee, and until last year he was my guardian." The sandwich was raspberry jam and clotted cream, the bread fresh.

"So purchase your own home," Mr. Pennrith said. "Your trust is doubtless written to allow the funds to be used for your basic needs, and if pretty dresses and a fancy coach meet that definition, so should keeping a roof over your head."

"I cannot maintain my own household, Mr. Pennrith. I am not yet thirty."

He glanced over at her between bites of his sandwich. "I'd put you at five-and-twenty. If you are old enough to marry and manage your husband's domicile, you're old enough to manage your own staff."

He'd guessed her age correctly, and from him it was merely a number, not significant of failed seasons and looming disaster.

"If I were a bluestocking spinster, perhaps I could establish my own household, but I am a ruined heiress. If I ever want to be received, I must accept the scolding my uncle will heap upon me. This is an exceptionally satisfying sandwich."

Mr. Pennrith dusted his hands together. "The honorable dunderhead took unpardonable liberties, didn't he?"

So much for allowing a change of subject. "He did not *take* liberties, I *permitted* him liberties." Society especially would see it in that light.

"You capitulated to stop his whining, then realized his ability to whine was reborn exactly ten minutes after he'd rebuttoned his falls."

"Twenty." When Matthew had demanded "a little encore," after their last coupling, Sarah had realized what he was about. "I suspect he was determined to get me with child, so that I could not cry off."

"No wonder you tossed him over. Are you with child?"

"That is an extraordinarily personal question." Though clearly not meant to offend.

Mr. Pennrith gazed out over the sparkling waves. "Do you know the signs of conception, Sarah?"

She did, thanks to Aunt Fletcher. "As determined as Matthew was on his objective, he was unsuccessful." Sarah told him the rest of it, though a lady never spoke of such things. "My companion abetted him, ensuring I was left alone with him at every opportunity, and that we were not disturbed. She reported to him on my... on the failure of his attempts in the direction of conception. While I might be halfway able to understand Matthew's scheming, my uncle encouraged him in it."

Mr. Pennrith was quiet for a time, perhaps shocked, though Sarah suspected it took a lot to shock him.

"How wealthy are you?"

The precisely relevant question, given her disclosures. "I am not sure. The solicitors send the reports to Uncle, but I've picked the lock in his desk drawer often enough to have a general idea of the sum." She named the figure, quietly, despite their deserted location.

"And all of that money becomes your husband's upon your marriage?"

"It isn't supposed to. Aunt says the money is to remain in trust, for me and my progeny, but I suspect Uncle has diverted a large sum into my settlements, and much of that would come under a husband's control."

Mr. Pennrith slanted a brooding glance at her. He was not a laughing god of the forge now. "You haven't signed the settlement agreements?"

"I was never asked to."

"But you are of age, and no longer under your uncle's guardianship. You would have to sign the settlements to make them binding."

"All of which suggests that Matthew's rutting was indeed an attempt to get me with child. To ensure my offspring were legitimate and well cared for, I would have signed half my fortune into Matthew's keeping and left the other half with my uncle. I never wanted a fortune anyway."

Mr. Pennrith passed her an apple tart. "I believe you, given what that fortune has cost you. Where is your auntie?"

"Cromer, twenty some miles past Norwich."

"And you cannot get to her as long as the road is washed out and your coach is unreliable. Promise me something."

"Of course."

His smile was crooked and fleeting. "You barely know me. Why promise so readily?"

"I *know* you. You've been honest with me, you trusted me with your real name but you don't ask for mine. You don't stare at my bosom, and if we were engaged, you wouldn't bend me over the nearest writing chair and not even bother to lock the door."

"A *writing* chair?"

Perhaps the fresh sea air had addled her brain, because Sarah could not seem to stop her tirade. "A wing chair is too tall, a vanity stool too short. Matthew prefers that I hold onto a writing chair while he enjoys himself. The angle is convenient for him. He also prefers that I not wear drawers even in cold weather, and when he is my husband, he will forbid me such scandalous underlinen."

"Did he ever speak to you of anything besides his convenience?"

"Not once we became engaged. As often as I was lectured about writing chairs, he could not be bothered to kiss me. He likes certain parts of my physique better than others, and felt the need to impress his preferences upon me."

Sarah passed the apple tart back uneaten, for Mr. Pennrith had finished his, and she abruptly had no appetite.

"They will make me marry him," she said. "He promised to give me a *jolly spanking* on my *splendid rosy bum*, to celebrate our wedding night, as if this is some great treat to look forward to, and he the master of the art. How can a spanking *be* jolly, and why would any woman marry a man who boasts of using violence on her person? He does not listen to me, he does not want me to even speak. I'm simply to bend over and hold still every twenty minutes for the rest of my life."

Mr. Pennrith passed her a handkerchief, though she hadn't realized she was crying. "They cannot make you marry him. You are of age, you have means."

"They can send me for a respite in the north until I come to my senses, Mr. Pennrith. Uncle was very clear about that. A great fortune inspires great ingenuity in those who covet it. I would give them my blasted fortune, but they want to take me prisoner too."

Mr. Pennrith was quiet for some time, a man at ease with female anger and female tears. He crumbled up her apple tart and tossed the bits onto a flat rock several yards away. Within moments, a dozen sea gulls were arguing over the feast, until the rock was picked clean.

"My family has some influence," Mr. Pennrith said. "My grandmother in particular is a force to be reckoned with. I'd like to put your situation before her without getting into specifics, and see what she recommends. May I have your permission to do that much?"

When had anybody asked Sarah's permission for anything? "Of course, but I doubt your granny can work miracles. Uncle is an earl. He inherited when my papa died without male issue—that's my fault too, that I failed to be male. I am in quite a taking, aren't I?"

Mr. Pennrith patted her arm. "You are doubtless overdue for a spectacular taking, and a temper puts roses in your cheek. I'm surprised you didn't bash Matthew over the head with one of those writing chairs."

The thought had not occurred to her, not until the coach had passed the last London turnpike and freedom had been in her hands.

"I used to like Matthew. He was funny and handsome and he said charming things as if he sincerely meant them. I was an idiot."

"You were cozened, and everybody you should have been able to trust conspired against you."

Sarah took a turn being silent, sorting through feelings, even enjoying the realization that she was angry. Not out of sorts, a bit testy, or in a mood—she was furious. Her trust and her person had been violated in an attempt to seize and carry off her future.

"If he had offered me one honest kiss," she said, "I might be able to see my way to some sort of affection, an accommodation, but he never has. He couldn't be bothered when he had a chance to toss up my skirts instead. Mrs. Matthew Tewksbury, whoever she may be, will go to her grave without having known the pleasure of one sweet, passionate, genuine kiss."

"And that woman will not be you," Mr. Pennrith said. "You are safe here in Fenwick, your aunt is barely half a day's journey away, and my grandmother will take your situation under advisement. You are not to lose hope."

"I have seen the vast ocean," Sarah said, rising and dusting off her backside. "I never thought that day would come. Hope is closer here than it was in London. Would you be scandalized if I took off my boots as you have, and let the water splash over my toes?" She had spoken to him of writing chairs and Matthew's plans for her splendid, rosy bum, and yet, she had needed to ask that question.

Mr. Pennrith gazed down at her without smiling, though his eyes held warmth and humor, possibly even approval.

"You could let the water splash you even up to your *ankles*, Miss Sarah, and I would not be scandalized."

She waded in the shockingly cold surf, letting it wet her clear up to her calves, and Mr. Pennrith waded right along beside her.

"This was all your idea," Matthew Tewksbury said for the eight-hundred-and-seventeenth time. "The whole bit, the flirtation, the engagement, the anticipating the vows, the..." he twirled a lace-draped wrist in an upward spiral. "You should have known she'd bolt."

Burton Weatherby, Earl of Bassham, did not so much as glance up from his steward's report. Reading in a moving coach was difficult enough without indulging the moods of a petulant, incompetent bridegroom.

"My dear young man, how was I to know your wooing would be so inept as to send my niece on a mad flight?"

"My wooing was enthusiastic," Tewksbury retorted, "as you insisted it be, and Lady Sarah was willing else I should have waited for the ceremony. She never raised more than an eyebrow at me when I sought a private moment."

"Spare me the details of your bumbling. We'll catch up to her soon enough."

"You said that in Alconbury. Nobody noticed a young woman traveling alone with a coach and four, and servants in London finery."

"Of course not."

The coach hit a rut, very likely the eight-hundred-and-seventeenth of those for the day as well.

"What do you mean, of course not? Young women of good breeding do not travel the Great North Road without proper chaperonage, but we haven't heard a word of her."

"The Great North Road sees all manner of traffic and lots of it. I daresay Sarah's coachy and grooms are not in livery."

"I'll sack the lot of them once she marries me. Damned nerve, abetting a runaway."

Bassham gave up on his steward's report. The news was never good, and it would keep for another day.

"The coachy and grooms are loyal to her, for it is she who pays their wages. They will keep her safe for you until such time as we can bring her home. You ought to reward their loyalty."

Tewksbury scowled, and even given his blond good looks, the expression did not flatter him. "Her solicitors pay their wages."

"And she pays the solicitors. Sarah herself might not understand all the roundaboutations, but those from society's lower strata grasp these things intuitively. She has only one possible destination, and that is my Aunt Fletcher's household in Cromer. We will doubtless find her there before the week is out."

The damned spring weather had made the going difficult, as had all the traffic heading for London. Despite the threat of renewed hostilities on the Continent, the London Season was already well underway.

"What if she's with child?" Tewksbury muttered. "I don't like to think of my future wife, in a delicate condition, racketing about the countryside all by herself."

"Now you turn up doting? I'm touched, Tewksbury."

"You think you know her," Tewksbury said, gaze on the rain-washed countryside of Cambridgeshire. "You think she's the meek, biddable, niece who would never gainsay you, but here we are, no Sarah and no idea where she's got off to. You should never have threatened her with a madhouse."

Much as broken clocks were accurate twice a day, Tewksbury had chanced upon a truth. "She was threatening to cry off before I mentioned a respite to settle her overwrought nerves. Your charm as a fiancé was sadly lacking and I grew impatient. You are not the only one with obligations that will go unmet if Sarah's fit of pique is indulged."

Bassham had chosen Tewksbury for three qualities. First, Tewksbury, as the younger son of a viscount, was of adequate social standing to woo a late earl's wealthy daughter. Second, Tewksbury was reported to be as randy as a four-year-old colt and had male by-blows to support that reputation. Third, he was hopelessly submerged in the River Tick. His gambling debts were part of the problem, but the true source of his misery was a father unable to check the fashionable excesses of his wife, heir, and daughters.

The whole Tewksbury family was headed for ruin in a fast chariot. Until Sarah's inheritance had come into Bassham's hands, Bassham's branch of the Weatherby family had been traveling toward the same destination.

"Why didn't that Framingham creature keep a closer eye on her?" Tewksbury muttered.

"Because the Framingham creature was told Sarah was spending the day with you."

Tewksbury's fine blond brows drew down. "Sarah told her that?"

"Left Framingham a note claiming you had invited Sarah out to Richmond for a picnic in the fresh spring air. From what Miss Framingham said, for you to tup Sarah on a blanket would have been a step up from your usual fumbling."

Tewksbury grinned. "Framingham likes to watch me? I'd happily swive her if she's been too long without. The sniffy ones always moan the loudest."

"You are, of course, free to make overtures to Miss Framingham, though I suspect you will find her less biddable than Sarah has been. Miss Framingham, unlike your handsome self, performed her duties without flaw. I'm told you had no less than a half dozen interludes with your bride in the space of three weeks, and that has proven insufficient to start a family with her."

"When Sarah and I are married, and we're not limited to two interludes a week, a baby will come along soon enough."

Bassham admitted to having committed a second error, this one more egregious than threatening Sarah with treatment for nervous hysteria.

Tewksbury was a mistake. He had all the attributes Bassham sought in a prospective husband for Sarah, but he lacked qualities that might have made him better suited to Sarah herself. Fiancés and new husbands were expected to be lusty. Their job was to be lusty, in fact. Tewksbury wasn't simply lusty, he was in thrall to his own pizzle.

Sarah was too much like her mother to find that quality appealing. She'd want weighty discussions, quiet walks in rural surrounds, tender words and all the romantic whatnot. Perhaps it wasn't too late to recruit a fellow to the campaign who had those qualities, and Tewksbury could be packed off to Rome, out of reach of his creditors.

"What if she took the coast road?" Tewksbury mused, gaze once again on the fields and farms bordering the thoroughfare. "She could have gone east from London instead of north. Taken the road through Chelmsford, traveled along the seacoast, and then angled toward Norwich."

"She has a London coachman, Tewksbury. For him it's the great north road or Town, period. The coastal route is longer, the inns humbler, and there's no reason on this earth why she'd do something so unexpected."

"No reason, except to elude you," Tewksbury said, sending Bassham a brooding look. "If Sarah thought you'd look for her along the Great North Road, she'd take a less traveled route and stand a greater chance of reaching her auntie. I keep telling you she's not stupid. She knows you'll simply marry her off to another nodcock if anything happens to me. You are the one she needs to outwit."

In that much, Tewksbury was absolutely correct. "It makes no difference to me how Sarah eventually makes her way to Cromer. When she arrives to Aunt Fletcher's home, you and I will be waiting for her with open and forgiving arms. Aunt Fletcher will see reason, as will Sarah. You will trouble yourself to be gallant and restrained for once, and all will be well."

"I can be restrained but you said the sooner—"

The coach hit another rut.

"Hold your damned tongue, Tewksbury. Recriminations get us nowhere. Sarah suffered a small attack of nerves—I was right that her disposition is a bit unsteady, wasn't I?—and she simply needs reassurances and some cosseting. Can you do that?"

"I can cosset with the best of them, as long as my bills are paid."

Most of Tewkbury's bills were paid. Bassham knew better than to pay them all before the vows were spoken.

The next few miles passed in blessed if bumpy silence, then Tewksbury spoke again.

"You ever travel along the coast, Bassham?"

"I have not had the pleasure."

"The inns are cheaper, there's less traffic. The ocean is pretty, though I don't care for the stink at low tide."

The sight of Sarah's signature on the marriage settlements would be beyond pretty. "If you don't mind, I'd like to get this report read before we turn east at Stilton."

Tewksbury slouched lower in his corner of the coach. "They get bloody awful storms along the coast. I heard they had one earlier this week. Half of Norfolk and a quarter of Suffolk flooded. Would be a shame if anything happened to Sarah."

"You are attempting to think, Tewksbury. The effort is doomed. I suggest you turn your thoughts to how you'll cosset your bride when the happy reunion takes place."

"She's not stupid," Tewksbury said again, crossing his arms and closing his eyes, "and though I adore a good romp, and I'll try to make Sarah a good husband, I am not stupid either."

CHAPTER FOUR

Road repair in a time of impending war was an urgent undertaking. Farming in spring was equally urgent, as was setting a village to rights after a major spring gale. Another gale was on the way, sooner or later, and the denizens of Fenwick knew to restore order as quickly as they could while the winds blew calmly.

Thad was thus at the forge until dark, and his back, arms, and legs had passed weary long before sunset. He'd shared his lunch with Sarah, and was famished as well as tired by the time he washed off at the pump.

The pump being at the back of the smithy, and Thad being filthy, he didn't merely sluice himself off. He stripped down to his natural state and had a good if chilly top to toes wash, donning only his breeches to climb the back steps to his room at the boarding house.

He really ought to go straight to bed, for tomorrow would be equally demanding, and a tired blacksmith was a blacksmith who grew short tempered with large animals and clumsy with hot metal.

The balcony beckoned, however, and—might as well admit it— the possibility of another quiet conversation with the prodigal heiress.

He donned a clean shirt and pajama trousers, and found a pair of house slippers to shove his aching feet into.

Sarah, covered from head to delectable toes in a green velvet night robe, had apparently waited for him, or so he hoped. She occupied her chair, which some obliging soul had positioned a mere six inches from Thad's. That same soul had put a cushion on Thad's seat, which in his present state loomed like a heavenly benediction.

"I saw you working," she said. "You didn't even stop for an evening meal, and I stole half your nooning."

"You did not steal anything." He sank onto the blessed comfort of the cushion, for which his tired fundament would have happily ransomed his soul. "You shared your company with a man much in need of conversation beyond, 'Hold still, there, Queenie,' and 'Give me your ruddy foot, horse.'"

"Does a lot of cursing go on in the smithy?"

He leaned his head back and closed his eyes. "It shouldn't. Most horses are willing enough to be shod if you're patient and reasonable with them. We're in a hurry to repair the road, though, and get the crops in, so patience is in short supply."

"Do you like to work so hard?"

Off to the west, the moon had already cast its silvery magic over the marshes, and a chorus of frogs sang to the night air. In the distance, the surf ebbed and flowed in a relaxing rhythm, and Thad's mind turned itself to Sarah's question.

"I do like to work hard," he said, "much to my surprise, though not as hard as we're having to go at it this week. When I arrived here, I needed the challenge. I needed to wrestle with iron all day and fall into bed each night insensate. I needed practical puzzles to solve and a list of tasks that would never end."

Sarah drew her legs up, wrapping her arms around her knees. "Were you angry?"

He'd been grieving, but he hadn't realized that. "I was angry, also sad. Both my parents and my older brother had died in the space of a year. My parents were taken by illness, but my brother... his death was stupid. A matter of honor, which is to say, drunken young men waving deadly weapons at each other."

And then Grandmother had started hounding Thaddeus to marry the instant the mourning duties had been fulfilled. In her way, she'd been grieving too, but Thad had been unable to see it at the time.

He began arranging the words in his head to explain how the title had made the whole business of grieving more fraught, when Sarah toed off her slippers.

"I pulled weeds this afternoon," she said, her bare toes peeking from beneath her hems. "I loved it. I yanked them up by their dirty roots and tossed them into the wheelbarrow to die. Why does nobody allow young ladies the opportunity to murder weeds? We'd be ever so much more even tempered."

Murdering weeds. Thad hoped she'd filled that wheelbarrow with her ire. "What else did you do?" *And might I kiss your toes?*

"Fifi came by again, chasing her pony. I caught him up and instructed her on not allowing him to snatch the reins. I took a few turns on dear Wellie, and I do not believe that pony has been so surprised since a saddle was first strapped to his lazy back."

"In your skirts, you took a few turns on Fifi's pony? I would have liked to have seen that." Not only because the pony was overdue for a comeuppance but also because Sarah had the prettiest ankles ever to wade on an English shore.

"I also helped Cook prepare for dinner. She said many hands make light work, or I think that's what she said. One could hardly understand her, but after an hour of trying, I had the knack of peeling potatoes. I will dream of peeled potatoes, a lovely great stack of them cut up for boiling."

Dreams of kissing Sarah had figured in the idle corners of Thad's mind. As he'd watched a horse trot up, or waited for iron to heat, his fancy had also turned to a pair of elegant sandy feet, and to a lady whooping with glee at the frigid sting of the surf on her ankles. On the way back to the smithy, he'd also taken a peek inside her elegant coach, and imagined her reclining on the well padded benches, a book in hand, her feet up on the opposite cushion.

He had not envisioned Sarah peeling potatoes, not ever. Nor pulling weeds, nor hiking her skirts to give a pony a lesson in manners.

"You enjoyed impersonating a peasant?"

"I have never had such an interesting, worthwhile day. I wasn't impersonating a peasant, Mr. Pennrith, I was being useful. Do you know how lovely it is to be useful? Fifi thanked me, Mrs. Peabody thanked me. Cook said I was welcome to help again tomorrow seeing as I didn't cut myself nor waste half the *tatties*. I think that means potatoes."

Sarah was reminding Thad of his own wonderment at adjusting to life in Fenwick. Idleness was not a virtue here, as it was in Mayfair, but rather, a privilege earned by honest labor and good fortune.

"You are proud of yourself," he said softly. "And that feels wonderful."

"Precisely. I've been thinking about what you said."

Not about another goodnight kiss? "I talk a lot. What particular bloviation inspired you to pondering?"

"About why not simply buy myself a house and take up the life of a spinster? Uncle was generous with my pin money, doubtless in hopes I would not grow curious about the rest of my funds. I had no place to spend what he gave me, and nine years of pin money is a lot of money."

"Nine years?"

"My mama's will specified that I was to have my own spending money from the age of sixteen. My come-out was delayed by deaths in the family, and I have thus arrived to the great age of five-and-twenty having had only five Seasons."

"Did you enjoy those Seasons?" He still could not envision her peeling potatoes, much less schooling Fifi's equine sluggard. Ladies did putter in the garden, but *murdering weeds* was a new perspective on that activity.

"One is supposed to enjoy one's come out," Sarah said. "One is supposed to feel special and as if life in all its sparkling potential awaits in the very next ride in the park or trip to the shops."

Thad propped his feet on the balcony. "You hated it." Very likely, nobody had known that. They'd seen the pretty heiress in the pretty ballgowns and envied her a prison made of money and family schemes.

"Wait here," she said. "One shouldn't sit in the chilly night air with wet hair. You'll develop an ague." She disappeared into her room and came out holding a shawl. "Sit forward."

Thad obeyed and she wrapped the shawl, a soft, closely woven merino, around his shoulders. The scent of roses clung to the wool, suggesting Sarah had recently worn it.

"Thank you." *I don't suppose you'd like to keep me warm by snuggling in my lap?* As tired as he was, he should not have been able to think of snuggling, but he suspected where Sarah was concerned, only death would part him from such wayward thoughts.

Thad was arranging his shawl when a thought occurred to him. "It's fairly dark on this balcony, Sarah. How did you know my hair was wet?"

She resumed her seat, once again tucking herself into a ball. "I watched you at your ablutions. You are quite well formed. One could wish one had more than moonlight by which to admire you." She sounded as if she was complimenting somebody's skill at pall mall. All proper and polite.

Perhaps with Sarah, the more polite she sounded, the more emotion she was controlling.

"Would you like to watch me make some cheese toast? I will likely keep my clothes on, though if you ask very nicely, I might give you back your shawl."

"I couldn't really see you when you washed," she said. "Not nearly as well as I wanted to. But I knew you were down there in the yard, not a stitch on, and I envied you how casual you can be about such behavior. The sea air is making me wicked."

"The sea air is waking you up," Thad said. "It can have that effect. Shall we to the kitchen, Miss Sarah?" He rose and extended a hand to her.

She accepted his courtesy, and kept his hand in hers. "I never want to leave this place, Mr. Pennrith. Do they have fairy mounds here in Anglia, because I feel that far removed from what I believed my destiny to be in London."

He wrapped her in a brief hug, not because he desired her—though he absolutely did—but because he knew that feeling of not wanting to leave, ever, and the sorrow that lay behind it. Ordinary people somehow made Fenwick an extraordinary place, a place worth cherishing.

"Let's raid the larder," he said, stepping back and draping the shawl around her shoulders. "And nobody is making you leave here, nor can they. You are of age, you have means, you should do as you please."

She squeezed him around the middle. "How I wish that were true. To the larders, Mr. Pennrith. Let's put the coastal trade to shame with our plundering."

Thad smiled and let her go, though if Sarah chose to plunder his personal treasures, he would not object one bit. He would volunteer, in fact, to become her prisoner for at least the duration of a few nights.

Hugging Thaddeus Pennrith was like hugging a venerable oak. He was that solid and sturdy, that formidable. Sarah hadn't been quite honest with him though.

She'd seen every detail of his wet, naked form gilded by moonlight. He was perfection on a grand masculine scale, roped in enough muscle to make the Mayfair dandies look like the prancing doddy-polls they were.

Making love with Thaddeus would be a glorious, passionate

undertaking, not some furtive interlude involving a writing chair. Sarah knew this by the way Thaddeus had frankly washed his parts, pausing to add a few affectionate strokes to his quiescent member, his head thrown back and the wet column of his throat exposed for her delectation.

She wanted to bathe him with her own hands, to explore his secrets and have him peel her out of her clothing, article by article. This was what came of peeling potatoes by the hour on the kitchen's sunny back steps, and of wading barefoot in the surf at high noon.

Sarah pushed those thoughts firmly aside and cast around for small talk. "Mrs. Pallant was safely delivered of a fine, healthy boy."

Mr. Pennrith paused on the landing. "What will they name this one?"

"Peregrine is among the possibilities, as well as a Percival, Parsifal, Peyton, Pompeii, Preston. Mrs. Pallant was hoping for a girl, for she did want to name the child Pandora." Not Charlotte, Elizabeth, or Georgina, as half of Mayfair was named. The girl would be called Dora and Dorie, and her husband would probably call her Adorable.

As Sarah and Thaddeus descended into the darkened kitchen, she realized she had never once considered what she might name a child conceived with Matthew. She hadn't, in fact, had much interest in bearing his child, viewing conception as simply his means of entrapping her in an increasingly distasteful union.

"Light a lamp," Thaddeus said. "And I will be about the cheese toast."

Sarah used the iron poker on the hearth to stir up the coals, touched a lit spill to the wick of the lamp on the mantel, and felt pleased with herself for mastering even such a pathetically mundane skill as lighting a lantern. She had not done even that much for herself for years.

"Shall I light another?"

"No need. I know what I'm about in this kitchen. Mrs. Peabody realized years ago that when I miss meals, I will forage."

The idea that a man knew his way around a kitchen should not surprise Sarah. The Regent's chefs were all men, most of the cooks in the military were men. But those men gave orders to underlings when it came to food preparation.

Thaddeus cut even bread slices off a half-loaf, then pared cheese from a wheel with equal precision. "The trick to perfect cheese toast is to get the cheese slices uniform." He popped a bite of cheese into his mouth, then sliced another and held it out to her.

When Sarah would have taken the cheese from his hand, he instead put it to her mouth. She took the bite, and he watched her chew.

Was this flirtation? It had nothing to do with fans, gloves, parasols, or bouquets. No poetry was involved, save for the poetry of Thaddeus's hands competently wielding kitchen utensils.

"Where are the plates?" Sarah asked.

"We're eating cheese toast," Thaddeus said. "Plates don't come into it." He arranged the bread slices on long toasting forks, and passed one to Sarah. "We'll wash this down with some lemonade, and if you'd rather we put butter and jam on a few slices, we can do that too."

He went through a quarter of the loaf, expertly toasting the bread to golden brown, and melting the cheese just so. The result was delicious and messy, consumed sitting side by side on the warm stones of the raised hearth.

Sarah finished the last of her lemonade some moments later. She was full and happy, but not content. "That was scrumptious. Thank you."

"That," Thaddeus replied, re-banking the coals, "was barely enough to hold me until morning, but I could not ask for better company." He took their empty mugs to a dry sink, and put them in a pan of water with other dishes awaiting the scullery maid's attention. "Shall we to bed, Sarah?"

He extended a hand down to her, and grimaced. "That came out wrong. Forgive me."

Sarah took his hand, and also grabbed for her courage. "I would like to go to bed with you. If that doesn't suit, I would be pleased to share a few kisses. Matthew doesn't like to kiss, and I found that honestly a relief. I'd always thought... that is... kisses should be special, and you are special, and this place is special, so I wondered if perhaps..."

She dropped his hand, and moved away to blow out the lantern. "I have made a complete gudgeon of myself, haven't I?"

The kitchen was cast in the deep shadow, only a lit sconce on the stairs shedding any light.

Thaddeus scrubbed a hand over his face. "Let's discuss this upstairs, shall we?"

That was not a yes, not a stolen kiss, not much of anything.

But it wasn't a no, either.

Sarah, licking her fingers by the meager light of the coals and a single lantern...

Sarah, reaching for the spill jar, such that her night robe strained across a generous, unconfined bosom.

Sarah, peeking at him as he'd washed off the sweat of the forge, and very likely watching as he'd considered a quick self-indulgence and discarded the idea for being a little too improper, even for a country blacksmith in the dark of night. And now she wanted to take him to bed.

The mind of a mere mortal male boggled.

He took her to his room, because if they were to make memories, he wanted them made in his bed. He also wanted her to be able to leave if and when she took a notion to quit his company.

"Here is my dilemma," he said, closing and locking his door. "You are a lady without escort at present, and I do not want to take advantage of you as you endure a low moment."

She peered around at his room, which was a temple to quotidian male needs. A wardrobe, clothes press, and cedar chest held his entire store of clothing. The writing desk was bare but for the implements needed to send Grandmother the twice-monthly reports she demanded. The bed was big, the quilts worn soft with age, the rug equally well used.

His hearth was swept clean, a fire laid in case a spring night turned chilly, and behind the privacy screen—yes, she peered around that too—she'd find everything needed to keep a fellow reasonably tidy and clean.

"I'm not having a low moment," Sarah said, coming back around the privacy screen. "I'm having an honest moment. They are rare in my experience, though here in Fenwick you probably see more of honesty than dissembling."

The comment stung, because Thad hadn't been entirely honest with his neighbors, or with Sarah. They knew him to be a Town swell who'd been passing through and had stayed. They did not know his lineage could be traced back to the Conqueror, and his fortune was more venerable still.

He could reset a pair of front shoes on a draft team in half an hour, and that was all the good folk of Fenwick needed from him.

What did Sarah need from him?

"I do not want to take advantage of you," Thaddeus said, "but I also do not want to leave you with the impression that I am indifferent. I nearly set my pants on fire twice today at the forge, because I was daydreaming about your toes."

She opened his wardrobe and peered inside. "My toes?"

Her hand stroking over his Sunday frock coat might as well have been caressing his cock. "Your toes—bare, sandy, elegant, like your feet, ankles, and calves. I found myself wondering if your knees would be elegant too."

She faced him and looked down, and then slowly, inch by inch, hiked the skirts of her robe and nightgown. Up, past exquisite ankles, up, past surprisingly muscular calves, and *up*, over the curious join of bone and muscle known as a lady's knees.

"Are they?" she asked. "Elegant? Nobody has opined on the matter previously."

She was trying for amusement, but Thad heard the courage—and the frustration—in her question. Her dunderpated fiancé had not *made love* with her, had not bothered to see to Sarah's pleasure, had not shown her the courtesy owed any woman, much less a wife-to-be.

"Sarah, your knees are the Creator's greatest testament to beauty, but are you sure? If we go to bed together, I will withdraw, and Mrs. Peabody keeps a store of the tisanes used to prevent conception, but you must be sure." *And please might you raise those skirts to your waist?*

Sarah let her skirts drop, which was a kindness to Thad's ability to form sentences. "I was *not* sure, with Matthew, but I let him convince me. We were to be married, after all—why delay the inevitable when he would simply pester me until I capitulated?"

She paced closer to Thaddeus, and he fisted his hands at his sides.

"Then," Sarah went on, "Matthew went about the business with no more finesse than a boar rooting in the midden, and again, I was not sure. Perhaps that was simply how men go on, and the poets have been embellishing reality rather more than I'd been led to believe. I was not sure when I left London, knowing my uncle would follow, and fearing scandal would as well, but I saw no other course."

She stopped before him. "When I behold you, Thaddeus, I know my own mind and body. I am sure in my bones of my preferred course. The feeling is marvelous. I want more of that feeling, and I want it with you." She slipped her arms around his waist, and gave him her weight. "I will not beg, but I am asking to become your lover."

Thaddeus had no illusions about his charms.

He was far from handsome, but he was big and fit. Just as some men wanted to ride impressively large horses, some women wanted a roll in the hay with a man well equipped to pleasure them. If that fellow was low-born that only added to their adventure.

As far as any of the merry widows tooling through Fenwick knew, Thaddeus was simply a town blacksmith with decent manners, a flirtatious smile, and a sizeable and occasionally willing prick. Of late, he'd been less inclined to accommodate the ladies passing through because the whole exercise put him in mind of furtive couplings in Mayfair alcoves.

Sarah didn't want a furtive coupling, she did not want to feel naughty or wayward. She wanted lovemaking and cherishing, and she hoped to explore that lovely and fraught terrain with him.

Thaddeus gently wrapped his arms around her and rested his cheek against the top of her head. "What if there's a child, Sarah? I will not allow my firstborn to be raised as a cuckoo in another's nest."

"Matthew tried diligently to get me with child. He failed. I am not all that worried about conception."

"You should be. Promise me you'll tell me if there's a child. I know you won't tarry but a few days in Fenwick, and I will probably quit the town myself before too long, but a child deserves legitimacy and two loving parents."

She shifted to look up at him. "This is why I am drawn to you, Thaddeus Pennrith, because I am all but throwing myself at you, and you think about the consequences to an innocent child. You might labor all day at the forge and eat your luncheon from a sack while sitting on a sandy rock, but you are more of a gentleman than all the strutting peacocks in London combined."

She met his gaze, gave him a moment to protest, demure, or babble, then kissed him squarely on the mouth.

Before Thaddeus unwrapped the great gift Sarah had made of herself, he had the presence of mind to open the draperies so the bedroom was full of moonlight.

"I want the bed," Sarah said, as Thaddeus draped her shawl across his reading chair and undid the belt of her robe. "I want to be lying on my back, facing you when you join your body to mine. I want to touch you everywhere, not just hang onto a chair arranged at the proper height. I want... so much. I want *you,* Thaddeus, all of you."

"You will have all of me," he said, peeling her robe from her shoulders. "I promise, all of me and more. You will leave that bed knowing what you like, what pleases you, what tickles. You will have satisfaction from me such as you will never forget. Never again will a man leave you *not sure* about your due."

If he thought he was giving her something—a benchmark, a frame of reference, some truth with which to battle against the ignorance she'd been subjected to—he could more easily allow himself the great selfishness of becoming her temporary lover.

So he gave her kisses, by turns delicate and voracious, to her mouth, her cheeks, and temple, then lower. She liked to have her neck kissed, and—thanks be—she adored having her breasts fondled. She arched into his touch like a demanding cat, until Thaddeus eased off her nightgown, and she stood panting, naked, and pale in the moonlight.

"You too," she said. "All of you."

By Saint Clement's forge, she was lovely. Also blushing.

"Undo me," Thaddeus replied, when he wanted to toss her onto the bed and commence pleasuring them both. "Undress me. I want to be skin to skin with you, and I want your hands on me everywhere."

She smiled, and if her stupid *former* fiancé and all the other witless fortune hunters distracted by her riches could have seen that smile, they'd have known her wealth was pocket change compared to the passion she possessed.

She unbuttoned Thad's shirt and pulled it over his head, then undid the drawstring of his pajama trousers and went exploring.

"Sit," she said, urging him into the reading chair angled toward the window. She retrieved her shawl from the back of the chair and draped it around her shoulders.

He kicked off his slippers, took his assigned seat, and prayed for fortitude. Sarah extracted his half-hard cock from his clothing, her touch tentative at first—but not for long. By the time she'd licked, kissed and otherwise explored the object of her curiosity, Thad was in the hands of bold lady indeed.

"Would you like to sit in my lap?" he said, when she rested her cheek on his thigh and was using just the tip of her tongue on the tip of his cock.

"Sit in your lap?" Sarah's tongue found *that spot*, that wickedly sensitive spot...

"Sit *on* my lap, rather. We face each other, you take me inside of you, and much of how we move and pleasure each other is up to you. You could tell me to tease your nipples for example, or put my mouth on them. You might like a few kisses from me, or—"

She peered up at him and used her thumb on his wet flesh to mimic the action of her tongue. "I'd rather be on the bed. I've had enough of chairs for the moment."

"Then take me to bed, Sarah, and have your pleasure of me." The words should have been naughty, but what Thad felt as he watched emotions play across Sarah's face, was a tenderness too vast for words.

She had been manipulated and threatened by the people who should have kept her safe. She had fled everything familiar to take her chances on the unknown. For her to entrust Thad with this night of loving was to honor him deeply. He would be worthy of her trust, if it took him until dawn and broke his heart in the process.

CHAPTER FIVE

Lovemaking was not intended to be a hurried or furtive process. Sarah had suspected as much, as she'd become intimately acquainted with the writing chairs in her uncle's home. Her suspicions had bloomed into near certainty when Matthew had concluded his rutting with a pat and a pinch to her derriere, then a hasty rebuttoning of his falls.

His next tender gesture was usually to remove himself to the nearest mirror, where he'd apply a comb to his artfully styled curls, while Sarah fumbled beneath her skirts with a handkerchief and fumbled in her heart with dismay.

Surely *that* was not the marital act?

That hopeless indignity could not possibly be the motivation for sonnets and ballads without number?

That perfunctory awkwardness wasn't the pleasure for which many a lady had sacrificed her good name?

Beholding Thaddeus Pennrith clad in little more than moonlight and exhaustion, she knew that patience and consideration were the essence of lovemaking, and whatever Matthew had been about, nothing of love had informed his behavior.

More fool he.

"You would sit in that chair, clutching the arms until they splintered if I asked it of you, wouldn't you?" she asked.

"In another two minutes, either the chair arms will splinter with force of my grip, or I will come undone with the cleverness of yours."

Sarah wanted to keep touching him, particularly his intimate parts. The contrasts fascinated her. Hard and silky, mighty and vulnerable, hot and sensitive. She wanted to consume him, with her mouth, her hands, her body, everything.

She contented herself with more of the first, but something about the tension coiling in Thaddeus's big body warned her to desist.

"I like having you in my mouth," she said, sitting back. "I am truly becoming wanton."

"A trifle bold perhaps," he said, cradling her jaw against a callused palm. "I long to be the man with whom you become bolder still. You might like having my mouth on you too, Sarah. Shall we find out?"

She rose, not exactly sure what he was proposing. "The sheets will be cool."

"No," Thaddeus said, getting to his feet, "they will not."

His pajama trousers had been pushed down to reveal his rampant arousal—pushed down *by her*—and the silk stretched tight over his hips and buttocks. That provocative dishevelment and his complete ease with it, made Sarah want to snatch him up and toss him onto the bed.

Thaddeus stepped out of his pajamas and laid them across Sarah's robe and nightgown.

"Now what?" Sarah asked, a frisson of uncertainty threading through her anticipation. Surely Matthew had not been equipped as generously as Thaddeus was. Not nearly.

Thaddeus folded the covers back, piled pillows against the headboard, and climbed onto the bed. "Now we take up where you so mercifully left off." He patted his thighs. "Your chariot awaits."

He had described this to her: making love facing each other, her straddling his lap. The opposite of her experiences thus far. Sarah got herself onto the bed, her shawl still about her shoulders, and settled herself in Thaddeus's lap. A length of hard male flesh arrowed up along his belly, and her ignorance once again threatened to swamp her ardor.

"That goes inside me, if I recall the particulars correctly."

Thaddeus cupped her elbows and kissed her. "We'll get to that part. No need to rush." He palmed her breasts, a marvelous pleasure given the warmth and calluses of his hands, then teased at her nipples with skillful fingers and an even more skillful mouth.

Sarah winnowed her fingers through thick, damp hair, and at some point—perhaps when he'd used the rough texture of his beard on the underside of her breasts?—she began to move. She slid her sex along the thick column of male flesh between her legs, and nothing— not anything, ever—had felt as shocking or as pleasurable.

"I like this," she panted. "I like this exceedingly."

"I like it rather a lot too," Thaddeus countered. "Say when you want more, Sarah, and that will please us better still."

He was asking her something, even as he kissed her throat and sketched the contours of her back with his hands. Sarah became dimly aware that for their bodies to join intimately, somebody had to touch somebody, and Thaddeus was leaving that initiative up to her.

A battle ensued, between the part of Sarah that was having a spectacularly good time riding his arousal, and the part of her that wanted him inside her.

"I don't want to stop," she said. "I like..." She sank her weight more tightly over him. "That feeling."

"Take me inside you. We can make that feeling more intense."

Had Matthew given her that assurance, she would have scoffed. He'd made her all sorts of promises. *I'll be done in five minutes. You'll get better at it with practice. You'll learn to love it. You'll beg me for this.*

Nobody should learn to like, much less tolerate, being bent over a chair for a man's convenience. Sarah could envision no sane moment when she'd beg Matthew for anything so tedious.

Thaddeus waited, his hands on her hips, and once again his patience did what passion could not. Sarah took him in one hand and started the joining.

"Go slowly," Thaddeus said, when she had placed him snugly against her opening, and dropped her hand. "Take your time."

He was barely seated, not even truly penetrating, and she'd expected him to start thrusting away. Apparently not. She tried a small, tentative undulation of her hips.

"Slowly," Thaddeus said again, two syllables conveying iron self-discipline.

Sarah could not help but go slowly, for Thaddeus was generously endowed and the sensations were too delicious to be rushed. She hung over him, attuned to her own body in a way that was new and fascinating.

"You were right," she said, withdrawing almost all the way before sinking back down. "This is scrumptious."

He laughed, a low rumble that Sarah could *feel* because they were so intimately connected. "Make a feast of me, Sarah. Gorge yourself on the sweetness."

His hands glided up from her hips to her breasts, where he applied a diabolical combination of caresses, pressure, kisses, and even his teeth, until Sarah's desire became as frantic as an ocean gale. The pleasure broke over her in a tempest, and when she would have gone still with shock, Thaddeus took over the rhythm of their joining.

He swept her past mere pleasure into a realm of transcendent, unimaginable sensation. The intensity of the cataclysm overpowered thought, and all Sarah could do was fling herself against Thaddeus until satisfaction battered desire into submission.

And yet, the storm was not over. Emotions flooded in even as the aftershocks of pleasure ebbed. Sarah was suffused with a joy that had no name. Perhaps the glow in her heart was simply the effect of a celebration of animal lust, for she and Thaddeus had celebrated wildly.

Behind the happiness came an urge to weep, for this moment with Thaddeus was stolen and could have so easily been missed. His hand in her hair was tenderness incarnate, his hard presence in her body a consolation for the parting to come.

He had not found satisfaction, and that he should deny himself made the tears creep closer.

"I am about to wax lachrymose," Sarah said, mashing her nose against his muscular shoulder. "I cannot credit such a thing."

"Cry if you want to," Thaddeus said quietly. "*...thy eternal summer shall not fade,*" he quoted. "*Nor lose possession of that fair thou ow'st/Nor shall death brag thou wand'rest in his shade/When in eternal lines to Time thou grow'st...*"

He quoted the Bard, gently implying that Sarah's interlude with him here by the sea might end, as the glories of a summer day did, but he would treasure his memories of her forever.

Thaddeus shifted them, so Sarah lay under him, sheltered by his body. She did cry then, for the foolish woman formerly engaged to a silly young man, for a family distracted by greed from what really mattered. She cried for a future she could not share with the man who had stolen her heart.

After Thaddeus had dried her tears and embroiled her in an orgy of kissing, he began to move again inside her, and Sarah moved with him. She would conjure a storm of passion for him as he had for her, and together they would glory in the gale.

Making love with Sarah had forced Thaddeus to think of his future, not in an abstract, vaguely grumbling allusion to *someday soon*, but as that future encompassed the rest of his fleeting and precious life. Did he truly want to live out his days wrestling hairy equines and sweating at the Fenwick forge? Was that truly his best option?

How much longer must his grandmother harangue him to take up the duties of his birthright?

He'd arisen from the bed he'd shared with Sarah resolved to put an end to Grandmother's waiting, and had written to her accordingly. To his surprise, she'd answered by return post that he was to join her not at her London residence, but at her girlhood home and dower property in East Runton. She'd directed him to attend her at once, and he was not to do anything foolish regarding the Errant Heiress.

Attending her *at once* would be foolish indeed. Grandmother had harangued Thaddeus for five long years, she could hold her horses for another few days.

As he'd waited for Grandmother's reply and slogged through the furious demands at the smithy, he'd also developed the habit of sleeping with Sarah. Over the past week, she'd been corresponding with her solicitors, though Thaddeus didn't pry into those details. He could draw the relevant conclusions: If her solicitors knew where she was, her uncle could find her easily enough.

She too was reconciling herself to her fate.

She did not ask Thaddeus to buy her passage to the Continent, and truly, she was safer in Britain.

"You repaired my coach springs today, didn't you?" Sarah asked, as she took Thaddeus's jacket from him.

"I did. The job took some effort, because the metal has to be tempered, but it's done. You are free to leave at any time." He'd also lingered over his inspection of her vehicle, noting the details of comfort and design, inside and out, and making certain the rest of the undercarriage was sound.

She leaned into him. "I don't want to go, but I must resolve matters with my family."

Let me resolve them for you. Except Thaddeus had his own family matters to resolve before he was free to make that offer.

"I could put you on a packet for Edinburgh," he said. "Your family won't think to look for you there."

"My funds come from London," Sarah said, stepping back. "My

solicitors, much to my surprise, have been responsive to my queries, but I doubt they will withhold my location from my uncle. Here, I have an ally in Aunt Fletcher, and I need that."

"You have an ally in me," Thaddeus said. "I too have funds, Sarah. More than you'd think, and they are at your disposal. If you want a house in Scotland, I will cheerfully buy you one. Don't capitulate to your family's demands because of the money." It was on the tip of his tongue to tell her the rest of it: *I have means mostly because I have a title, you see...*

But that title was an earldom, and Sarah had on many occasions made scathing references to her uncle of the same rank.

She gazed up at him, her expression unreadable. "Would you come to Scotland with me?"

He was a peer of the realm, he had responsibilities, and they did not lie in Scotland, and after five years, Grandmother was out of patience.

"I could come to you there, for a time, but first... Do you recall telling me that you fled London because you did not know what else to do?"

She hung his jacket in the wardrobe and sat on the bed. "I do, and I am so very glad I did flee London."

"I fled London too, and that was the right choice for me as well. I have sorted myself out here in Fenwick on Sea. You provided me with the last bit of sorting that I needed to face a situation I ran from years ago."

Sarah unbelted her night robe and untied the bow of her nightgown's décolletage. "Does that situation involve a woman?"

"Yes, in a sense." Grandmother was female, though she was more dragon than human lady.

"Do you love her?"

"I do."

"And she has waited patiently for you all of this time?"

Thad had to focus on the question, because Sarah had raised her skirts to her hips, scooted to the edge of the bed, then spread her legs.

The view was spectacularly distracting. "She has waited," Thaddeus said, "not patiently. Sarah, what are you doing?"

She parted the fabric of her nightgown, so her breasts were all but displayed. "Saying good-bye."

"Not good-bye," Thaddeus said, crossing the room to stand between her legs. "Not that, Sarah. I must deal with matters relating to my family, as you must, and then I will beg you for an audience, if you are willing to receive me. I will come to you in London, I will call upon you at your aunt's, but please do not say good-bye."

And pray God, Sarah would not take a Cornish earl into dislike because she'd fallen in love with a Suffolk blacksmith.

"You are not engaged to another?" Sarah asked, leaning back on her elbows.

Two nights ago, Thaddeus had sat Sarah on the edge of the bed, the better to share with her the pleasures of his mouth on her sex. They had also discovered, though, that the bed was the perfect height for copulation if she lay on her back and he stood at the bedside.

Thaddeus undid the buttons of his falls. "I am not engaged to anybody. Never have been. Will you break it off with the ninnyhammer?"

"I am convinced he will break it off with me."

Thaddeus took his aroused cock in hand and stroked himself along Sarah's damp folds. "Not good enough, Sarah. Tell me you'll send him packing." Thad had no business making that demand, but his store of gentlemanly delicacy was rapidly washing out to sea.

"If he doesn't toss me over," Sarah said, jiggling on the bed a little, "I will cry off. Stop teasing me."

"When you wiggle like that, it makes your breasts bounce. I love it when your breasts bounce."

She looked him right in the eye, and began twiddling a nipple. In mere days—and nights—she'd gone from a prim and proper lady to a houri of the bedroom, and Thaddeus had the sense she was still—*still* —barely getting started on her erotic vocabulary.

He eased into her heat, more slowly than she usually liked,

because he owed her the pleasure of anticipation. "Did you peel potatoes today, Sarah?"

She eyed him balefully, though this was a game they played. Small talk to make the passion flare hotter.

"I made pie crusts and jam tarts. I brought Mrs. Pallant some fabric and thread to make baby clothes. I separated irises, and planted some in the yard of your smithy."

Sarah had a surprising aptitude for village life, another reason she might prefer a blacksmith to an earl. Thad set that troubling thought aside and sent his thumbs exploring the russet curls between Sarah's legs all while he kept up an easy, relaxed rhythm.

"Sarah, if I were not a blacksmith, but some other sort of fellow, from some other station in life, would you still want me?"

"If I were not an heiress, awash in money and running from my family, would you still want me?"

He bent over her and gathered her close. "Yes, I absolutely would. I will want you to my dying day and beyond. I will cherish every moment spent with you and long to return to your side when we are parted."

The lovemaking changed, from mutual teasing to a focus on not only desire—desire was ever present between them—but on closeness. Sarah lashed her arms around his neck, and her legs around his waist. She met him thrust for thrust until the bed was creaking and Thad's thighs were burning. Still they pushed each other, straining both toward and away from the moment of completion, until Sarah began the soft panting that signaled her release.

Thaddeus held out, barely, until Sarah was once again moving in a lazy, replete rhythm. He withdrew and spent on her belly, though it nearly cost him his sanity. He would not take choices from Sarah as her family had tried to do, and foreclose her options with maternal guilt.

"I want you again," she said, when he was spooned around her in bed some minutes later. "I am still humming inside, and I want you again."

If I were an earl, would you want me? If we had to bide in London for a portion of the year while I voted my seat, would you want me?

"Shall I escort you to your aunt's home in Cromer," he asked, "or would you rather your family not realize you've formed a friendship with a village blacksmith?"

Sarah was quiet for a time, while Thaddeus once again mentally arranged ways of announcing the truth to her:

I have this little earldom in Cornwall, quite pretty, a mere 30,000 acres if you count only the Cornish properties.

There's this title I've been meaning to mention—my own, as it happens.

I realize your uncle is an earl and you probably detest all things earl-ish, but I hope you'll make an exception in my case...

"I did not know how to ask you," she said, "but I am very much afraid Aunt Fletcher will try to talk sense into me, or that Uncle will simply have me carted off to the north unless I marry Matthew by special license. I am not a coward, but I think the escort of an ally would be a prudent measure."

"We will call on your aunt first," he said, "but I'd also like to introduce you to my grandmother. She's just down along coast from Cromer in East Runton, and she will be less uncivil if I bring a proper lady with me."

That wasn't half of the story, but Thad would take on one set of difficult relations at a time. He made love with Sarah again, slowly, tenderly, hoping it wasn't the last intimacy they'd share.

Sarah was more determined than nervous, or so she told herself, until she saw Thaddeus crossing the thoroughfare to join her beside her coach. In the sparkling morning sunshine, he looked not like the village blacksmith, but like the largest and most exquisite exponent of Bond Street's sartorial arts ever to saunter down a high street.

His boots were polished to a champagne shine, his morning attire was cut to lovingly flattering perfection, and the paisley embroidery on his waistcoat found the exact balance between extravagant needlework and elegant good taste.

"My finery is a few years out of date," Thaddeus said, bowing over her hand, "but will I do?"

He had assisted her to dress, then sent her to make her farewells to Mrs. Peabody, so his splendid turnout was a case of first impression for Sarah.

"You will dazzle Aunt Fletcher," Sarah said, fluffing the snowy lace of his old-fashioned jabot. "You dazzle me." Even Uncle would take Thaddeus seriously attired thus, which was more reassuring than a determined—but *not* nervous—woman should admit. Aunt Fletcher had sent a note warning Sarah that both Uncle and Matthew were imposing on her hospitality, and they did not intend to leave until Sarah joined them.

Thaddeus had declared that development to be a relief, for it allowed Sarah to settle matters without returning to her uncle's household.

Her uncle's household, from which Sarah could be sent, bound hand and foot, to some walled estate where hysterical women were interned with orders to *come to their senses.*

"Let's be off," Thaddeus said, tossing a valise to the footmen at the boot. "The roads will be the worse for the storm, and delays and detours are likely." He handed Sarah up, climbed in after her, and joined her on the forward-facing seat.

A sharp rap with Thaddeus's fist on the coach ceiling, and MacAdams gave the horses the office to walk on.

Because Thaddeus chose the route that turned inland toward Norwich rather than keeping the coach traveling along the coast, the going was lamentably uneventful, and the coach passed through Norwich well before noon. Sarah spent the first part of the journey dozing against Thaddeus's side, but her sleep was fitful.

"You are worried," Thaddeus said, stroking her hair. "Don't be. I won't let them bully you, Sarah. You state your terms, and your family complies with them. This is not a negotiation."

"They aren't in the habit of complying, and I am not in the habit of stating my terms."

He bent near enough to whisper. *"Touch me here, Thaddeus.... Faster... Not like that, like this.* You state your terms quite firmly, and I love it when you do."

"That's different."

"No, my love, it is not. The same woman who takes me by the hand and shows me exactly how I'm to please her can be equally clear and firm with meddling relations. In mere days, you have Fifi's disgrace to the equine species trotting docilely up and down the lane, and I see that your solicitors have been prompt responding to your queries. If you can make the lawyers attend you, a troublesome uncle will be of little moment."

"An uncle and a fiancé. I did accept Matthew's proposal."

"Crying off is a lady's prerogative. Leave me to my forge in Fenwick if you must, Sarah, but never tell me that you'll allow a man like that to call you wife."

"Do you intend to remain at your forge?" she asked, taking his hand.

"For the near term, while the Arbuckles sort out how to go on when I leave." He took Sarah's hand, and she had so often joined hands with him over the past week, she noticed that his grip felt different.

Still callused, still warm, still a pleasure... but he wore a ring. A *signet* ring.

"Why would you leave Fenwick?" Sarah asked. "You seem so happy there."

The coach slowed as he peered down at her, and then he gently kissed her. The kiss held no heat, no offer of an erotic distraction, but a wealth of tenderness.

"I have been happier in Fenwick on Sea in the past week then I thought it possible for a mortal man to be, but my grandmother will not leave me in peace until I set her straight on a few points."

"Exactly," Sarah said, "I must set my uncle straight on a few points."

"And your fiancé?"

"I pity him." Sarah could say that honestly. Matthew was a rutting boy with nothing to offer the world but charm, good looks, and bumbling skill with an unimpressive pillicock. "I watched you at the forge, yesterday. You work without your shirt."

"The forge is hot, and fabric can catch fire."

The forge was also dark, the better for a smith to assess the exact color of heated metal or hot coals, and Sarah had tarried in a shadowed corner after bringing Thaddeus his nooning. He'd been fashioning a new set of horseshoes from a straight iron bar, curving the metal blow by blow, then reheating it to bend it yet more.

Thaddeus working at the forge had stirred all manner of emotions, and not a little arousal. He was a magnificent specimen, also skilled, patient, hard-working, good-humored, kind, and determined. Sarah would never regard horseshoes, herself, or the working man in the same light as she had before leaving London.

"You toil without your shirt, but you work with your mind as well as your hands," Sarah said. "I found that impressive. I would like to work with my mind too, Thaddeus, to be of use, and not merely a means to the end of my uncle's laziness and greed."

The coach slowed further and made a turn off the road.

"Of use how?" Thaddeus asked. "Your fortune could be of great use, but perhaps that's not what you meant."

"I don't know, except that I would like to find a worthy charity or three to support. Peeling potatoes is useful, though I hope I can aspire to more than that. Schooling Fifi's pony was useful. Taking the air in Hyde Park so other ladies can criticize my bonnet and gentleman can ogle my bosom is not useful."

"We are agreed. Who are these other gentlemen?"

The coach halted, and the time for private discussions was over, which was fortunate for the gentlemen whose names she would have listed.

"We have arrived," Sarah said. "Aunt can be a dragon, but I hope she breathes her fire on Uncle rather than me. And Thaddeus?"

"My love?"

Oh, she adored his endearments. "I suspect given the chance you could be of even greater use to the realm than you are when serving at Fenwick on Sea's forge. When we have more time, perhaps we ought to discuss that topic as well."

Thaddeus looked pained, and as close to out of sorts as he ever became. "Agreed, but if your aunt breathes fire at you today, you simply singe her eyebrows with your own flames. Once or twice and she'll get the idea." Thaddeus preceded Sarah from the coach and handed her down.

Aunt's cottage—a rambling three-story edifice of eighteen bedrooms—sat on a rise overlooking the sea. The white columns of the front terrace were still gleaming white, and red pots of salvia still adorned the steps. The same venerable butler Sarah recalled from her childhood admitted her, and the same scent of lemon oil and sea breezes wafted through the house.

"May I take the gentleman's hat?" the butler asked.

Thaddeus passed over his hat, and Sarah noted the beat of awkwardness when no calling card accompanied the hat.

"Mr. Pennrith has kindly escorted me from Fenwick on Sea," Sarah said. "Where might we find Aunt Fletcher?"

"Madam is in the guest parlor," the butler replied, setting Thaddeus's hat on the sideboard. "Your uncle and Mr. Tewksbury are with her. Today is her day to be at home, and I am certain she will welcome you with open arms."

The butler twinkled at Sarah, then led her down the corridor past familiar paintings and a sparkling pier glass Sarah did not recall seeing before. Thaddeus paced at her elbow, silent, and oddly of a piece with the elegant surroundings.

He wasn't nervous, and Sarah borrowed from his calm as she waited for the butler to announce her.

"Lady Sarah Weatherby," the butler intoned, "and Mr. Pennrith, late of Fenwick on Sea." He bowed and withdrew.

And abruptly, Sarah was very nervous indeed.

CHAPTER SIX

"Your ladyship?" Thaddeus winged an arm at Sarah, and if he was dismayed that she claimed an honorific, he hid it behind a warm, even mischievous smile.

Sarah took his arm, angled her chin up, ignored the flock of demented butterflies in her belly, and let Thaddeus escort her into the parlor.

Uncle stood near the window, his expression radiating banked annoyance. Matthew struck a pose near the piano, a cross between wronged suitor and eager lover. He kept one hand on the lid of the piano, and half-turned toward her, as if forces beyond his control kept him from going to her.

Or perhaps common sense did that, when he caught sight of Thaddeus at Sarah's side.

"My darling girl." Aunt Fletcher, tinier than ever, came out of her seat. "I have been so worried about you. And here you are, quite in the pink and on the arm of as impressive a fellow as ever graced my parlor. The gentleman bears a resemblance to your grandson, Sephronia. Isn't Pennrith an old Cornish name?"

Aunt addressed another older woman, who reposed in a rose velvet wing chair near the unlit hearth.

"Unless I mistake myself, which I almost never do, that is my wayward grandson. Thaddeus make your bow."

Good heavens. *That* was Thaddeus's grandmother? She rose from her wingchair with all the dignity of a grieving queen, and extended a beringed hand to him. He moved forward and some perverse impulse led Sarah to keep her hand entwined with his arm.

Even as he bowed to his grandmother, Sarah did not let him go.

"Thaddeus," Sarah said, "might you introduce us?"

The older woman glowered down her nose at Sarah. On Thaddeus that nose was splendid. On his grandmother, the effect was not nearly as attractive.

Aunt Fletcher rang a little bell that chimed merrily enough to be heard in the corridor. "Introductions are hardly necessary, Sephronia. You know my Sarah and I know your Thaddeus, though I do believe he was frolicking naked in the surf when last I met him, and an exasperated nursemaid or three was begging him to come back to shore. We will need a fresh pot of a certainty. Mr. Tewksbury, shut your mouth, lest you catch flies, and Bassham, do stop pouting by the window. Our Sarah is here, safe and sound, and we rejoice to see her."

"Bassham?" Thaddeus said. "Earl of?"

Uncle bowed. "At your service, and you would be?"

"Thaddeus Pennrith. And this must be the *honorable* Mr. Matthew Tewksbury."

Matthew mustered a bow. "At your service. Sarah you are looking none the worse for your ordeal. You will be pleased to know I brought a special license. We can return to London as a married couple, and nobody need know that you indulged in a mad flight due to your bridal nerves."

Matthew smiled, and the kindly promise of forgiveness in that smile, the smug confidence, lit the fire of Sarah's temper. He was graciously offering to bend her over an endless procession of writing chairs, while setting her abigail to spy on her, and spending her money on stupid wagers.

"I have made arrangements to give away my fortune, Matthew. Are you still interested in returning to London as my husband?"

The only sound was the soothing rhythm of the distant surf, breaking on the beach far below the windows.

"You are mad," Uncle said. "Clearly, unequivocally mad."

"I might be," Sarah replied, as Thaddeus rested his hand over the fingers she'd wrapped around his arm, "but I am well within the terms of the trust when I make that decision. Mother gave generously to charities, and I merely intend to follow her example. I have also reviewed an accounting of all disbursements made from my funds since you became the trustee. You are either excessively greedy or a very poor manager. The solicitors have been scolding you for years because you waste my money."

"Sarah," Matthew began, taking a step toward her. "You must be reasonable. In times of war, investing is uncertain, and I'm sure Lord Bassham has done his best to preserve—"

"Whatever he has preserved," Sarah said, "I am giving the bulk of it away. Injured soldiers strike me as a worthy cause. Life boats appeal to me, as do widows and orphans. If you have any self-respect to your name, Matthew, you will take yourself off for a repairing lease in the West Riding and never blight my day with your presence again. Uncle paid a number of your gambling debts, and you provided *nothing* of value in return."

Thaddeus's posture shifted subtly. He went quietly from standing at Sarah's side to *looming*. Matthew retreated to the piano.

"You're crying off," Matthew said, nodding once, and glowering at Uncle. "A gentleman does not argue with a lady."

"I am not crying off," Sarah said, "I am casting you into the nearest muddy ditch like the rubbish you are. Aunt, Mr. Tewksbury will not be staying the night."

Thaddeus' grandmother harrumphed. "Be off with you, puppy.

Thaddeus has a taste for a good brawl, I am ashamed to say. In this case, one is inclined to indulge his unfortunate proclivities."

"But Sarah," Matthew said, sounding genuinely bewildered, "*why*? I'm reasonably good looking, of suitable station, and I would have let you buy all the fripperies you cared to buy. I could keep Bassham from being too big of a pest, and give you some babies to spoil. Why throw that away and a fortune as well?"

Sarah did drop Thaddeus's arm. "You would have let *me buy frip-peries*, and I am supposed to be grateful for that? When it's my money I'd be spending—while you fornicate the afternoon away with my lady's maid? What woman in her right mind would choose that future when she can instead make a difference throughout her day and share a bed at night with a man who thrives on honest work? I could slap you."

"Why don't you?" Thaddeus's grandmother asked.

"Because," Thaddeus replied, calmly, "to slap him, she'd have to touch him, and Sarah decided before she left London that Tewksbury isn't worth even her anger."

Sarah felt as if she'd been about to trip, but a strong hand had prevented her from stumbling. "Exactly," she said. "Away with you."

Matthew jerked down his waistcoat and marched from the parlor, though his show of affronted dignity was undermined by the speed with which he scampered past Thaddeus.

"We are well rid of him," Uncle said, "though I had hoped to avoid the scandal of a broken engagement. I will take you back to London, Sarah, and we will sort out your funds to your satisfaction. To disburse a fortune—and it remains a sizable fortune—in a display of pique is not the behavior a rational woman."

The exhilaration of casting Matthew aside collapsed into cold dread. "I will not return to London with you, Uncle. I refuse to."

Aunt remained silent in the face of that declaration, when Sarah very much needed her to speak up.

"Nonsense," Uncle replied. "You were foolish, but I agree that Tewksbury lacked the intellectual stature to keep you amused. We'll find you another fellow, one willing to overlook a broken engagement in light of your means, and this will all be forgotten."

Thaddeus did not cross the room so much as he rolled forth like a storm making landfall from the North Sea.

"Shut your stupid mouth," he said, stopping two paces from Uncle's place by the window. "Sarah is of age. You are no longer her guardian, and if her Aunt will not provide a home for her, *she can provide a home for herself.* You have offered her nothing but a gilded cage and selfish manipulation. You turned a rutting bounder lose on her in a further attempt to steal from her. Tewksbury is pathetic, but you are disgusting."

And Thaddeus was absolutely lovely. Sarah's resolve had slipped with Uncle threats, her courage had flagged. Thaddeus was simply pointing out the truth, though. Uncle was no longer her guardian, and he had stolen from her.

"Who the hell are you, sir," Uncle sneered, "to be insulting a peer of the realm? I have no doubt you've been sniffing around Sarah's skirts in an attempt to get your own brutish hands on her money. I will take her back to London, and she will thank me for sparing her from your advances."

The old women were exchanging a glance that to Sarah looked quietly amused.

"Uncle, hush," Sarah said, not amused in the least. "You have pilfered the last coin from my coffers. I would rather be a black-smith's wife in Fenwick on Sea than your niece in Mayfair. I am happy to sever relations with you if you insist on clinging to your arrogance."

"The arrogance," Uncle snapped, "is yours, my girl. Those damned solicitors had clear instructions, and—"

"And lately, they have obeyed them," Thaddeus said, "because those instructions came from Sarah, and her mother, their clients, while you are a parasite and a disgrace to the peerage. You either apologize to Sarah or run along back to London to explain to your glovemaker, coalman, mistress, and jeweler, that you have no legal means of paying your bills."

The very calm with which Thaddeus offered those options settled something inside Sarah that had needed settling.

"I do not want to see you ruined, Uncle," Sarah said. "I will bring your accounts up to date, but then you must manage within your means. I expect you will quit London and let out the townhouse at least for a few years."

"Burtie," Aunt Fletcher said, "you'd best take that offer, for I have neither the means nor the inclination to bail you out."

Uncle looked down his nose at Sarah, using an attitude of disdain that would have turned her to knees to blanc mange only a few short weeks ago.

"And you will rusticate in some seaside swamp with this, this..."—he waved at hand at Thaddeus—"jumped up stable boy?"

Thaddeus was watching Sarah, his eyes conveying his admiration for her, and something else, something that reminded her of his pained expression in the coach.

"I will gladly become the wife of the Fenwick on Sea blacksmith, and spend my days weeding our garden and raising our children rather than subject myself to an earl's high-handed meddling."

Uncle strode for the door. "That you would make such a choice proves that the last of your wits have gone begging. Marrying a blacksmith. For shame, Sarah. I can assure you that Chancery will see me re-appointed as guardian of your property the moment I inform the courts of your proposed folly. And to think, I took you in, when you hadn't a roof over your head or a—"

Thaddeus had shifted during this tirade to block the door. "And what if, instead of marrying a lowly blacksmith, the young lady is planning to marry an earl?"

"I am the only earl foolish enough to endure this company," Uncle said, "and I can easily remedy that sad state of affairs." He swanned out the door, and Sarah frankly never cared if she saw him again.

To think his approval had ever meant anything, when in fact, he ought to have been earning Sarah's respect. The comfort of that insight was fleeting, however, when she grasped the significance of Thaddeus's words.

"Thaddeus," she said, "what are you going on about? I want nothing to do with earls or honorables or even baronets. I shall have my blacksmith, if he will have me."

Thaddeus should have given her a broad, mischievous smile, maybe even a wink. Instead he looked a bit sheepish.

"I blush to inform you, Lady Sarah, that your plan to marry a village blacksmith has become slightly problematic."

"Quite," Grandmother said, as Thaddeus searched for the words that would explain his situation to Sarah without making him sound like another manipulative, untrustworthy, titled male.

"You cannot expect a peer of the realm," Grandmother went on, "the sole male exponent of the earldom's line, to marry a hoyden who goes racketing about the countryside because she's lost her patience with a strutting dandy and his dollymops. Dollymops are a fact of married life, and I am surprised that Eudora Fletcher's great-niece would quibble over such a detail."

"Grandmother," Thaddeus said as gently as he could for a man who wanted to clap his hand over a querulous old woman's mouth, "please hush."

"Sephronia,"—Mrs. Fletcher chose a tea cake from the tray—"your grandson has apparently done a fair bit of racketing himself."

Grandmother thumped her cane. "Men are always racketing. That's most of what they are good for, but the least Thaddeus can do is take twenty minutes to speak his vows and secure the succession. I have made a list, a carefully researched list, and now that he's done with Frolic on Sea, he will subject himself to my guidance—"

Thaddeus might have let Grandmother's temper blow itself out, but across the room Sarah was looking again like the bewildered young woman whose coach had pulled up on damaged springs outside The Queen's Barque.

"Grandmother, if you do not cease prattling, I will take Lady Sarah by the hand, quit this parlor, and never open another letter from you."

"I never prattle."

Thaddeus reached for Sarah's hand and she caught him in a firm grip. The effect was the same as if his spine had been a length of iron glowing with the heat of the forge, then plunged into cool water for tempering. Every strength he possessed became focused on the same end, casting mere determination into the shade.

"Sarah met me as I labored at the Fenwick on Sea forge, where I have earned a wage these past five years. She did not disdain me because I labored with my hands, but she might well disdain me for allowing you to berate me as you did my brother. There is more to life than securing the blighted succession."

Another grandmother might have resorted to tears, or at least made a dignified retreat.

"Had your brother listened to me, my lord, I would have seen him married to a decent young woman whose steadying influence would have prevented his lamentable excesses. I would have great-grandsons by now, and you would be free to dirty your hands all you pleased."

Sarah slipped her arm around Thaddeus's waist, and her silent support—without hearing Thaddeus's apologies or explanations—reminded him of the families he knew in Fenwick on Sea. They loved one another, they accepted one another. They argued and fumed and pouted, but they found their way back to high, sunny ground when the domestic storms moved on.

Respect was evident in those families, as it had not been in Grandmother's dealings with Thaddeus.

"Grandmother," Thaddeus said, tucking an arm around Sarah's shoulders, "had you not carped at my brother so ceaselessly to marry the biddable cipher of your choosing, he might not have been driven to those excesses in the first place. Your days of pestering and shaming and haranguing me are over. If you ever want to know your great-grandchildren, you will cease meddling *now*."

Sarah leaned against him. "When Thaddeus uses that tone of voice, I daresay draft horses ten times his size know better than to argue. God willing, he will be papa to any number of darling children. I'm sure he would hate for them to have no idea *at all* who their great-grandmother is."

Grandmother inhaled through her nose. "You are comparing me to a *beast?*"

Mrs. Fletcher munched on her tea cake. "You are as stubborn as a mule, Sephronia. You'd best listen to your grandson."

Grandmother rose. "Send for my coach," she snapped at the footman. "There is no good company to be found here."

She made an exit worthy of Mrs. Siddons when upstaged by the ingenue, while Mrs. Fletcher poured herself another cup.

"Sephronia drove your poor father to eloping, my lord," Mrs. Fletcher said, dropping a lump of sugar into her tea. "Best thing that could have happened. Inbreeding invariably results in feeblemindedness and weak nerves, as my late husband often observed."

"My parents eloped?" That was news to Thaddeus.

"Sephronia fumed about it until your brother showed up. Once you came along, the match was very nearly Sephronia's idea, despite your mother's people being *in trade*. Owning half a dozen foundries isn't exactly the same as selling posies on a street corner, but Sephronia thrives on being affronted. Will you have some tea, my dears?"

"Sarah?" Thaddeus wanted to hear more from Mrs. Fletcher about his parents' courtship, but his own courtship matters had become pressing. "Will you walk with me by the water before we sit down to tea?"

"Take a parasol," Mrs. Fletcher said. "The sea air is fine for invigorating the animal spirits, but a lady must protect her complexion."

Sarah gave Thaddeus a measuring look. "Are you truly an earl?"

"I am afraid so. Are you truly parting with your fortune?"

"Most of it."

"My title wasn't making me happy, but I could not escape it entirely. If your fortune is making your miserable, then toss it into the sea for all I care."

"You mean that?"

He offered her his arm. "With all my heart. Let's enjoy some fresh air, Lady Sarah, for there's more I would say to you."

Sarah did take a parasol, because the sun on the water was fierce. "I will pay off my uncle's immediate debts, but are you horrified that I'd give away my fortune?"

"Are you horrified that I'm an earl?"

The beach was a wide expanse of fine white sand, but here too, the shore turned to rocks a hundred yards on. Sarah headed for the rocks, because she and Thaddeus could sit and talk there, and because they'd be out of sight of the cottage.

"You told me you were a London dandy, and those fellows tend to come from a notably few well set-up families. I did see the finery in your wardrobe but I was too interested in seeing more of you at the time to puzzle over your clothing. Your diction is public school, and your size is also indicative of aristocratic breeding."

"My size is indicative of Viking blood blending with my Norman antecedents. I didn't mean to lie to you Sarah. I am sorry for that, but discretion has become my habit. What I have in Fenwick on Sea has saved my sanity, and I protect it instinctively."

That dear, decent Thaddeus had sought refuge by the sea as Sarah had sought refuge, suggested he'd been in dire straits indeed.

"I did not exactly announce my lineage to you when I climbed into your bed either, Thaddeus. I thought you would run from the room in dismay, gentleman blacksmith that you are."

He took her hand. "Your coach sat in the innyard for days, Sarah. I had a closer look at the springs and also noticed the turned crests. I also saw the solicitors' letter to you, and being solicitors, they addressed their mail properly."

"You knew I was the daughter of a peer?"

"I figured that out eventually, but you deserved to be just yourself for a few days in Fenwick on Sea. I'd had that privilege for five years. I wasn't anybody's *lucky spare*, I wasn't a nob. I was simply Thaddeus Penn, a competent hand at the forge. I'd earned some respect with hard work, honest dealings, and skill. That was balm to the soul of a man who'd been raised to be a reproductive insurance policy dangling idly from the family tree."

"Can we be honest with each other going forward, Thaddeus? We had reasons for guarding our privacy before, but I don't want to keep secrets from you."

He stopped walking and faced her, their hands still joined. "You want to go forward with me? I will understand if I was simply a means of blasting your future free of the course your uncle had set for you."

The breeze whipped his dark hair about his shoulders, and his grip was the same warm, firm, callused grip Sarah adored.

"Thaddeus, I will *not* understand if you merely wanted a farewell frolic with a willing woman in Fenwick on Sea. I'm glad we met without family trappings—or traps, to use the more accurate word. I'm glad you took me to bed on the terms I set for myself, glad you were willing to come to me simply as Thaddeus Pennrith, the real man rather than the title. I will treasure the memories of our early days for all my life, and I want that life to be shared with you."

He looped his arms around her shoulders and held her in a loose embrace. They were still visible from the cottage, and Sarah did not give a hearty damn who saw her in the arms of her beloved.

"I love you," Thaddeus said. "I wish I could say, I will be anybody you want me to be. The village blacksmith, an Anglian country squire, a Cornish earl, a London swell... but the more I saw of village life in Fenwick on Sea, the more I realized that the labor of people like the Arbuckles and Pallants is what drives this land, and their needs and priorities should be heard in Parliament."

Sarah leaned into him and slipped her arms around his waist. "And your earldom?"

"I miss Cornwall. I miss my home, I miss being able to visit the graves of my family, Sarah. I love Fenwick on Sea in part because it reminded me so much of home. For five years, I've contented myself with the reports of stewards and factors, but the land deserves more from me. The Corsican will not wreak havoc forever, and adjusting to peace will take ingenuity and tenacity. I have those qualities. You have them too, and I want us to be part of forging a better future for Britain."

"I am not to have my marriage to the village blacksmith, then?"

"And I am not to become the adoring spouse of a wealthy heiress. I will adjust to my changed circumstances as long as I can still be married to you. Will you have me, Sarah?"

She closed her eyes and let the sound of the sea merge with the steady beat of Thaddeus's heart. "I would like to have you right here on the beach, Thaddeus. To cast off our clothes and get sand in inconvenient places and then wash off frolicking naked in the surf. I will settle for a kiss—for now."

He kissed her with all the tenderness and passion she could have wished for, and they sat on the rocks for a long time, talking of summers in Cornwall, an annual honeymoon in Fenwick on Sea, and how to forge a future for their homeland as happy as the future they envisioned sharing with each other.

TO MY DEAR READERS

To my dear readers,

I hope you enjoyed Thaddeus and Sarah's happily ever after! This tale originally appeared in the Bluestocking Belles *Storm and Shelter* anthology. If you like true love by the sea, you can purchase the **whole anthology,** and get to know more of Fenwick on Sea's damsels and swains.

The Belles also have a new collection out, **Desperate Daughters**, which looks to be every bit as much fun as **Storm and Shelter**.

When I'm not figuratively frolicking in the surf, I'm busy writing both historical mysteries and Regency romances. My next **Mischief in Mayfair** title, *Miss Devoted*, comes out in February 2023, and my most recent **Lady Violet Mystery**, *Lady Violet Says I Do*, came out in January 2023.

If you'd like to see what else I have in the works, please do drop by my **website**, or follow me on **Bookbub**. The BB folks will let you know when a title goes up for pre-order, releases, or is discounted as a Bookbub featured deal. I also put out a periodic **newsletter** highlighting a new release or blathering on about works in progress. I never, ever sell, swap, give away, or otherwise let your email addie out of my sight, and unsubscribing is easy-peasy.

And finally, I **blog** most Sundays, and usually do a weekly give-away of some sort in conjunction with those posts, so please do stop by and join the conversation!

Happy reading (by the sea or elsewhere)!

Grace Burrowes

Read on for an excerpt from my next Regency romance, **_Miss Devoted_**!

MISS DEVOTED—EXCERPT

Chapter One

To be naked in a room full of intently staring strangers had become a sort of relief. Michael Delancey—vicar's son, ordained priest, and rising star at Lambeth Palace—shrugged out of his dressing gown and let his mind go quiet.

The drawing instructor made a few remarks about the difficulty of accurately rendering hands and feet and the need to pay attention to the smallest shadows—beneath the chin, below the ankle bone— and then Michael was posed, semi-recumbent on a chaise, one foot on the floor, one arm flung back to rest beside his head.

The posture was restful, though after twenty minutes, Michael's arm began to tingle. The only sounds in the room were the soft scratch of charcoal or pencil against paper, the occasional cough, or one page being set aside so another could be begun.

Berthold, a fussy old Frenchman with a meticulous eye for detail, murmured critical comments to this or that student, and time drifted along in a peaceful trickle of moments.

"And now, *mes prodiges*, we draw more than the fingers and the toes," Monsieur Berthold said. "We have noted before the regularities of our model's features—the nobility of the brow, the fine angle of the chin, the lovely musculature, and the perfect symmetry of the dark brows. This man is quite attractive." Monsieur's remarks, while flattering, might have been describing a marble effigy, so dispassionate was his praise. "Now I pose him thus..."

Berthold demonstrated for Michael a sitting posture, one elbow braced on a thigh, gaze on the floor.

"The handsome face is hidden. Draw this man so that without seeing the quality of his gaze, without knowing the set of his mouth or the angle of his nose, he conveys merriment. He is about to spring up and give a shout of joy, to laugh with great glee."

Michael, staring at his feet—scrupulously clean, second toe longer than the great toe—could not see the consternation in the room, but he could feel it in the silence that greeted Monsieur's challenge. Berthold had a whole speech about the difference between an artist and a draftsman. The draftsman rendered accurate likenesses and could make a fine living doing so.

May the good God bless and keep the draftsman, and may every artist aspire to at least a draftsman's skill.

The artist, though, put truth on the page. The visual truth, the emotional truth, the moral truth. All a bit high-flown when the audience was a room full of young men, many of whom were more adept at draining a bottle than drawing that same bottle sitting on a sunny windowsill.

One lone stick of charcoal began scratching away. High up, farthest from the center of the room. That would be young Mr. Henderson, who preferred the longer perspective. Slight, blond, barely emerging from adolescence. Henderson never said much, but when he did pose a question to Monsieur, the answer came without the usual garnish of sarcasm and criticism.

Henderson had talent and didn't feel compelled to bruit that about. Lord Dermot Anthony, by contrast, had sizable talent and an even bigger mouth. Always in the front row, close enough that

Michael could smell the sour aroma of debauchery blended with expensive shaving soap.

Everybody professed to like Lord Dermot, and even Monsieur offered him the occasional encouraging remark. Lord Dermot's mama, the Marchioness of Stanbridge, was a noted patroness of the arts, as was Dermot's auntie.

As the minutes crept by, Michael mentally steeled himself for his next obligation—dinner with his sister and her doting husband. Dorcas had chosen well, and she set a fine table. Alasdhair MacKay, Michael's brother-by-marriage, was a lovely fellow with a sly sense of humor and a fondness for smooth whisky.

The drudgery, though, of being polite and mannerly toward some pretty widow or spinster-in-training for three or four hours... The hope in the lady's eyes, the determination in Dorcas's, and the sympathy in MacKay's... A penance, the lot of it.

The session came to an end, and Berthold passed Michael his robe. "Our thanks, as usual. We will see you again on Tuesday, sir."

Michael donned the dressing gown and belted it loosely, then took himself to the changing room. Clothes maketh not the man, but rather, the masquerade. A priest wore sober attire, though he need not be shabby.

Michael enjoyed fine clothes. Perhaps if he showed up at Dorcas's with a stain on his cravat and a smear of charcoal on his cuff... But no. Dissembling for personal gain would not do.

He was making his way through the academy's grand foyer, wondering if he had time for a quick stop on Circle Lane before he was due for dinner. Just fifteen minutes, not really a visit, more of a sighting. He was too intent on his plans to watch where he was going, and thus he and Henderson collided right in the doorway.

"Beg pardon," Henderson muttered in his signature husky tenor. "Entirely my fault. Do go on." He tugged down is hat brim and gestured with a gloved hand.

"My apologies," Michael said, bowing. "I was preoccupied. After you."

Henderson bustled through the door and jogged down the steps, soon disappearing among the pedestrians thronging the walkway. Michael stood on the terrace, the chilly evening breeze wafting about him as he reviewed what he'd just learned.

Henderson, who preferred to sit in the studio's most shadowed corners, who rarely spoke at all, and who never joined with the other students in the general jockeying for status, was distinguished by more than talent and eccentricity.

Henderson had the unmistakable bodily endowments of a well-formed woman.

Order your copy of **Miss Devoted**!

Made in the USA
Columbia, SC
20 April 2024

34655866R00124